EMERGENTS ACADEMY

ACADEMY OF THE APOCALYPSE: BOOK 1

K. A. RILEY

NOTE FROM THE AUTHOR

The events of the *Academy of the Apocalypse* series take place immediately following the conclusion of the *Conspiracy Chronicles.*

Although the *Academy of the Apocalypse* draws upon characters and references some events in that nine-book series (made up of three interconnected trilogies), this is a stand-alone series and doesn't require intimate familiarity with what's come before.

(But it couldn't hurt, right?)

Either way, enjoy!

KARiley

SUMMARY

The year is 2047.

It's been more than five years since Kress and her Conspiracy defeated Krug and his Patriot Army, traveled through Europe and back, completed a cross-country rescue mission, and made it home alive.

Things were looking up for the future of the nation...until the Cult of the Devoted and the teenagers of the Army of the Unsettled decided to light the fuse for an all-out civil war.

Now, a special Academy—hidden high in the Rocky Mountains and designed as a school to train young Emergents in the use of their abilities—is being forced into the fight.

On the brink of a new global apocalypse, the tenacious raven-whisperer Branwynne and the techno-genetically enhanced teenagers of the Emergents Academy find themselves entangled in a three-way battle for power, where survival is doubtful, peace is impossible, and death is inevitable.

EPIGRAPH

"Teaching would be impossible unless students were sacred."

— Henry Higgins, *Pygmalion*, George Bernard Shaw

"You're off to great places. Today is your first day! Your mountain is waiting, so get on your way!"

— Dr. Seuss, *Oh the Places You'll Go!*

PROLOGUE

I WASN'T alive when the world ended.

By the time I was born, the Eastern Order and their drones had already blown up most of London.

They destroyed lives, monuments, roads, buildings, bridges, and worst of all, hope.

And they didn't stop until London—the only home I'd ever known—was a flat, smoldering mess of death.

Most of the adults got killed or cleared out. The Royal Family legged it up north, and the city was left in the hands of the survivors—mostly kids—who couldn't or *wouldn't* leave.

Until I was twelve, I lived in the Tower of London with my parents, Llyr and Penarddunne, the resident Ravenmasters.

Other than the radiation storms and the occasional drone strikes, we got along okay. The Banters and the Royal Fort Knights were too busy fighting with each other to bother us, and the Scroungers were too superstitious or too scared to try to attack the Tower.

I used to think my parents lived a pointless sort of life, fussing over seven ravens—six jet-black and one ivory-white—

thing else in between is a wasteland of disease, carnage, and cannibalism.

Instead of a country, now it's just dozens of warring factions, all fighting and killing each other in the shadow of the skyscraping arcologies the Wealthies are building up in the ruins. Maybe there never was any real unity. Maybe it was just propaganda or a hoax or a marketing trick.

I didn't grow up here, so maybe I shouldn't talk.

On the other hand, I spent the last five years here, so maybe I should.

Back in London, when I found out the whole terrorist global threat known as the Eastern Order was made up, I cried. I don't know why. I'm not the most emotional girl in the world. I think I was upset because of how dumb I felt for falling for the world's biggest lie.

The governments, the enemies, the need for some people to have all the power while everyone else had to suffer and starve... it was all based on one big load of rubbish. A giant myth. Like the weird, made up stories that gave me my name.

Which I guess makes me a myth *inside* of a myth.

It's crazy how two lies can make each other seem like the truth.

Since learning the facts about the wacko way the world's been run, I've actually felt more complete. Like I have a purpose. Like I'm more than just a character in an old story.

When they left London, Kress and her Conspiracy of friends brought me back to Washington, D.C. with them. My parents insisted. They said Kress would "save" me. They said my future was tied to hers and that the fate of a new nation would one day be in my hands.

Thanks for not putting any pressure on me, Mum and Dad!

From D.C., I joined Kress and her Conspiracy on a cross-

1

FIRST CLASS

"HEY, Branwynne! Are you ready for class?"

Bracing myself in the long hallway against her bonkers bubbliness, I give Libra my best get-away-from-me glare. But she's not fazed. "Come on!" she urges, tugging me by the arm.

Her beaming white smile is happy. Her walnut-brown eyes are happy. Her smooth, unblemished mocha skin is happy. Even her bouncy coils of silky, licorice-black hair are happy.

Ugh.

It's like someone melted down puppies, sunshine, birthdays, and babies into a giant vat and poured the whole mess into the mold of a way-too-pretty teenage girl.

She's so cheery, it's all I can do not to punch her in the throat.

Almost all of us at the Academy have special abilities to one degree or another, although not all of us know our full potential or limitations.

I know about Lucid and Reverie from the other Cohort. They can combine their abilities to open a portal to another dimension called the *Lyfelyte*. I've seen them do it.

In my own Cohort, I've heard Sara can do something

unusual (and possibly dangerous?) with her voice, and Ignacio has some sort of affinity for electricity. I don't know about Arlo or Mattea yet.

Libra's powers seem to include being super annoying, pointlessly cheerful, and totally oblivious to the fact that she's about to get her face bashed in.

Of course, if I didn't want to get my hands dirty, I could always sic Haida Gwaii on her. With one good telempathic request, my sharp-taloned, occasionally over-protective white raven could carve some seriously deep trenches into this giddy kipper's perfect, perky face.

But I doubt that would dampen her enthusiasm.

So I let Libra grab my hand and drag me along down the hall. Not because I'm excited about the first official day of classes at the Emergents Academy. And not because I'm desperate to bond with this chuffed-up, human-shaped chatterbox.

No. What I'm looking forward to is some serious combat training.

And not just *any* combat training.

Our teachers for First Semester Unarmed Combat are Kress and her boyfriend Brohn.

They're the school's power couple, the ones everyone knows about and wants to be like. Brohn is tall and handsome with insanely watery blue eyes that dare you to look at them and then dare you to even *try* to look away. He's got broad shoulders, thick dark hair, just the right amount of stubble on his square jaw, and a rumbling baritone voice that soothes you and snaps you to attention at the same time.

Oh, and he's bulletproof.

And Kress...well, she's a legend.

Sometimes known as *Kakari Isutse,* "the girl who dreams in raven," she has her own super-powered telempathic bond with Render, her personal raven companion since she was six years old. She's probably the most powerful Emergent around. She downplays it, though.

Over the past few days of orientation, I've seen her—with Render perched like a glossy-black gargoyle on her shoulder—walking around all casual, chatting with her friends, making last-minute improvements to the Academy, and tinkering with our class schedules like she's the most normal twenty-three-year-old woman in the world.

That's a laugh.

I've seen her kick ass, dodge bullets, and walk through walls.

(I can walk through walls, too sometimes. She's just way better at it than me.)

She's even been known to fly from time to time. But when I ask her about it, she blushes, calls it "gliding," and changes the subject.

I've been studying with her for the past five years, mostly learning focus, patience, and how to be an expert Ravenmaster with a deeper mental bond with Render, Haida Gwaii, and their brood of six raven offspring. So far, all I've been able to manage from the lessons are vague feelings, blurry images, brain-splitting migraines, and an unfortunate craving for carrion.

When Granden showed up with the six Emergents we left behind in Washington, D.C., Kress and her team of teachers decided it was time to start having proper classes—with schedules, assignments, lectures, seminars, and even homework.

So, altogether, there's Chace and her twin brother Trax, the other set of twins— Lucid and Reverie—the six new arrivals, and me. That makes eleven of us in the first class of the Emergents Academy.

We're all in awe of Kress and her Conspiracy. And why wouldn't we be?

We've heard the stories about how, on the day they turned seventeen, Kress and her friends were recruited away from the

Valta—the bombed-out and annihilated town just down the ridge on this very mountain. How they escaped from the Processor where they were being trained as genetically enhanced super soldiers. How they went on the run.

We know bits and pieces about what happened after that. The work they did to free San Francisco. Their experiences in Chicago where they met War and Mayla, two of our other teachers. Their victory in D.C. when they catapulted that wanker President Krug off a roof. The way they turned themselves into an unstoppable reconnaissance, infiltration, assault, and rescue team.

And I know first-hand about their experiences after that in London, England because that's where I first met them, and it's where I first found out that I'm not the only person in the world who can share minds with a raven.

After returning to the U.S., we rescued a bunch of Kress's kidnapped friends from a Midwest Processor, battled our way past the Army of the Unsettled in a Colorado desert, and escaped from the eerily friendly clutches of the Cult of the Devoted.

All the while, Kress protected me like I'm her baby sister.

As an only child growing up behind the high stone walls of the Tower of London, I always dreamed of having a big sister, someone to mentor me, train me, and show me the ropes. I dreamed of a special place where I could be taught how to discover, enhance, and control my abilities.

Now my dream has come true.

Only it seems to have come with a price: I have to deal with annoying classmates.

Giggling and yakking away, Libra drags me through the open doorway of CSTR-1—the primary Combat Skills and Training Room—the largest of the third-floor training rooms where the other four members of our six-person Cohort are already gathered in a nervous huddle.

The room is clean, well planned-out, and fully stocked. Basically, the opposite of the chaos and violence in the dodgy world outside.

Anxious to get away from Libra—and afraid that her over-the-top cheeriness might be as contagious as the Cyst Plague—I make a beeline to where Kress and Brohn are standing side by side, waiting to start the class.

I greet my adoptive big sister, my fellow raven-whisperer, and my dear friend with a smile and a big wave.

She returns my greeting by leg-sweeping me off my feet and hammering her fist into my sternum on my way down.

Perfect, I think as I try not to black out. *First day of class, and I get body slammed by the teacher.*

After this, the rest of the school year should be a breeze.

2

LESSON

Brohn hooks his hands under my armpits and hauls me to my feet.

He's big and strong, which makes me feel small and weak.

I *hate* that.

I try to shrug him off, but my muscles have decided to ignore my orders and have opted to fall asleep on duty, instead.

I've been in some pretty intense fights before, and I know full well how to handle myself. But right now, my legs have gone wobbly, my eyes have gone wonky, and the room looks like someone slathered it in six layers of Vaseline-coated plastic wrap.

By the time I start to blink the world back into focus, Kress has her back to me and is pacing panther-like in front of the rest of the class. In my throbbing head, her voice sounds like it's coming from the far end of a train tunnel.

"Here's your first lesson: Don't drop your guard. *Ever.*"

Great. Now you tell me.

I look up from where I'm still bent over and trying to catch my breath. The five other kids from my Cohort are standing there wide-eyed while I feel my cheeks go hot and red.

I've known Kress longer than any of them. If anything, I should get special privilege. So it's not fair that they get to stand around and gawk while I take a personal inventory to determine how many of my internal organs are still where they're supposed to be.

I don't know if the room is spinning or if I am, but either way, I *really* wish it would stop. It's bad enough getting the wind knocked out of me. I'd rather not add a round of uncontrollable public vomiting to top it off.

Brohn holds me at arm's length until he seems satisfied I'm not going to spew up my guts all over him. Patting my shoulder, he says, "You're alive. That'll have to be enough for now." Then, turning his back and leaving me wobbling on my own, he walks over to join Kress.

So much for special privilege.

Render flutters over from his perch on a ledge on the far side of the room and lands on Kress's shoulder.

She flicks a treat up to him with her thumb, and he gobbles it down.

The other members of my Cohort—Libra, Sara, Mattea, Arlo, and Ignacio—are standing in a line now, frozen in military attention, as Kress continues to pace.

The eleven of us in the Academy's first class have been divided into two Cohorts, cleverly called "Cohort A" and "Cohort B." Apparently, originality isn't an Emergent ability anyone around here possesses.

I don't know the new girl Roxane from Cohort B, but I know both sets of the twins pretty well. I should have been placed with them. It's my bad luck I get stuck with all these Newbies in Cohort A.

Like me, they're wearing the Academy's standard issue combat kit:

Form-fitting black cruiser pants with gray trim, flexible

fabric joints, and Kevlar inserts. Matching military-style vests. Black field boots. And white, half-sleeved compression tops with the Academy's seal—a black raven on a blue shield with the school's Latin motto, "Corvus Oculum Corvi Non Eruit," on a crest over the heart to complete the school uniform.

I once asked Kress what the motto meant. She told me it translates as, "A raven will not pluck out the eye of another raven."

I thought she was kidding.

She assured me she wasn't.

"In the best and worst of times, we stay united in word, purpose, plan, and soul," she told me. "That's what makes a Conspiracy strong."

I'm not feeling especially united or strong at the moment.

Standing at rigid attention, Libra looks nervously happy. Sara looks bored. Mattea and Ignacio look like brainwashed military recruits. They *all* look terrified.

Slouching in front of Kress, Arlo is sporting the same, grubby gray hoodie he eats and sleeps in. And I've got on my favorite red leather jacket, which I zip up with trembling fingers as I limp over to take my place with my classmates.

"There's a lot of fear out there in the world," Brohn bellows to the six of us with a wave of his hand. "And a lot of desperation. The first step to surviving is knowing and respecting that fact."

"The rules in here will largely be the same as the rules out there," Kress tells us. "*None.*"

Render ruffles his hackles, stares at the six of us with those button-black eyes, and makes a few clacking sounds that I swear sound like laughter.

"There's no room for error in here," Brohn explains. He directs everyone's attention to the areas of the room dedicated to sparring, training, assessment, competitive fighting, and combat skills analysis. There are no mats, no roped-off rings, and no equipment—just a few sections of the room divided into quadrants by strips of pink and white holo-lights embedded at right angles in the floor.

In neat stacks off to the side, only partly concealed by a red, ceiling-high sliding curtain, there are more stretchers and first-aid kits than I've ever seen in my life.

"Some of you might remember being taught things by your parents. Or by friends or by older brothers and sisters. Some of you might have even heard stories about what regular school was like before the wars." Brohn scans our Cohort and crosses his arms hard across his chest. "This isn't that."

"We're not here to train you to survive," Kress adds. "Our mission is much bigger than that."

"We're here," Brohn says evenly, his voice a gentle but powerful rumble, "to teach you how to help *others* to survive. Saving yourselves out there will be easy. When you're in trouble, all you have to do is *run*. Sticking around, saving others...*that's* heroic."

"You're going to save the world," Kress promises. "But first, you need to know how to save yourselves."

"And that starts," Brohn continues, "with alertness, not as something you turn on when you think you might need it..."

...but as your default setting," Kress finishes.

Render tilts his head back to *kraa*! his agreement.

Like a church bell ringing underwater, his guttural voice peals out in blaring, metallic-sounding clangs in the huge room.

Kress and Brohn guide us over to the side of the room where one of the practice spaces has been sectioned off. I don't want to show weakness, so I walk as straight and upright as possible, even though the vibrations from the shot Kress gave me a minute ago are still rattling through my bones.

The back of my head hurts, my lungs haven't decided if

they're going to start working again, and the air in the room is still shifting and hazy.

I've known Kress for over five years now, and I've seen her in action out there in the world—here and in England. I've seen her shred enemies with her razor-sharp Talons, the special gloves she wears with the built-in switchblades. And I've seen her fire all kinds of weapons and break out all kinds of martial arts moves.

But I never knew she could hit quite that hard.

Mattea, the exotic, boyishly thin girl with the dark skin and wide-set eyes, clears her throat and asks if we at least get head-gear and gloves for whatever lessons we're about to learn. "It's how I've seen soldiers training," she explains. "It's what they wore in the Processor." Her voice is crisp and confident.

"Are you going to have headgear and gloves in the field?" Kress asks quietly. "Are you going to raise your hand and ask the wild, cannibalistic kids of the Unsettled to take a time-out while you outfit yourself with proper sparring equipment?"

Mattea tilts her nearly-shaven head down about half an inch. "No."

"Are you going to ask the True Blues to take a break from loading their shotguns while you look for a good place to hide? Or hope the Devoted decide not to brainwash you into their cult?"

Mattea's head drops a bit more. Her eyes dart side to side before settling back onto Kress's boots. "No."

Kress takes two full steps until she's nearly nose-to-nose with Mattea. Even though she's got a dead-serious squint to her eyes, her voice is somehow even quieter than it was before.

"Are you going to ask the Survivalists or the Syndicates to go easy on you since they're organized and armed and you're just a seventeen-year-old girl who's spent most of her life as a helpless lab rat in a Processor?"

Mattea's chin is now fully buried in her chest, her eyes fixed firmly on the floor. "No."

"No," Kress repeats. "Good answer."

Kress goes back to pacing in front of us while Render gives us all terrifying evil eyes and mocking, squelchy clucks from his perch on her shoulder. "We can't afford to have you confuse training with real-life combat. The split-second it takes for you to figure out which is which is the split-second where you wind up with your head on one side of the battlefield, your body on the other, and a great big pool of your blood and a long line of your internal organs in between."

Libra, pouty and clearly a little stunned, raises a shaky hand. Her perky smile isn't quite as bold as it was when she dragged me in here. "So...um...this *training* you're going to give us...it's... um... life or death?"

Kress winks at her. "Libra, if you can't survive the training in here, you can't survive the world out there."

Libra gulps, nods, and takes such a big step back that I think for a second she might bolt for the door.

Brohn gestures us toward the center of the room. I've never seen a person offer up such a charming smile and look so rip-your-head-off deadly at the same time, but he's managing it. "Come on," he tells us with a wicked grin. "Class is in session."

3

KRAV MAGA

FOR THE NEXT SIX HOURS, we fight.

And I'm not talking about little kid Judo class with stops and starts and gentle words of encouragement from a kindhearted sensei.

Kress and Brohn are serious.

Deadly serious.

First, they run us through some of the most basic elements of Jeet Kune Do, Tae Kwon Do, and Muay Thai kickboxing. "Just to give you a taste of what you'll be doing in this class," Kress tells us, "and in some of the follow-up classes over the new few terms."

Then, the two of them launch into a rapid-fire volley of lessons.

Their demonstrations are a whirlwind of control, precision, and power. Gathering us around them, they run us through movement after movement—kicks, punches, grappling techniques, blocks, attacks, and counter-attacks—until we're all doubled over, hands on our knees, gasping for breath.

After what feels like forever and with my lungs scorching hot and dust-dry, I'm sure we've got to be almost done with the lesson.

Class has got to be nearly over, right?

We've been at it for *hours*. But Kress and Brohn plow right along, leaving us with no choice but to dig deep and do our best to keep up.

"Those are some of the basics," Brohn says with smooth calmness and with a dismissive flick of his hand. "Just a preview. But today, we're going to start with Krav Maga."

Wait. Did he say, "Start"? How long have we been at this?

"Krav Maga is a practical, real-world fighting style," Kress explains. "It's designed to give you the skills you'll need to hurt, incapacitate, disarm, and, if necessary, kill an opponent. Speed and lethality will be your goals. Situational awareness will be your friend. Your body will be your weapon. Like with Wing Chun—which you'll learn later—defense is also offense."

Kress and Brohn usher our Cohort into a circle around them.

With the six of us clutching our sides and struggling to stay focused, Kress and Brohn go into a blindingly fast display of hand-to-hand combat that I'm sure is going to end with one or both of them dead in the middle of the room.

With quick punches, impossibly fast knee-strikes, hammer fists, forearm presses, and ferociously applied wrist-locks, they grapple, lunge, and attack each other with the viciousness of a life-or-death situation. And this is just *sparring*.

When they stop, they're not even winded.

These two are working on a whole different level.

As they break us into three pairs for partner training, they toss around terms like "soft tissue," "pressure points," "instant incapaci-tation," and *retzev*—which they tell us means "continuous motion."

"No time to think, pause, or plan," Kress warns. "It takes

about one-tenth of a second for your central nervous system to get a signal from your brain to your muscles. Whether it's throwing a punch, dodging a strike, or pulling a trigger...we need you to cut that time in half."

We all stare, and I know they're waiting for one of us to object, to claim that what she's asking is impossible. But we don't say a word. We don't dare.

They expect us to be tireless, fearless, and to absorb every speck of information they throw at us. It's only the first class of Unarmed Combat, and they're already teaching like our lives depend on it.

After another demonstration, something occurs to me:

They're not just fighters. They're dancers, choreographers, strategists, scientists, athletes, and artists.

I've fought alongside Kress and Brohn before, but I guess I was too busy enjoying the adrenaline rush to realize how much I was missing.

For the past five years, Kress has been trying to teach me to connect with Haida Gwaii, to channel the white raven's natural skills and adopt them as my own. I thought I was doing okay. I thought my evolving coordination, strength, speed, and senses were making me a superhero.

I thought wrong.

After hours of relentless lessons, my head's spinning worse than it was when Kress nearly knocked me out at the beginning of class.

The other members of my Cohort aren't faring any better.

We work with partners for this part of class, but Kress and Brohn bounce from pair to pair, stopping us, telling us what we're doing wrong, and showing us how to do it right.

Their instructions come at us as fast and ferociously as the combat moves, themselves.

Poor Arlo—quiet and shy—gets paired up with Libra and

her constant happy chatter. Even exhausted, she finds a way to blather on about nothing.

Sara and Mattea seem to make a good team and are picking up this style of fighting faster than the rest of us. They're not at Kress and Brohn's level yet. Not by a long shot. But at least they're making a pretty good show of it.

I get paired up with Ignacio.

At well over six feet tall, he towers over me. He's toned and glossy-skinned, and I can make out each bulge, ridge, and ripple of every muscle in his body.

He keeps smiling at me, flexing under his tight white tank top, and giving me little winks like he thinks I'll be distracted by his dishy good looks.

Let's see how pretty that face of yours is after I'm done with it.

I'm fast but undisciplined. At least that's what Kress always tells me.

In the center of one of the lighted sparring squares, I do my best to stay focused in my Krav Maga battle with Ignacio. I'm able to tag him with some pretty good body shots, but when he charges at me, I panic myself into a purely defensive posture, which I know I'm not supposed to do. He catches me with a forearm to the side of my head, and I drop to a knee.

He adds insult to injury with another sassy smile and another smarmy wink as he reaches out a hand, with a glimmer in his golden-amber eyes, and offers to help me up.

Bloody hell, he's cute.

Okay. Maybe I was a *little* distracted.

I smack his hand away, and we go at it again. I'm faster than he is, but he's doing something that makes my muscles twitch in a weird way from tense to relaxed and back again. For a second, it feels like I might be having a heart attack.

I know he's an Emergent, of course. And I've heard he can do something weird with electrical impulses. I wonder if he's doing something cheeky to my central nervous system right now.

The thought of him screwing around in my head makes me mad.

You can beat my body. But no one mucks around with my brain!

Technically, we're not really supposed to be using our Emergent abilities in class, not until we get more training in how to use them without accidentally killing anyone, including our teachers or ourselves. But since our abilities are a part of us, it's next to impossible *not* to access them from time to time.

Especially in times of pain or stress. Which this is.

Whether he's cheating or not, Ignacio gets me on the ground and winds up on top of me with my arms and shoulders pinned under his knees.

"Looks like I win," he gloats, one hand curled over my throat, the other balled into a ready-to-strike, cocked fist by his shoulder.

I take a second to point out that the blood on his face and pooling around on the floor next to us is his, not mine.

When he presses his fingers to the corner of his lip and inspects them for blood, I take quick advantage of the distraction, buck my hips up, and give him a thunderous knee to the goolies.

Groaning in pain, he rolls to the side, and I scramble to my feet, fully prepared to kick his face into a pasty dough.

But I'm stopped by Brohn who tells me, "Nice job, Branwynne. You can chalk this one up as a kill."

I grin and reach out a hand to help Ignacio to his feet, but he snarls at me and grunts himself up, his eyes still crossed from my shot to the pills.

With all of us now breathing hard and begging for water, Kress and Brohn drag the six of us into a ring surrounded by a glowing border of pink holo-lights. They tell us we can have a break as soon as we force them out of the circle.

"One at a time?" Sara pants, her short blond hair dark with sweat and matted to her forehead. Her chest is heaving, and her cheeks are cherry-apple red. Like me, she's trying to conceal her fatigue, but she can barely get her words out.

"One at a time," Kress grins, "or as a team. We don't care."

So we leap at them—all six of us—and are knocked back just as fast.

Sara and Mattea are both taller than me and pretty strong but with no real combat experience. Kress has them doubled over and teary-eyed before they know what's hit them.

Oddly, Arlo barely puts up a fight. With his head down and his eyes unfocused under his sweat-soaked hoodie, he throws a couple of weak, telegraphed punches that wouldn't bruise a butterfly. He reaches for Kress's wrist, but she slips away while back-kicking Libra halfway across the room at the same time.

Turning, Arlo makes a half-hearted lunge at Brohn. Brohn rewards him for his gentle restraint with a sharp fist to the ribcage and an almost simultaneous elbow strike to the temple. I'm pretty sure Arlo's unconscious before he hits the floor.

Even Ignacio, who's nearly as big as Brohn, is embarrassingly out of his league. A fist-swinging flurry in Kress's direction ends with him flying across the room and sliding to a crashing stop in a helpless tangle of limbs against the wall.

Kress and Brohn are Emergents, like us. Like us, they have certain abilities. *Unlike* us, they know how to use them.

Of the six of us in this class, I think I'm the only one who's been in actual, life-or-death combat before.

My real-world experience plus my work with Kress has given me a confidence the others don't have. That gives me an edge.

Brohn, though, looks determined to dull that edge.

Grinning, I dance around and slip away from his attack before launching one of my own.

Already congratulating myself in my mind, I strike with blazing speed at all his pressure points: throat, bridge of the nose, floating ribs, instep, solar plexus. Hoping to replicate my success against Ignacio, I even take a shot at his groin.

He's not happy about that, and he lets me know it with a spinning back fist I never saw coming.

You can be big, you can be strong, or you can be fast. It's not fair that Brohn gets to be all three.

And bulletproof on top of it all, I remind myself. *Totally not fair.*

For the second time today, I wind up gasping for breath on the floor.

The fact that I'm the last of my six-person Cohort to get pummeled to the ground isn't much comfort.

"That'll do for today," Kress tells us. "You can head to the Infirmary to get fixed up. War and Mayla will meet you there. Then, get yourselves to the Tavern. Cohort B will be there soon, and you can all eat together." Without waiting for a response, she and Brohn stride out of the room. At the door, Kress turns back to her gasping, bruised, and bloodied students. "Get some rest. You've got an hour until your next class."

She's not even breathing hard.

Great. It's the first day, and I get the stuffing beaten out of me. Twice. If this is a sign of what's to come, I might not just be one of the Academy's first students. I might also be its first to leave in a body bag instead of in a graduation gown.

4

INFIRMARY

AFTER THE BRUTAL humiliation of Unarmed Combat Class, my Cohort limps downstairs to the Infirmary where War and Mayla are all set up to attend to our assorted wounds and injuries.

The large room and the smaller lab and tech rooms connected to it are bathed in pure white light from banks of holo-panels embedded in the walls. Every surface—from ceiling to floor and from wall to wall—is cold, sterile, and completely uninviting.

With all the flat white light, there aren't even any shadows.

I think alarms might go off if so much as a speck of dust found its way in here.

In the middle of the room, War and Mayla are dressed in matching powder blue scrubs with clear surgical shields covering their faces and transparent nitrile examination gloves on their hands.

Mayla's long, dreadlocked hair is threaded through with a colorful array of beads, clips, and ribbons.

War, all four hundred pounds of him, is glistening with a light sheen of sweat and is glittering next to Mayla, his hands on his hips like someone carved him out of a giant block of ice.

Considering his size, I'm wondering how they managed to rustle up a pair of scrubs big enough to fit him.

Maybe they used some of the extra bed sheets?

Our two teachers—and for now, our nurses—look fresh and clean...unlike the bin of bloody clothes, towels, bandages, and gauze sitting over in the corner.

Gruesome and sticky-looking, it's the only thing out of place in this otherwise completely hygienic room.

Well, the bin and *us*.

Our clothes are a Rorschach test of rips, sweat, scuff marks, and blood. We look like we've been dragged through Hell by our tongues.

"You just missed the other Cohort," War tells us, flipping the lid closed on the bloody bin and scanning us up and down. "If it makes you feel any better, I think they got it even worse than the six of you."

"Don't listen to him," Mayla laughs. "Terk just ran them through their first class of Demolitions and Explosives in the Weapons Lab. No big deal."

"Sure," War chuckles. "Just a few flash burns, jangled nerves, and some temporary hearing loss. And I'm sure Trax's eyebrows'll grow back in a few weeks."

Mayla gives him a playful smack on his bulging inner-tube of an arm. "Don't scare the kids."

Grinning, War taps his wrist-mounted holo-scanner to life. He invites us to have a seat on the row of hovering examination tables lined up in the middle of the room under a bank of tendril-like sensors hanging down from the ceiling. "Now...let's see how the six of you fared. You lived through the first day, so that's something, eh?"

"Only two broken ribs," Mayla tells Ignacio as she applies a liquid-blue gel wrap around his midsection.

"It's two more than I had this morning," he groans, wincing

as he pulls his blood and sweat-soaked tank-top back down.

"You've still got twenty-two good ones left," Mayla grins. "If I were you, I'd start protecting them a little better."

"It's just going to get tougher from here, kids," War warns us. "We didn't set up the Academy to kill you. Just to give you a sneak peek at what death might look like if you're not one-hundred percent prepared for it."

Sara cringes as Mayla circles around behind her, prodding her neck and back, looking for damage.

"Don't worry," Mayla tells her, "death is still a long way away. And the good news, while you're waiting for it, is that you've only got one bruise."

"And the bad news?"

"It covers pretty much your entire back. And your shoulders. And some nice spots here on the backs of your arms." Sara gives Mayla a dirty look, but Mayla doesn't seem to notice. Instead, she hands Sara an icepack-vest and pats her knee. "Don't worry, kid. Black and blue suits you."

War runs his huge hands over my shoulders and down my arms as Mayla slips over to the table next to mine to treat a gash running the length of Libra's forearm. She tosses a silver penlight to War and tells him to check my pupils for dilation.

Swinging around in front of me, he shines the penlight into my eyes.

Frowning, he calls over to Mayla. "She doesn't have any."

"No dilation?"

"No pupils."

"Oh, right."

I can feel the others looking at me. It's no secret that my eyes are...unusual. It's not like I can hide that fact.

But I forget sometimes that my eyes don't look like other people's.

While Ignacio has his amber golds, Mattea has her murky

browns, Arlo has his emerald greens, and Sara has her baby blues, my eyes—even the parts that are supposed to be white—are outer-space black with pinprick specks and atomically thin swirls of silvery light shifting around in tiny, dancing galaxies.

I'm not self-conscious about my eyes. Never have been. After all, I'm the one person in the world who can't see them. But being reminded that they're one—or rather *two*—of a kind isn't something I've learned to take pride in just yet.

"Trust me," I say, squinting and swatting away War's brick-sized hand. "I can see just fine."

"It's not only about your vision," he explains. "We need to check for concussions as well."

"I'm *fine*," I assure him, hopping off the table, sliding my hair into a ponytail, and slipping back into my red leather jacket.

I drop my head down so he can't see me cringe at the bursts of pain running through my body.

Leaning in to scan Arlo, Mayla says, "Hmmm" loud enough for all of us to hear.

"What is it?" Mattea asks, stepping over and hovering above him like a protective mother hen.

"His cuts. His bruises."

"What about them?"

"They're already healed," Mayla says, half to herself. "Kind of."

"What's that mean?" Mattea leans in close to see what Mayla is talking about. She says, "Oh" and takes a step back.

That piques my curiosity, and I inch over for a closer look. "What is it?"

With Mattea already stationed by his side, Arlo is sitting quietly hunched over, surrounded now by Libra, Sara, and Ignacio, who have all clambered over to join me in a huddle around his lab table.

Absently fiddling with his hoodie that's draped over his lap and with his chin tucked into his chest, Arlo doesn't seem to notice or care that we're gathered around him, leaning in with wide eyes and inspecting him like he's a specimen in a zoo.

"Weird," Sara mutters, and I have to agree.

Thanks to Kress's training and my growing ability to channel Haida Gwaii's metabolism, my injuries are already healing. Arlo's are, too. Only not the same way.

It's been less than twenty minutes since class let out, but my cuts and bruises are fading. His seem to be growing thicker and more permanent right in front of our eyes.

On anyone else, the long cut on his cheek would normally start healing by itself after a few days. On Arlo, it's darkening and closing up, rising up into a thick, rubbery ridge.

As we stand there gawking, the bruises on his shoulders and upper arms turn *more* purple, not less.

Mayla excuses herself and steps over to where War is checking a scrolling holo-display of rising and falling graphs for any major anomalies in our vital signs. Her voice isn't loud or clear, but I hear it all the same from across the room.

"It's advancing faster than we thought. We better report this to Wisp and Granden."

War glances over at Arlo before turning back to Mayla and nodding his agreement. "I think they're in Wisp's office upstairs."

"Okay. We'll go up. But let's get these six heroes off to the Tavern first."

Mayla plops six stacks of clean Academy uniforms on one of the examination tables and tells us we can change in the Infirmary annex rooms before heading down to the Tavern.

The clean, dry clothes feel nice against my skin, although they don't do much to alleviate the muscle cramps or the aches and pains throbbing through my body.

Back in the Infirmary's main examination room, War and Mayla take a few final minutes to fuss over us. They advise us about getting enough rest, changing our assorted bandages, using the antibacterial spray they give us, and they request that we try not to get quite so beaten up next time.

"We'll do better," I tell them on behalf of my Cohort. "Easy-peasy."

Once we're as bandaged up as good as we're going to get, War and Mayla head upstairs, while my fellow students and I limp our way downstairs to the Tavern.

Mattea makes it a point to walk next to Arlo, her long, thin arms at the ready in case he stumbles or something.

But Arlo doesn't seem weak or shaky. Maybe just a little sad.

His face is back to being hidden under his gray hood, but every few steps, I catch a glimpse of the furrow of scars and the patchwork of dark bruises lining his face and neck.

He can heal, but his injuries just look worse? What kind of Emergent ability is that? And why do I get the feeling that the damage runs deeper than the surface of his skin?

5

TAVERN

BACK TO BOUNCY, Libra leads the way into the Tavern, skipping like a little girl into the huge room of low-hanging lights and walls of brightly polished cherry wood.

The rectangular lunch tables are set up in orderly rows with slatted, leather-cushioned cherry wood chairs and matching benches tucked under them.

When we enter the paneled, high-ceilinged room, Roxane is already there with Chace, Trax, Lucid, and Reverie.

Together, they make up Cohort B.

Like us, they're wearing the Academy uniform, only their compression tops are cobalt blue instead of white.

The two sets of twins and I have been here for five years now, but I barely recognize Lucid and Reverie at the moment. Their normally jet-black hair is crusted and drab. Their usually pale white faces are streaked with ash and singed with patches of angry red flashburns.

The other twins—Chace and Trax—look like they've aged ten years since this morning.

War wasn't kidding about Trax. That boy really did lose his eyebrows.

Demolitions and Explosives class must've been a shambolic shite-fest.

And I get to take it next term. Great.

Completely ignoring the sparse meal on the plate in front of her, Chace is hunched over, writing and drawing on the holo-pad projected in the air in front of her. Trax, being deliberately annoying, keeps leaning over her shoulder and asking, "What's that? What's that?"

"They're drawings," she tells him, shoving him away with one hand while she continues her flurry of creative activity with the other.

We call Chace the Chronicler. She says she's drawing pictures and keeping detailed notes about what we do. "So there'll be a historical record for when we save the world," she constantly reminds us.

Lucid and Reverie are sitting next to each other at the far end of the bench seat, eating in silence. Even after five years, I still don't know them all that well. I don't really want to, either. But Kress tells me I have to. "They'll be the key to helping you reach the next stage in your evolution."

That's the problem with evolution: It just keeps going, so you never get a chance to rest or to rejoice at reaching the end.

Sitting on the far end of the table, Roxane is part of the new arrivals, too. She's pink-skinned and shy, her white hair always hanging down over one part of her face or another. As far as I know she hasn't said a word since they got here.

For the past few days, she and the other new kids spent most of their time in one of the fourth-floor Med-Labs, being taken care of by Wisp and the others and recovering from whatever they went through to get here.

I haven't gotten the full story yet.

All I know is that Granden got them here and that he says they're important to the Academy's mission.

With the eleven of us from the two Cohorts seated together at a single long table in the middle of the room, we eat in mostly silent exhaustion.

Granden and Kella are sitting across from each other at one of the tall bistro tables on the far side of the room.

They finish eating just as we're all settling in. Standing up and walking hand in hand, they give us polite nods on their way to the door where they disappear into the corridor.

I'm not surprised that Kress and Brohn didn't follow us down. They almost always skip meals. Instead, they spend their down time exercising in the gym, doing research in the bio-tech labs on the fourth floor, or battling realistic enemies in one of the high-tech VR-sims.

I don't know if they're in competition with us or with each other, but—as they so clearly demonstrated in today's class—they work, train, and teach like their lives depend on it.

Or, maybe, like *our* lives depend on it.

Wisp, our school's dean, spends almost all her time in her office in the Administration Wing. I think she sleeps there.

She's small, thin-boned, and frail-looking. She's also as driven and determined as anyone I've ever met, and I know from sharing time in battle with her that she's tougher than she looks.

Our other two teachers, Rain and Terk, spend most of their time up in the Communications Hub on the top floor of the school.

As a Modified, Terk has an integrated computer system called "The Auditor" fused into his neural network. The three of them—Rain, Terk, and the disembodied voice of the Auditor—handle almost all of the tech issues in the Academy.

With all of our teachers off doing their own thing, that leaves us, the two Cohorts, eating alone in the large cafeteria we call the Tavern.

Other than the occasional grunts and groans, we eat in

silence. Except for Libra, that is. Despite a cut lip, a shredded forearm, and a swollen jaw, she manages to waffle on about how great it is to be here and about how excited she is to get to learn so many new things.

I give her a glare that she returns with a smile and a happy, one-armed hug, which I shrug off.

I don't do touchy-feely.

She's lucky looks can't really kill or else she'd be nothing more than a chalk outline on the floor right now.

As a little girl in the Tower of London, I used to fantasize about going to a proper school. Now that I'm in one, it's not exactly how I imagined. It turns out, being around this many people all day, every day, is harder than I expected and possibly more than I can handle.

On the other hand, take away the classmates and the pain of getting beaten up by our teachers, and I guess it's not all that bad.

6

BROUHAHA

AFTER LUNCH, we make our way upstairs to the Dormitory.

The fifth floor of the Academy is divided into a dozen separate, round rooms, each with six beds set up in a semi-circle, with an island of six rattan armchairs. two plush loungers, and a glass and chrome coffee table in the middle.

The Dorms take up the entire floor and spoke out around the Lounge and a hub of common bathrooms and shower rooms.

A ring of windows in an interior balcony lets us look all the way down to the first-floor Atrium far below or up to the bank of snow-covered skylights two floors up.

Right now, twenty of the Dorm Rooms are empty—Kress says the goal is to fill them with more students like us. The other two round rooms are occupied by our two Cohorts with one group assigned to each room.

For now, though, we all cluster into the Lounge, the huge central rec room—filled with games, activities, and comfortable furniture—with doors leading out to each of the ten Dorm Rooms.

We're barely through the sliding silver door from our own

Dorm when Libra leaps onto a couch, bouncing herself onto her knees.

I wonder how perfect her smile would be if someone knocked out a couple of her teeth.

Sara collapses back into a reclining leather chair, her arm slung over her eyes. "Libra, how can you possibly still have so much energy?"

"Are you kidding?" Libra gushes. "Today was great!"

"Getting beaten up for six hours straight...*that's* your definition of 'great'?"

"But think about how much we learned!" She makes a dramatic show of throwing air punches at invisible enemies.

Dropping gingerly onto a four-footed, linen-covered ottoman, Ignacio pokes at his ribs and winces. "I learned that Kress's knuckles are made of synth-steel."

Holding a pack of ice to her badly swollen cheek, Mattea moans her agreement. "Be glad. They went easy on you. I can't feel anything below my hairline."

"How about you, Arlo?" Libra calls out from across the room.

"How about me, what?"

"Back me up. That was great, right?"

Arlo seems to sink even deeper under his dark hood. "Sometimes...I miss pain."

"What?"

Arlo answers Libra by curling up on his side with his back to us.

Sitting cross-legged on one of the four soft, orange-cushioned chairs in the middle of the room, Roxane flips her ivory-white hair back and giggles.

Grunting as he tries to work out a cramp in his leg, Ignacio asks her what's so funny.

"Pain."

"Pain?"

Roxane stands up and walks over to stand right in front of him. He sneers and glances over at me before turning back to look into the pale blue eyes of the small, blank-faced girl in front of him.

"Suffer," she says. It sounds like a command.

"Is that a threat?" Ignacio hisses through clamped teeth.

Roxane presses a fingertip to his chest but doesn't say anything.

Offering up an uncomfortable laugh, Ignacio smacks her hand away.

"Die," she says. This time, she presses the palm of her hand to his forehead and pushes his head back, *hard*.

Furious, Ignacio bounds to his feet and shoves Roxane with both hands, sending her dainty-limbed body sprawling backwards, arse over elbow.

Small and waif-like, she crashes through a pair of armchairs before stumbling and collapsing to all fours on the floor. Peering out from behind her platinum hair, she stares blankly for a second through empty, emotionless eyes as Libra and Mattea leap to their feet and jump in between her and Ignacio.

"Hey!" Mattea shrieks at him. "What'd you do that for?"

Ignacio puts his hands up, palms out. "You saw what she did. She's crazy."

"She *did* start it," Sara offers from the reclining chair where she's stretched back with her fingers laced behind her head and doing an excellent job of looking completely bored.

"And I finished it," Ignacio snaps at Libra and Mattea. "Any questions?"

The two girls in front of him pause and exchange a look before retreating, with Mattea muttering, "What a jackass" as they go.

Trax is over on one of the thick, high-backed loungers, his eyes wide as he takes in the scene.

Chace is sitting on the floor at his feet where she's been scrawling away with her holo-stylus on the shimmering pad of yellow-white light hovering above her wrist. Now, she's open-mouthed and wide-eyed.

Ignacio throws Chace a sinister glare and flicks his thumb toward Roxane. "Be sure your little historical record there shows that we've got a psycho among us."

Standing side by side and still as stone against the wall, Lucid and Reverie watch it all, their dark eyes flashing back and forth across the room. I can't tell if they're scared, pleased, or if they're just comparing telepathic notes about the sudden burst of violent drama.

As for me, I'm watching everything too, only I'm sort of amused.

The two sets of twins and I have been living here for five years. I got used to that. If the six new kids want to kill each other and return things to how they were, who am I to stop them?

Trax pushes himself up from his seat and walks over to where Roxane is still sitting in a crouch on the floor. He offers her a hand, which she accepts, and he lifts her to her feet.

"We better get to our room," Trax announces. "We don't have a lot of time before our afternoon class."

His sister flicks off her holo-pad and nods.

Gathering up Lucid and Reverie from their stoic posts against the wall, Trax ushers their Cohort through the doorway and into the adjacent Dorm.

Watching them go, Ignacio scowls and cracks his knuckles, staring daggers at the back of Roxane's head as she disappears into the next room.

With Cohort B off in their own room, Libra, Sara, Mattea, Arlo, Ignacio, and I head in the opposite direction toward ours.

We sit down on our beds or in the rattan armchairs, but I can tell we're all too wound up to even *think* about resting before our next class.

"Well, that was quite the argy-bargy," I say.

Ignacio scowls in my direction. "The what?"

"You know. A go Have at arms. A punch up. A corking row."

"A corking what?"

"A brouhaha. A fight. Does anyone speak English in this country?"

He stares at me for a second. I'm guessing he's trying to figure out if I'm psychotic, sarcastic, or on his side.

"You should've gone ahead and killed that psycho," Sara tells him.

He glares at her before his gaze softens and his fists unclench. "Roxane may be a first-rate, top of the line lunatic, but I'm not killing anyone."

"You heard what Kress and Brohn said about the world out there," Sara shrugs. "I think we're going to be doing a lot of killing before this is over."

"We're supposed to be *saving* the world," Libra reminds us all from her bed, which is adjacent to mine. "We're not killers. Especially not of each other."

"Speak for yourself," Sara growls.

I hate admitting I'm curious, but I ask Libra, "How'd you all get here, anyway? I never did get the whole story."

"You mean how did we get here from D.C.?"

"Yeah."

"Our truck," Sara yawns, crossing her legs and tucking herself deeper into her chair. "You saw it."

"I saw what was *left* of that wonky clunker."

"It got us here," Libra says. "That and Granden. The GPS conked out after about two or three days, so we didn't really know where we were going after a while. Mattea was able to get us on track—"

"And stop anyone we came across from killing us," Ignacio adds.

I swing around to face Mattea.

I don't really know any of these new kids that well. I can tell she wants to brag, but her eyes drop, and she just offers up a modest shrug.

"Mattea is a communicator," Libra explains with far too much squealy enthusiasm for my taste.

"A communicator?"

"She can speak any language, practically instantly."

"You mean like English, French, Spanish...?"

"Not just *that* kind of language," Mattea says under her breath.

I swing around to face her. With our six beds set up in a semi-circle around the perimeter of the room like this, it's easy to see each other. "What other sort of language is there?"

From her chair, Sara rolls her eyes like she can't believe how stupid I am. "She speaks literal languages. But also figurative language, body language, colloquialisms, jargon, slang, regional dialects...you name it."

"She can read between the lines," Libra explains. "Intentions, desires, threats...all the stuff behind the words."

Sara gives an exaggerated yawn, arms spread wide and everything. "Sounds pretty useless in a scrum."

"It is," Mattea whispers.

"But boy, does it come in handy for talking our way out of trouble!" Libra gushes.

I look over to Ignacio for confirmation, and he offers up a reluctant nod. "It's true. She talked us all the way here."

"I like how *you* talk," Mattea says to me. "You've got strength and fear. A little bit of queen. A little bit of commoner. There's a balance to you—an eyeful of talent and an easy-peasy way of being in the world—I don't think you even see."

Her voice sounds oddly familiar, and then I realize, it's *my* voice.

"Wait! Are you mocking me?"

"No."

"Good. Don't. And how come you sound like me?"

"I'm imitating you."

"Well, don't do that, either."

"Sorry."

"What are you apologizing to *her* for?" Ignacio sneers. "You can talk however you want."

"She's not mocking you," Libra assures me.

"It's true. I wasn't mocking," Mattea pleads. "I sometimes can't control it."

"Can't control how you talk?" I ask.

"The accents, the imitations...they just...happen."

"Well," Arlo says. "That's why we're here, right? To learn how to control our abilities."

Sara sits up straight. I think she's going to respond to Arlo, but she swings around to face me instead, her unblinking eyes on mine. "Hey, Branwynne. Speaking of abilities, where's that dumb pigeon of yours?"

"Her name's Haida Gwaii. She's a raven. And she's a damn sight smarter than you."

She rolls her eyes so hard I think they might leap from their sockets and make a run for the door. "Fine. Where's that super genius dumb pigeon of yours?"

I glare at her, but she just grins back at me, which makes me want to leap over and pound her to a bloody pulp.

Instead, I remember my training and take a breath. "She prefers to stay outside most of the time."

"Do you two communicate like Kress and Render?"

Nodding, I tell her, "Yes. But I'm not as good at it. *Yet*."

Arlo clears his throat. "I heard you can walk through walls."

I hold up my fingers in a "V" and tell him, "Twice."

He says, "Marvie" and starts to ask me what that was like, but Sara seems intent on getting me miffed up. Leaning in, she jumps back into her interrogation, her eyes sparkling, her voice laced with acid.

"I heard you've got superhuman reflexes," she scoffs.

"Mm-hm."

"Enhanced coordination?"

"That, too."

"And some pretty deadly strength."

"Yep."

"I'd like to see that."

"Keep talking. Maybe someday you will."

I head to the doorway leading to one of the communal bathrooms, making sure to give that trollopy slag Sara a nice, hearty flip of my middle finger on my way out.

7

WAR

OTHER THAN THE middle of the night when we're asleep, our two-hour, midday break is the only real unsupervised time we have to ourselves.

For that all-too brief window, we're free to rest, recover, study, relax with a holo-text in the Reading Nook, or hang out in the Movie Room.

If we want, we can even leg it back down to the Tavern for a snack.

One thing we're *not* allowed to do is leave the Academy.

"*Ever*," Wisp stressed to all of us at Orientation two days ago.

When I raised my hand in the Auditorium and reminded her that, unlike the six newcomers who just joined us and the two sets of twins who spent most of their lives in captivity in techno-genetic military Processors, *I'd* already fought and survived in the "Divided States of America," she stared at me for a long time. Long enough for me to gulp and find something else to look at.

"This isn't a comic book," she said, her voice cotton ball soft, her eyes on mine before scanning the ten other teenagers making up the Academy's entire student body. "The dangers out there are real. The fact that you've seen them first-hand, Bran-wynne, should be enough for you to understand why we need to stay secluded. For now, at least. Out there, good guys don't always win, and bad guys don't always lose. The ones who died to overthrow Krug might be nothing more to you than faceless names in a story. For *us*," she finished, tilting her head toward Kress and her Conspiracy seated on the stage behind her, "they were friends."

So, I dropped my hand, shut my mouth, and sulked all the way up to my Dorm Room where I buried my face in my pillow and vowed to toughen up.

Now, two days later, battered and beaten from my morning class, I spend my two-hour break lying in bed, my arm draped over my eyes, as Libra chatters with Ignacio and Sara, Arlo naps, and Mattea sits and reads a holo-book, her back pressed against the side of Arlo's bed.

At 2 PM, the blue and white lights flash to signal the start of afternoon classes. Cohort B mumbles their goodbyes to us before heading out to their Drone ID, Detection, & Avoidance class.

I'm a little jealous. Growing up in London, I got to see the drones and their attacks up close and personal, and I always wanted to know how to kill them.

And now Cohort B gets to learn exactly that.

I know I'll have the same class soon—maybe even next term —but I *really* want to do it now.

Instead, I head off to my own Cohort's afternoon class: Transportation and Mechanics.

Along the way, I grumble to myself inside my head.

What's the point of learning transportation if we're not allowed to go anywhere?

I wind up in the front of our procession with the other five members of my Cohort padding along behind me. We walk all the way down to the Sub-Basement, through the dark corridor with the weak wall lights, past the monstrous banks of humming mag-generators, and into the cavernous, domed maintenance room and vehicle storage hangar.

The class is taught by War. As the oldest of our teachers—and by far the biggest—he commands total respect and a fair amount of distance. While most of us feel comfortable asking our other teachers questions and even joking around with them from time to time, we all turn into mice in the presence of War. Even Libra keeps a pretty tight seal on her incessantly flapping lips.

Only Ignacio seems unafraid of him.

When War, standing over the husk of a disemboweled mag-jeep, tells us about the problems with arc-dynamos and integrated solar cells, it's Ignacio who thrusts his hand in the air to challenge him.

"According to my research," Ignacio boasts, clearly quoting something he probably read five minutes before we came down here, "the degeneration rate of the solar cells spikes in the presence of the exact radiation levels measured in the drone strikes."

I have to give War credit. He's twice Ignacio's size and could probably rip his head off and floss his teeth with his spine if he wanted. But he pauses and treats Ignacio's challenge like it's the most reasonable thing in the world.

"That's under laboratory conditions," War explains through what's slowly morphing into a menacing frown. "You're not here to learn how things work in the lab. You're here to learn how things work—or don't work—out *there*." He takes a breath, his boulder-sized shoulders and inflated chest rising and falling as he reins himself in. "The solar cells you're talking about are always compromised by environmental conditions, age, wear-and-tear, irradiated dust and sand, airborne particulate matter, and a host of other problems you won't find in any research center. And the drones you're talking about are mostly second-generation Demolition Drones. The ones *I'm* talking about—the ones that'll kill you—are the newest generation of Assault Drones. Two totally different animals. If you're not convinced, I can always take you to Chicago where I grew up, and you can visit the tens of thousands of burned bodies stacked up in nice, crispy piles along what's left of the river. At one time, I fought for, with, or against a lot of them....before they were just bodies, that is."

Ignacio's mouth opens like he's planning to launch a counterargument, but he seems to think better of it and takes a half-step back.

"If there are no other...*questions*," War says with a resonant rumble I can feel rippling on my skin, "let's get down to business."

According to our syllabus, we're down here in the Sub-Basement for a lesson in how to cannibalize parts from one vehicle for use in another.

War leads us over to a second battered military jeep and a line of tables filled with an assortment of scavenged auto parts. After lining us up and ensuring we're paying attention, he calls up a holo-display outlining our tasks.

The long list of lessons floats in a glowing block of text and graphics next to him.

"Transportation is limited out there," War reminds us. "It used to be there were mag-cars rolling off assembly lines faster than people could buy them. When the economy collapsed, no one bought. With no one buying, no one was building. Supply chains got cut off. Auto plants and parts factories got blown up in the drone wars. And make no mistake. They weren't *accidental* casualties of war. They were part of an entire infrastructure that got deliberately targeted to keep us poor, scared, and too ignorant and afraid to fight back. Not that we knew who or what to fight back *against*. Our fear left us with nothing. But see...that's the thing—that'll be the foundation for every lesson you learn in this class."

He holds up a bundle of frayed wires that look like the stems of badly wilted flowers in his massive fist. He slips the bottom end of four of the wires into a housing in the base of a small black box and presses a button on its side. A holographic gauge materializes in the air with a weak indicator light showing a flicker of power. The wilted wires quiver and pulse with a hesitant but visible glow.

Libra's mouth hangs open. "You got power out of nothing."

War shakes his head. "There's no such thing as 'nothing.' There's always *something* to salvage. It might be hope. It might be luck. It might be a bouquet of dead plasma leads. The point is, don't give up. Just because something *looks* dead doesn't mean it is."

The next six hours are filled with War timing us, running us through drills, quizzing us on the names and uses of a wide range of auto parts, barking orders, hurling assignments, and whipping tools at us when we mess up.

When we're too slow or when we puncture a patch or get ham-handed and break a seal, we get yelled at.

Surprisingly, Libra is the only one of us who really excels. She gets pretty much everything right.

That doesn't stop War from growling at her, too, from time to time.

Ignacio leaps to Libra's defense, asking War why he's being so mean to her when she keeps getting the lessons right.

War towers over Ignacio, who stands rigid, his eyes fixed on the middle of War's chest.

"Getting it right's not good enough, kid," War growls down at Ignacio. He whips around to loom over Libra whose proud smile drops in time with her slumping shoulders. "While you're busy being happy with yourself because you managed to re-route that circuit," he thunders at her, pointing toward the wall at the far end of the room, "a convoy of the Unsettled just clicked on a Systems Diode Dampener, undid your work, and shot you in the face!"

I'm two workstations down, but I can hear Libra gulp from here.

"You can't give your full focus to the task at hand," War bellows. "You have to fix the problem *and* protect yourself at the same time!"

His bald head glistening with sweat and with his face twisted into an angry knot, he storms over to where Sara is buried torso-deep under the hood of a skeletal, stripped-down military lorry.

Once he's out of earshot, Libra comes over to my workstation and pokes me with her elbow. "This is almost as much fun as combat class was this morning."

I know I'm supposed to hate her—after all, she's a first-order plonker. But I clamp my hands over my mouth to stifle a giggle. Not because I'm afraid War might yell at me, but more because I don't want Libra to think I'm encouraging her brain-frothing nuttery.

She leans over the systems-generator I'm working on and asks if I want a hand.

I tell her, "No," but she plunges in like I've offered her an engraved invitation.

Fiddling with the acid-encrusted power pack on the work-table, Libra's eyes flit over in War's direction. "You really fought next to him?"

"Uh huh."

"And you survived?"

I stare at Libra for a second before letting my eyes roll in a looping, sarcastic arc.

"Oh. Right. Of course you did," she whispers with a self-correcting moan. "Sorry. But he makes me nervous."

"Who—War?"

"He's twice the size of anyone I've ever met. Bigger than Terk, even."

"He's got a few soft spots," I whisper back.

"War? Really?"

"He once cried when he lost his pet vulture."

Libra stops, her hands frozen in the air over the bundle of green and white wires spilling over the top of the micro-fuse port of the systems-generator. "You're kidding."

"Nope."

"Vulture?"

"Its name was Jeff. I never met him, but I hear he and War were as close as a person and a bird could be."

"Kind of like you and Haida Gwaii?"

"Well, War's a Typic. So he didn't have the same sort of connection Haida and I have. But Jeff was definitely more than a pet to him."

"Speaking of pets, have you caught how Mattea's been fussing over Arlo like he's a wounded puppy?"

I'm about to say, "Yes," but then I decide I'd rather not get sucked into any of Libra's blathery gossip. "We'd better get back to this," I tell her. "War might have had a soft spot for Jeff, but I'm pretty sure that's where his sympathy ends. And I'd rather not be the first person to get knocked out in two classes in a row."

"Don't worry about it," Libra says, directing my attention to the generator, now tidy and humming with life on our workstation. "It's fixed."

"How—?"

Libra shrugs. "Haida's more than a pet to you. Mechanical systems are more than just a collection of random parts to me."

Libra may be annoying and a gossip, but she might also be a good person to have as a lab partner in Transportation and Mechanics.

Not a friend, I remind myself. *Just a convenient classmate to have sharing my workstation. And if her talent helps me get a decent mark and stay on War's good side, so be it.*

After another few hours of taking things apart and putting them back together—all under the furious gaze of War and his relentless, angry barking—I'm starting to miss being out in the world and fighting for my life.

8

CHALLENGE

AFTER TRANSPORTATION and Mechanics lets out, my Cohort and I, under a chorus of complaints, slog our way through a very groggy dinner before plodding back upstairs to the Dorm.

I never thought walking up a few flights of stairs would be quite this bone-crunching, muscle-mashing, or soul-sucking. But it's all three.

"Well," Mattea sighs, her hands on her knees with every aching step up the never-ending flights of stairs. "That's Day One behind us."

"How many more to go?" Arlo asks, his voice muffled from deep within his hood.

Libra counts off on her fingers. "Two classes per day. Four terms per year. That's about eighty or ninety more classes of getting wrenches thrown at us by War."

"And eighty or ninety more classes of Branwynne getting beaten up by Kress," Ignacio jokes.

"Not funny," I tell him with a growl and a two-handed shove that knocks him off balance and against the wall but doesn't send him crashing down the stairs like I'd hoped.

"It could be worse," Mattea announces to our Cohort. "At

least with regular classes, there's an end. With the one-on-one Emergent lessons...those could go on forever."

She smiles when Arlo asks her what she means.

"It means there's no timetable. We keep going until our mentor says we're ready."

"Ready? Ready for what?" Ignacio asks.

Mattea scrunches up her face and shrugs.

"Who do you have for your one-on-ones?" I ask, thankful that I get to have Kress as my personal mentor.

Mattea tells us she's got Rain. "She's helping me with identifying logic patterns in languages."

"So how long do we have to do these...what did Wisp call them?" Libra asks.

"Apprenticeships."

"Right. How long?"

"Rain says it's for as long as it takes," Mattea sighs.

"What's that mean?"

"Well, she refers to our apprenticeships as 'mastery learning.'"

"Mastery?"

"It means we don't get passed along just because the Apprenticeship is over or because we've completed all the lessons and assignments. We have to keep going until we've each demonstrated mastery *and* retention."

"That means we have to be experts?"

"Yes. In our individual Emergent skills. And we have to stay that way."

"Oh," Sara groans as she heaves herself up the final flight of stairs, her hand gripping the handrail. "Is that all?"

After what feels like a Himalayan level hike, we get to our floor, limp down the hall, and collapse in the Lounge.

In addition to the couches, chairs, and ottomans, the spacious room of wide-planked, yellow birch floors is furnished with all kinds of games and activities—a pool table, a ping pong table, foosball, darts, pinball, chess, holo-sim consoles, a set of VR goggles, and one entire wall that turns into a giant movie screen.

But we're all way too tired to take advantage of anything recreational at the moment.

Instead, we spend a full ten minutes melting into the furniture in chest-heaving, clamp-eyed exhaustion.

When I'm finally recovered enough to form words, I ask why Ignacio would challenge War like he did back in class.

"We're here to be wolves, not sheep," he replies, patting his chest with his fist.

"I hate to say it," Sara says through a pout. "But I've got to agree with Ignacio. You've heard what Wisp and the others have been saying. This isn't boarding school. It's boot camp."

"More like gladiator finishing school," I giggle. "Easy-peasy."

Chace looks up from her holo-pad. "What's 'finishing school'?"

"They were big in England," I tell her. "Apparently, some old relative of mine went to one a long, long time ago. They were supposed to teach young women etiquette, social manners, grace, charm...things like that. Basically, a school to teach young girls how to be grown-up slaves."

Sara says, "Ugh" and follows her grimace of disgust up with a derisive snort.

While Chace hunches over her holo-pad, writing frantically and chuckling to herself, Ignacio groans himself up and walks over to the pinball machine.

He plants his hands on either side of the console, his fingertips pressed lightly to the flipper pads, but he doesn't actually play. Instead, he stares for a second before swinging his gaze over to where Lucid and Reverie are sitting hip-to-hip on the deep purple sofa.

"So...What's with you two, anyway?"

Lucid and Reverie answer Ignacio with blank stares, first at each other, then at him.

"I heard you once brought someone back from the dead."

"You heard wrong," I interrupt.

But Ignacio ignores me and plows along with his interrogation. "And that you had something to do with Cardyn and Manthy getting killed."

"Strike two," I tell him. "They weren't killed. Why don't you leave them alone?"

"It's okay," Reverie says quietly, taking her brother's hand in her own.

"No," I insist, standing up and drilling my eyes into Ignacio's. "It's really bloody not."

Ignacio puts his hands up and gives us all what I'm assuming is supposed to be an innocent look, but it comes off as mocking. "We're supposed to be in training to bring justice and truth to the world. How are we supposed to do that when we can't even be just and honest in here?"

"And how, exactly, does nagging the twins and being a chuffing wanker accomplish that?"

"Don't you think it's time we were all honest about what we can do?"

I don't answer at first, because honestly, I sort of agree with him.

For the most part, we're eleven strangers in a confined space. We have abilities whose origins we don't know, whose uses we haven't fully explored, and whose potential has gotten most of us imprisoned and all of us nearly killed at one time or another.

It's an entire herd of elephants in the room. It's like the questions only a bunch of teenagers would wonder about the virgins in their ranks:

Have they, or haven't they? Who's done what, and how far did they go?

I'd be lying if I said I wasn't curious about what my classmates were capable of. I know some of my own strengths and a lot of my own limits. But I don't know *theirs* at all.

Is there someone in this room who can save the world? Is there someone in here who might one day destroy it?

Finally, I remind Ignacio about how Kress doesn't want us using our abilities without proper training.

"Says little Miss Teacher's Pet," he laughs. "You think you're better than me just because you've been living here like a nun for five years while the rest of us were stuck back east, going to sleep and wondering if tonight's the night when the True Blues make their move and blow the city up for good?"

"No," I tell him, my voice steady and controlled. "I think I'm better than you because you're a bully and a barmy arse."

Ignacio swings away from the pinball machine and beckons me forward with a curl of his finger. "Kress went easy on you. I won't."

Although I'm not connected to Haida Gwaii or channeling her abilities, I skim across the space between me and Ignacio like a skater on ice.

Leaping up, Libra locks onto one of my arms, and Mattea locks onto the other before I have a chance to start swinging.

"Don't waste your time on him," Libra advises.

Mattea snaps a vicious glare at Ignacio. "He's an instigator. He's been like this as long as we've known him."

Ignacio cracks his knuckles and tells the girls to let me go. They do, slowly.

He folds his arms across his chest and leans back against the pinball machine. "I hear you once walked through a wall."

"That's true," Reverie whispers from the sofa. "It's how she helped save me and Lucid in London."

Ignacio stops and flicks his eyes toward her before locking them back onto me. "Think you can walk through a punch to the head?"

I push up the sleeves of my leather jacket and ball up my fists. "Try me."

This time, he takes a giant step toward me, the muscles in his shoulders and arms twitching.

The lights in the Lounge flicker, and we all blink and stare up at the holo-strips running along edges of the ceiling. The lights dim, flicker again, and then go out completely.

In the dark, I hear Ignacio say, "What the hell?" and then shriek and swear when he bangs his shin against the steel corner of one of the glass-topped end tables.

The lights flicker for a third time, and it's like they're trying to decide if they're going to go back to normal or else give up and die.

They must not have the strength to go on because they fizzle and fade, leaving the entire Lounge soaking in murky, near total darkness.

After several minutes of back and forth murmuring and nervous questions about what the frack is going on, I hear the lounge chair Sara is sitting on squeak as she hops to her feet. She tells me to go check the door.

I'm not a fan of being bossed around, so I tell her to go check it herself.

She swears at me under her breath and clomps across the Lounge toward the main door, which slides open to reveal a huge figure bathed in the harsh red glow of emergency lights in the corridor.

9

FLICKER

SARA STEPS BACK as the figure lumbers past her into the long, thick shadows of the busy room.

"War!" I call out. "What's going on?"

Grumbling from somewhere deep in his barrel chest, War runs his palm over his bald head and asks if we're all okay.

We tell him we are, and he does a quick head count in the near-dark to make sure we're all present and accounted for.

"So what's going on?" Mattea asks. "Power surge?"

War shakes his big bald head. "Not sure. Rain is downstairs right now checking on the mag-generators. Kella's upstairs to see if there's a break in the solar cells."

"We can help," I tell him.

"No. You all stay here. Wisp just sent me to make sure you're okay."

"We're fine," I assure him. "We've been through a lot worse than a barmy little power-flicker."

War surveys the eleven of us. With his back to the open doorway, he's entirely in shadow, and I can barely make out the expression on his face.

Apparently satisfied, he gives us all a little nod and says, "Okay then."

Bulky and slow as a cargo ship, he pivots on his heel and lumbers back out of the room, leaving the door open and leaving us in the dim halo-red of the hallway's emergency lights.

"It's just a power outage," Sara sighs as she crosses the Lounge and hops up onto the edge of the pool table. "No biggie."

"I don't like this," Trax whines, wrapping his arms around himself.

"You're not scared of the dark, are you?" Ignacio teases.

"I'm not afraid of the dark," Trax protests. "I'm afraid of the monsters that leap *out* of the dark and suck out your eyeballs."

"Forgive my little brother," Chace sighs, her face a rainbow glow of neon over the top of her holo-pad. "He's been watching old horror movies on his ocular viz-screen."

"I'm not little," Trax pouts. "I'm only six minutes younger than *you*."

Chace lifts her eyes. "I lived a lifetime in those six minutes, Baby Bro."

Mattea plops down into one of the Lounge's deep, plush armchairs, her eyes focused on the open doorway and on the weak but fiery light that's cast all of us in a web of eerie, angled shadows. "It's not the dark. But War's afraid of *something*."

I shake my head. "I've known War for five years. Have you *seen* him? That man is not afraid of *anything*."

"Trust Mattea," Libra tells me evenly. "She reads people like we read words. If she says he's afraid, he's afraid."

"Mattea's right. War's afraid. Something's wrong." Lucid seems stunned when we all swing around to look at him.

He runs his fingers through his black hair and clears his throat. Because he's usually so quiet, to hear him talk at all is a bit of a shock. To hear him announce, with such casual indifference, that something—*anything*—might be wrong with War or with the Academy feels like a sledgehammer to the gut.

There's just enough light for me to make out a crease of worry between Arlo's eyes. He pushes back his hood and asks Lucid what he means by that.

But Lucid just stares and slips his hand into his sister's.

Reverie squeezes his hand and seems sort of sad when she raises her eyes to meet ours. "My brother's not wrong. There's a hole in the Academy. There's a thunderhead on the horizon."

We all stare at her and lean in, fully expecting her to elaborate. But she doesn't. And neither does her creepy twin brother.

Instead, they stand up and walk, hand in hand, over to their Dorm.

Muttering about "getting some straight answers," Ignacio gets ready to chase after them, but Mattea reaches out to lock her hand on his forearm. "Don't."

"But..."

"They know something's wrong, but they don't know what. Confronting them isn't going to make them know any more than they do."

"Then what do *you* suggest?"

"I can't speak for anyone else, but I suggest sleep. A good, long night of it, if possible."

Mattea walks through the Lounge door leading to the showers with Libra, Sara, and Arlo right behind her.

"I guess that's our cue," Trax says, pushing himself up and nodding to Chace and Roxane. "Let's try to get some sleep. Tomorrow's a new day. With lots of new challenges...and pain."

Trax and his Cohort disappear through the door leading to their Dorm.

Libra leads Sara, Mattea, and Arlo through the door on the opposite side of the Lounge and into our own wing.

Alone in the Lounge, Ignacio and I watch as the two Cohorts file out.

Standing side by side, I don't look over at him when I ask, "Are you sure it wasn't you?"

"Am I sure what wasn't me?"

"The power flicker."

"What makes you think I can do something like that? Or that I'd even want to?"

"I heard you can disrupt electrical impulses." When Ignacio doesn't answer, I press on. "Is that what you did to me in Unarmed Combat this morning?"

He tilts his head toward me just enough to let me see his scowl in the near-dark. "If I wanted you dead, Branwynne, you'd be dead. And I don't want you dead. *Yet.*"

He strides off toward the shower rooms, leaving me alone in the Lounge, my mouth open, my fists clenched for the fight I know will have to happen.

10

MORNING ADDRESS

I SPEND most of the night in my bed, restless and fidgety.

I don't know how the five other members of my Cohort can sleep so soundly.

Unfortunately, they don't all sleep *soundlessly*.

Libra giggles in her sleep. Sara grumbles. Ignacio snores.

Mattea and Arlo sleep quietly at least, although Arlo keeps his hoodie on all night. I'm not even sure he takes the thing off to shower.

When I can't stand lying still any longer, I push my blanket off and slink out of the Dorm.

The dim, nightlights are back on in the hallways.

I make my way down to the fourth floor where I hear voices coming from one of the Bio-Tech Research Labs.

A halo of light from the seam around the door seeps into the corridor.

The voices coming from inside the room are muffled, so I concentrate, trying to connect with Haida to borrow some of her heightened senses. Unfortunately, nothing happens.

It's a problem I've been having forever, and it's not getting any better. When Haida's asleep, I have trouble accessing her. It's tricky when I'm nervous or stressed, too. Kress has been working with me for a long time now, and I've made good progress in a lot of areas, but this is one of the things I just can't get the hang of.

When I hear bootsteps approaching the door from the inside of the room, I backpedal down the hall and toward the stairs, slipping back up to the Dorms and into bed.

The voices, it turns out, belonged to Kress and Brohn. I couldn't tell what they were saying, but they sounded exactly like War did earlier: *afraid*.

That thought alone is enough to keep me wide awake for the rest of the night. I lie there, biting my lip and staring at the ceiling until the holo-lights along the top edges of the walls flash gold and white to wake us up.

At least the power's back on.

Brohn's voice rumbles out from the narrow speech-amplifiers built into the top of every doorframe in the Dormitory. "Cohort A and B. Please meet in the Assembly Hall for Morning Address."

Somehow, after all we went through yesterday, Libra manages to sing herself awake, leap up from her bed, and throw herself into her uniform.

She slips into combat pants and a form-fitting white compression top before sliding her hands along her hips.

"You have to admit," she gushes, "these fit great!"

"It's an organic, stimuli-response polymer," I tell her. "They're designed to adjust to our bodies."

"Really?"

"There's a storeroom full of them downstairs."

Libra toggles her thumb back and forth between the two of us. "You've been here the longest. Maybe later you could give some of us a tour?"

"I thought Wisp and Granden already did that."

"They did. But this place is *massive*. I want to see the secret places. You know, the nooks, the crannies."

"That sounds like a great idea. Only..."

"Only, what?"

"I don't want to."

Libra throws her arm around me and pulls me close. She whispers, "I think you do" into my ear.

I push her away, but she just laughs and tells the others to get moving and to stop being such lazy bums.

Ignacio groans his disgust at her chipperness and swings his feet to the floor.

Mattea is groggy and grumbling, but she seems to get a burst of competitive energy when she sees Libra already up and ready to go.

Dragging from my lack of sleep, I sling on my red leather jacket. Technically, it's not part of the official Academy uniform. Neither is Arlo's shabby hoodie, but Wisp lets us get away with it.

Sara is the last one up. Unlike Mattea, she doesn't seem to get any sort of energy boost by seeing the rest of us up and about. In fact, she tugs her blanket over her head and curls into a human nautilus shell.

"Come on Sleepy-bones!" Libra beams as she steps over to shake the Sara-shaped lump.

"Go away."

"Wisp said she'd have Terk break our arms if we showed up late." Libra's sprightly smile drops down into a rigid line. "I don't think she was joking."

Grumbling and cursing under her breath, Sara rolls out of bed and trundles off to the Shower Room.

A few minutes later, she emerges, dressed and groggy-eyed, but apparently ready for class.

Cohort B is already out in the hall when we step out of our room.

They're huddled around Trax, who seems to have slipped into the leadership role for their Cohort.

I guess that makes sense. He's an expert on directions and tracking, so it's reasonable for him to be in the lead, especially in a group with four other kids looking as lost as they do.

Besides, his sister spends all her time writing and drawing, Roxane is a monosyllabic, brain-muddled nutter, and Lucid and Reverie more or less live in their own world.

That leaves Trax—usually shy and a little fragile-looking—to run the show.

Like the proverb says: In the land of the blind, the one-eyed man is king.

With our two Cohorts together and the soreness from yesterday kicking back in, we start down the hallway—all of us looking like a bunch of geriatric tree sloths slogging through a marshy bog.

Although there are several mag-lifts in the Academy, we're supposed to take the stairs. "To keep you in shape," Kress told us at Orientation a few days ago.

I know that's not entirely true, though. For a while now—ever since the new Emergents arrived, actually—the mag-generators have been as glitchy as the lights.

They won't say it out loud, but I know Wisp and the others are worried about us getting stuck in one of the lifts or stepping into a malfunctioning one and plunging to our deaths.

On the glossy wooden stairs, I can feel a lightning strike of pain shooting through my legs with each step, but I shrug it off and muscle through.

Passing through the big double doors of the Assembly Hall, the eleven of us clomp down the aisle and take seats scattered throughout the first few rows.

With its comfortable red-cushioned, fold-down seats, the auditorium-sized room is designed to hold almost three hundred people. Plus there's room for another fifty or so in the balcony.

But, right now, the eleven of us barely outnumber the teachers.

So, like the rest of the Academy, there's an open, echo-y feeling to the big hall, and I can clearly hear every breath and squeak of the seats as my classmates and I settle in.

On the stage, Kress and her Conspiracy are sitting on mag-chairs in a semi-circle behind the podium where Wisp is standing next to Granden.

Wisp is thin and small. Her baggy combat jacket hangs on her like an oversized pelt. But there's something about her that makes her a great leader. It's like she says the right things at the right time, and you just sort of want to do what she tells you.

"And how was everyone's first day?" she asks us with a pleasant smile.

We answer with a disjointed round of sleepy grumbles.

Except for Libra. She says, "Great!" and I roll my eyes and start a silent count in my head of the number of ways I could kill her right now.

"Well, you survived," Wisp says. "So that's a good start." She pushes up the sleeves of her jacket and brushes back her feathery brown hair.

"I've spoken with the two Cohorts separately, but this will be the first time I've had a chance to address all eleven of you together. I know we provided schedules for you a few days ago at Orientation, but after consulting a bit, we've made some changes to the course list. Your final schedules are now in place. As you know, your classes are arranged into five Disciplines: Weapons and Combat, Survival, Governance, Medical, and Espionage. In the hopes of giving you the best chance to succeed out there in the world, we've added a few classes to each Discipline. We'll go over those in just a minute. Time will be allotted for each of you to have Apprenticeship—that's your one-on-one private mentoring sessions—with one of your instructors in the use and development of your individual abilities as Emergents. Some of you have already started that training. The rest of you will meet with your mentors and start today. Plus, there will now be some time scheduled in for you to catch up on your books and movies."

"I *love* movies," Libra whispers to me. "Don't you?"

I shift in my seat to be as far away from her as possible, only that puts me shoulder to shoulder with Ignacio.

Great. I can be annoyed by Miss Blabbermouth on my left or harassed by Mr. Conceited on my right. Am I doomed to be the meat in an imbecile sandwich?

On the stage, Wisp taps the bracelet on her wrist. "Here is the revised list of courses. As I noted, you'll see some classes we went over at Orientation a few days ago as well as some new ones the Conspiracy thinks are essential to your training."

As she talks, the names of the classes and of the assigned teachers appear next to her in a floating holo-display:

5 DISCIPLINES

I. WEAPONS & COMBAT
    Unarmed Combat (KRESS, BROHN)
    Sniper, Marksmanship (KELLA)
    Alternate Weapons Training (BROHN)
    Demolitions & Explosives (TERK)
    Blacksmithing (TERK)

Strategy & Tactics (RAIN)

2. SURVIVAL SKILLS
Hunting & Foraging (WAR)
Topography & Navigation (RAIN)
Outdoor Survival (BROHN)
Communications Skills (MAYLA)
Transportation & Mechanics (WAR)

3. GOVERNANCE & PHILOSOPHY
Transhumanism (GRANDEN, WISP)
Rhetoric & Propaganda (GRANDEN)
Diplomacy & Negotiation (WISP)
Rights, Duties, & Laws (GRANDEN)
Politics & Power (WISP)
Apocalyptic History (GRANDEN)
End of the World: Fiction & Fact
(GRANDEN, WISP)

4. MEDICAL
Field First-Aid (WAR and MAYLA)
Surgical Techniques (MAYLA)
Pharmaceuticals & Vaccines (MAYLA)
Exercise & Fitness (WAR)
Coordination & Reflex Skills (KRESS)
Bioethics (TERK / AUDITOR)

5. ESPIONAGE
Puzzles, Codes, & Game Theory (RAIN)

Surveillance & Reconnaissance (KRESS)
Infiltration (KRESS)
Drone Detection, & Avoidance (WISP)
Intelligence Ops (KELLA)
Counter Terrorism (KELLA)
Digital Tech (RAIN, TERK/AUDITOR)

EMERGENT APPRENTICESHIP
Specialized Mentoring (VARIOUS)

WISP TAPS HER BRACELET, and the holo-display sizzles away into a fading, pixilated cloud. "If you have questions about any of the changes, please let me or one of the other instructors know. Remember, this is your first time being students, but it's our first time being teachers. We may be older and have a bit more experience, but we're all in this together, okay?"

Our two Cohorts nod our understanding as Wisp clears the holo-display.

"Make sure you check the announcement board posted in your Dorm each morning for any changes to the schedule."

Granden clears his throat, and Wisp gives him a go-ahead nod. "And be sure to consult with your Mentor to set up a schedule that will work for both of you." He gives a sideways flick of his eyes toward War and Mayla who are sitting behind him with our other teachers. "Some of us are Typics, but we'll be acting in a Mentoring capacity as well. At least as much as we can," he chuckles, "until your Emergent abilities exceed our ability to help you. After that, you'll be assigned to one of your fellow Emergent instructors for advanced training."

"Contrary to what some of you might think," Wisp adds,

"you're not just here to learn how to become expert fighters. You will also be taught the arts of survival, diplomacy, medicine, and espionage. And you'll be taught how to use your abilities as Emergents. As you know, some of these classes will include all of you. Most, however, will be taught to each Cohort separately. You'll be together for meals and for your downtime in the Dorms and in the Lounge upstairs."

Holding up his fingers in a "V," Ignacio leans toward me and whispers, "I can't believe we have to take two classes every day."

"Nothing to whinge about," I whisper back through the corner of my mouth. "It's less than I thought they'd give us."

"Branwynne!" Kress snaps from her seat on the stage. "Pay attention!"

I snap back in my seat like I've been electrocuted.

Wisp nods her thanks to Kress before turning her attention back to us. "I see from the bumps and bruises that your first class was a roaring success. I'm sure the rest of your time here will be just as productive."

Taking a half-step to the side, she turns the center of the stage over to Granden.

Square-jawed, clean-shaven, even-tempered, and cold-eyed, he's a total field general. Like Wisp, he commands respect and attention—almost magically—and gives off a total *Pay Attention and Don't Frack with Me* aura.

I don't know him that well, but the six new arrivals—the ones he took care of for the past five years and escorted across the country—all sit up straight and lean forward as he talks.

"As you know, Wisp is your dean. If your teachers are busy, you should feel free to consult with her if you run into problems. I'll be around as well. Some of you will see me when you have my class on Post and Transhumanism." He rubs his hands together with pretend glee. "Not as much fun as getting beaten up in Combat Training, but I'm sure we'll have some good times tracking the past, pondering the present, and predicting the future of techno-human evolution."

"For today," Wisp adds, sliding back to the center of the podium, "review your schedules, set up your mentoring sessions, listen to your teachers, and never forget why we're all here at the Emergents Academy. Our mission is simple: Save the world."

11

TIME PASSES

THE NEXT COUPLE of weeks are a blur of classes, exhaustion, and pain.

The routine is essentially the same:

Snap awake at 6 AM to the rapid-fire, wake-up blast of gold and white holo-lights.

Follow the bouncing Libra into the Shower Room.

Fortunately, there's plenty of space, so we don't have to fight over toilets or shower stalls, although Ignacio still likes to be a territorial wanker and keeps trying to claim the best sonic shower as his own.

After we're dressed in our Academy uniforms—complete with Kevlar armor for the full-contact and weapons classes—we stumble down five flights of stairs to the Tavern where we scarf down our breakfast.

It's bland-looking and thin on flavor, but at least there's not much of it.

Then, at 6:45 AM, it's back up two flights of stairs to the Assembly Room where we plunk down in front of Wisp and some or all of our other teachers for Morning Address.

With classes set up in modules of two per day over a period of what we're told will be about three months, our two Cohorts go our separate ways from 7 AM to 1 PM for Morning Module—the first of the day's two ridiculously intense classes.

After Morning Module, we get an hour of "down time" from 1 to 2 PM when we can get a snack in the Tavern, grab a catnap upstairs in one of the Academy's reading nooks or, more likely, spend that time getting patched up by War or Mayla in the Infirmary.

The flash of blue and white lights signals Afternoon Module, which runs from 2 PM to 8 PM.

Then, it's one more stop at the Infirmary if necessary (and it often is), a quick and unsatisfying dinner, and then back up to the Dorms for a few hours of chit-chat, debriefing, comparing notes, showering up, or playing games in the Lounge—if we're not too buggered out—before finally drifting off to sleep.

And then, at 6 AM, the gold and white lights blast us awake, and we start the routine all over again.

No one in my Cohort has ever been to a real school before, so it's all new to us. Other than our lives in hiding, imprisoned in Processors, or isolated in the Tower of London like I was, we don't really have a lot to compare it to.

But sometimes, one of our teachers—usually War or Mayla —regales us with stories about what school *used* to be like.

"Before the Eastern Order, before Krug, before the drone strikes, the techno-genetic experiments, and the Atomic Wars," Mayla tells us one day when we're gathered in the Infirmary for our daily dose of medications, casts, and bandages, "kids your age went to school for around six hours a day."

"That's all?" Ignacio asks with a snooty grunt. He jumps up from his floating mag-table and inspects the biotic plasma stitches Mayla just threaded through the length of his right thigh.

"Well," Mayla sighs, "they were usually training for citizenship or careers or for university. They weren't training to fight to save what's left of a post-apocalyptic wasteland."

"Did they live in their schools like we do?" Mattea asks.

Mayla shakes her head but doesn't look up from the thin blue stitches she's now weaving into my forearm. "Not usually. And they mostly went to school for five days a week."

She looks up from my arm when she realizes we're all staring at her in quiet anticipation.

"Oh, right. You don't really know about weekends, do you?"

Libra thrusts her always-enthusiastic hand into the air. "I do. Kids didn't go to school on Saturdays and Sundays, right?"

The words sound strange to me: *Saturday. Sunday.* Sure, my parents used to talk in terms of days, weeks, and months—all with a specific name to designate a certain block of time.

But that faded over the years. When every sunrise means a new threat and every sunset inspires a silent prayer of gratitude for not being dead, things like names for days of the week sort of go out the window.

It's not like we've never heard of the names for days of the week and for the months of the year. Kress and her friends still use them from time to time.

But any real meaning they might have had in Mayla's day has been made mostly pointless in a world where time is measured in how long it will take for you to succumb to the Cyst Plague, get hacked to pieces and eaten by the Unsettled, get vaporized in a drone strike, or starve to death once your food and water run out.

As someone who spent the first twelve years of her life living with her parents and seven ravens in a thousand-year-old castle, the idea of a strict military routine is strange to me.

Growing up in the Tower of London, I was pretty much free to do what I wanted.

My parents took care of the ravens and tried to teach me as much as they could about the world.

But the world they knew—the one they talked about and kept hoping would come back—was long gone.

The stories they used to tell me about "the good old days" gave way to the reality of drone strikes, septic water, Cyst Plague, radioactive smog, murderous gangs, and all the disease and death that are bound to happen whenever a few people seek absolute power, leaving hundreds of millions to scrounge for scraps.

In the Tower, we had a storeroom full of rapidly aging, canned rations and skunky but drinkable water.

Because of the drones and the gangs that started popping up, leaving the Tower was strictly forbidden.

"Under *no* circumstances," my mother always told me. "Stepping beyond the Tower's walls...you might as well just kill *yourself* and save the Banters, the Royal Fort Knights, and the Roguers the trouble."

"Listen to your mother," my dad would inevitably add. "We may not have much behind these walls, but we *do* have life. That's more than we can say for the piles of corpses outside."

It was a terrifying, soul-sucking thing to hear and an even worse vision of Hell to imagine.

"You'll be safe here," my mother promised. "Just stick with us here on the castle grounds, and you'll be safe."

The first time I left, I was eight years old.

I was supposed to be securing the motion sensor on a perimeter fence as instructed by my mum. Instead, I got tempted by the outside world and gave in to curiosity and the possibility for adventure. I unlocked one of the small access panels, deactivated the motion sensor, peeled back the sheet of laser-wire, and slipped out into the night.

Easy-peasy.

A drone strike must have happened right before I left the Tower, because everything outside was quiet and smoldering.

I expected to hear screams and to see people running for their lives.

Because of the stories I'd heard from my parents, I was braced for explosions, battles, shrieks of agony, and rival factions fighting for survival.

But the quiet was creepier than all the noise of my imagination.

I didn't go far that first time. Just far enough to have a look around and see a bit of the world outside our walls.

The pavement was buckled into long, jagged-topped ridges with huge sinkholes pockmarking the roads.

The buildings and shops around the Tower were windowless and black with ash. In the distance, skyscrapers, most with their tops sheared off, stabbed up into the sky like shards of broken glass in an old, warped windowsill.

The south end of the Tower Bridge was in the Thames where it formed a horrific dam of twisted steel with a few hundred dead and bloated bodies pressed against it.

The slimy white corpses bounced and bobbed in the briny current, rolling and basking under a blistering hot sun. And I had the strangest thought—the kind only a little girl living in wartime isolation could have—that they must be happy.

The next time I snuck out, I saw living people for the first time and got a taste—from a safe distance—of what life was like.

I slipped into an abandoned building and watched from one of the empty windows as two groups of teenagers made a circle around a chubby boy with an iron pipe and a bone-thin girl with barbed wire wrapped around her hands and forearms. The two teens fought until they were both bloody and shredded and the girl was dead.

After that, I snuck a few blocks over and followed another

gang of kids, watching while they rummaged through the rubble of old stores looking for building supplies, food, and weapons.

When a small fleet of scissor-shaped drones with pulsing red eyes skimmed overhead, everyone scattered for cover.

I ducked down, too, and breathed a sigh of relief when the drones disappeared around a corner.

A split second later, the sound of explosions and screams startled me alert, and I poked my head up just enough to see another set of drones—bowl-shaped with a stem on top and larger than the first fleet—firing a hail of plasma bombs at dozens of fleeing kids.

I scampered down a set of broken stairs and found a place to hide toward the back of the building. I was fast enough to avoid being seen but not fast enough to escape the sound of the kids' screams or the smell of their burning, melting skin.

I don't remember being scared. Or even angry about the slaughter I'd just witnessed.

No. More than anything else, I remember being offended. After all, the sky was the true home for the ravens of the Tower. It belonged to them. To see it hijacked and violated by whirring, weaponized chunks of metal...that was the mother tragedy that spawned all the offspring tragedies that followed.

I think that's why I had revenge on my mind as I climbed down into a dried-up underground sewer line and made my way back home to the Tower.

I left the safety of the Tower a bunch more times after that. And I never got caught. Not by my parents. Not by the drones. Not by the roving bands of Scroungers and desperate teenagers doing anything they could to survive.

Back then, my life was my own. Which meant my routine was my own. Except for the daily tasks my parents assigned to me, I had almost total freedom.

Now, I've traded that in for the daily routine of the Academy.

And, honestly, I don't mind. Oddly enough—and I'm only realizing this now—what I was really escaping from before was safety.

For most people, safety's a good thing. For me, it always meant isolation, loneliness, boredom, and the feeling my life was being wasted and flushed down the loo.

The Academy may be safe from the outside world, but inside, we're under constant siege. And that's totally by design.

As dean of the Academy, Wisp has made it crystal clear that she's not pulling punches with us.

And, with the year divided into four terms under the instruction of some of what *have* to be the toughest and most powerful Emergents in the world, we have ample opportunity to be punched.

Every day, in fact, carries a whole new host of dangers.

Usually, it's Libra who wakes up first, stupidly excited to begin the day.

Today, it's me. And that's because today is the first day of the second term, which means Alternate Weapons Training and Weapons Selection with Brohn.

Sure, Unarmed Combat was a blast. And we all have the scars, sprains, and broken bones to prove it. But learning about Medieval and makeshift weapons—and then getting to pick our own—should be a whole new level of brillie fun.

"Are you excited?" Libra asks as we get dressed.

"Does it take as little as five seconds for a person to die from a severed carotid artery?"

Bare chested and in blue and white checkered boxing shorts, Ignacio steps out of the bathroom, a towel around his waist and a toothbrush jutting out from the foamy corner of his mouth. "There is something seriously wrong with you."

"Don't listen to Mr. Grumpy-bum," Libra says through a snarly smile. She tosses my red leather jacket over to me and heads for the door. "Come on, Branwynne. Let's go get some nice deadly weapons into those pretty little hands of yours!"

12

WEAPONS

WE'VE COME to know the Academy's third floor pretty well over the past couple of months.

From our Unarmed Combat classes with Kress and Brohn in the Combat Skills Training Rooms to our weight-lifting and cardio workouts in the Fitness Center, the third floor has practically become our home.

(Not counting the Dorms where we sleep or the Infirmary where we've become constantly wounded regulars.)

Today, we're introduced to one of the rooms we haven't been in yet.

The Weapons Training room is narrow but long, like an extra-wide hallway with floating target stations set up at the far end.

Brohn is down by the stations, and he turns and strides toward us to greet us as we enter.

Without missing a beat, he launches into the first lesson.

"Guns are getting harder and harder to come by," he tells us, his tone practically apologetic. "Krug destroyed millions of handguns and rifles to stop them from falling into the hands of people who would use them against him. Millions more weapons were scavenged, stolen, hoarded, stored away, damaged, or lost. The Wealthies kept most of what was left for themselves."

He gazes at the six of us, as if to ensure he's got our attention. Which he has.

"To survive, we've had to find alternatives. In this class, you'll learn about alternate weapons—where to find them, how to make them, and, most important, how and when to use them."

Brohn stops his pacing for a second and turns a stone-hard stare at Sara, who's fidgeting with one of the Kevlar plate-pockets on her combat vest.

She catches his eye, flushes coral red, and apologizes.

"Later on," Brohn nods, continuing with his slow, powerful pacing, "you'll select a weapon that feels best for you. Not the weapon that *looks* the best. Or the one you *think* makes you look the best."

He locks eyes with Ignacio, who puffs out his chest in silent defiance but who, like Sara, quickly blushes and averts his eyes.

"We're about function, not fashion. Your weapon of choice needs to be an extension of you. Of your mind, your body, and your style. It needs to reflect and amplify the way you move, the way you strategize and think. A good weapon won't just be an appendage, a back-up, or a means to gain an upper hand in combat. The right weapon for you will be one that has the potential to become part of your body, something that moves *as* you and not just at your command."

Brohn slaps a fist into his open palm. "I'll say that again. Your weapon is *not* a slave. You are *not* its master. Fighting of any kind—open hand or with a weapon—is a partnership, not a rivalry."

Trembling, Libra raises her hand halfway. "A partnership? You mean between us and the enemy?"

Brohn's lips turn up ever so slightly at the corners, and his eyes flash that glittering glacier blue. "No. It's a partnership between you and *yourself*. Between the self you are now and the self you have the potential to become. As you continue to develop your Emergent abilities, your weapon of choice should be one that can and will develop, grow, and evolve along with you."

Brohn points us to a rack along the wall. "You'll find a variety of bladed and club-type weapons, Medieval weapons, and even some makeshift weapons we put together and tested out over the past few years."

"This is our firing range," Brohn explains, tilting his head toward the far end of the long room. "We'll be using it for some of your long-gun sniper training in the future. But first..." He hauls an enormous crossbow out of a large black case on the floor and snaps its two arms into their open position. "Among other things, you'll learn about this."

"Crossbow," Mattea mumbles.

"It's called an arbalest," I correct her as Brohn passes the huge weapon to Sara who groans under its weight and looks like she might actually fall over.

I laugh out loud, and she glares at me. I tell her I'm not laughing *at* her, but who am I kidding? Of course I am.

Sara grunts the arbalest over to Libra who also struggles to hold it without having it drag her to the floor.

Ignacio snatches it out of her hands and smirks. "Light as a feather!" as Libra obnoxiously inspects her fingernails for cracks.

Showing off, Ignacio bounces the heavy weapon in both hands. I notice him glancing down at his own tight forearms and bulging biceps as he passes the arbalest to Arlo.

Arlo, quiet, sullen, and with his hood perpetually pulled up and shading his face, somehow takes the weapon with one hand, the handle of the huge arbalest pinched between his forefinger and thumb. He doesn't even look at it as he passes it to me like it's a stick of kindling.

The weapon is super heavy, and I hope no one hears the strain in my voice when I say, "Thanks" and lug it back over to Brohn.

I've seen him use it before. We all have. Back in London, when we were just kids, we got a small sample of what Brohn and this weapon are capable of.

But as the only one of us who traveled with Brohn across the divided nation once known as the United States, I've seen him use it more recently. I've seen him use it to save lives and to take them. Knowing for the first time that it practically weighs more than I do makes his easy use of it that much more impressive.

"The arbalest goes back to the twelfth century," he tells us. "The word 'arbalest,' comes from two Latin roots: *arcus* for bow and *ballista*, a term meaning 'a missile-throwing engine.' The same root that gives us the word 'ballistics.' And yes," he nods to Mattea, "it's in the same family as the traditional crossbow. But Branwynne's right. It's called an arbalest. I'll let you play with some smaller versions of it—actual crossbows—in a minute. Historically, the arbalest came along a little later than the cross-bow, and, as you'll see, it has its advantages but also some disadvantages. The goal for this course will not be about making you proficient in this *particular* weapon."

Brohn cradles the huge weapon to his chest like it's his newborn baby. "This is one of a kind," he says with a pretend scowl. "...and it's mine. Instead, you'll be taught to find the strategic capabilities of *any* unfamiliar weapon, overcome its drawbacks, exploit its advantages, and add it to your own personal arsenal."

Brohn has us line up behind a strip of pink holo-lights embedded in the floor and points us toward the target, which,

I'm guessing, as I squint down the firing range, is somewhere between five or six million miles away.

I've got great eyesight, and I can barely see the target at the end of the range. How the others are going to manage this exercise is beyond me.

First, Brohn demonstrates the arbalest. With rapid-fire hand-speed too fast for our eyes to follow, he loads the weapon and fires off bolt after bolt at the target at the far end of the impossibly long shooting gallery.

The targets at the end ding and plink with light as his bolts find their mark.

After that, we queue up so we can each have a go.

One by one, we line up, load the massive arbalest, and fire.

One by one, we miss by a mile.

Libra, Sara, and Mattea are terrible. I'm almost as bad. Arlo doesn't really try.

Ignacio isn't great, but he's better at it than the rest of us.

After getting a few tepid compliments from Brohn, Ignacio's head swells up like a hot-air balloon, and he gets a bit too keen on "helping" the rest of us.

And his help is annoyingly hands-on.

Brohn gives each of us our own fiberglass crossbow, much smaller and lighter than his arbalest.

While he's showing Mattea a trick for loading one of the crossbows, Ignacio stalks around the room, inspecting our technique and making "Hmmm" noises like *he's* the teacher.

One by one, he sidles up to each of us as we stand in a line facing down range.

At least he's an equal opportunity jackass.

When Arlo has trouble with the fast, double-bolt loading technique Brohn taught us, Ignacio shuffles over to help. He puts one hand on Arlo's shoulder and the other on his wrist.

"Here. Like this."

Arlo shrieks like he's on fire and lashes out, his arms spasming.

One of his elbows catches Ignacio in the solar plexus and knocks the wind out of him.

By the time Brohn gets over to check on them, Arlo is halfway across the room, cowering against the wall and tucked behind a wooden rack of knives, swords, mallets, axes, and hatchets.

Ignacio, meanwhile, is doubled over and busy trying to catch his breath. When he does, his eyes narrow, and he lunges across the room toward Arlo. He shoves the rack of weapons aside and towers over our quivering classmate. Grabbing Arlo by the scruff of his hoodie with one hand and with his other clamped into a beefy fist, he hauls him to his feet.

I'm expecting Brohn to intervene, but he stops in his tracks and stands back.

Ignacio blasts an uppercut to Arlo's ribs, and Arlo folds in half, crashing down face-first onto the overturned wooden rack. A jet of blood explodes from his mouth and sprays out over the floor.

His eyelids quiver as he tries to hang onto consciousness.

Ignacio's face is in a knot, and his fists are veiny with tight red bulges as he prepares to finish off Arlo, who's gagging and coughing up phlegm mixed with spatters of blood.

Before Ignacio can take his second swing, Brohn steps forward, catches his wrist, and spins him around.

"Don't."

"But—"

"One hit is justice, Ignacio. Two is revenge."

"But he—"

"We're not pacifists here. But we're not warmongers either. Don't let all the combat and weapons training fool you. Our goal is to *break* the cycles of violence, not to perpetuate them. The only thing more important than knowing when to use your strength is knowing when to stop."

Ignacio stares at Brohn with his steely golden-amber eyes, but then his gaze softens, and his eyelids lower.

To my surprise, behind him, Arlo stands up as easy-peasy as a morning glory rising up to meet the sun.

Just before he tugs his hood back up and over his head, I catch a glimpse of his face. It's always scarred and sandpaper-rough, but now it's pulsing with a weird purplish glow. In the space of half an eye blink, the fresh red cuts to his lip and jaw turn as dry, gray, and solid as stone.

He makes his way past Brohn and Ignacio to join the rest of us, who are gathered in a stunned huddle.

His voice soft and patient, Brohn grips Ignacio's shoulder and asks if he's okay.

I notice he doesn't ask Arlo.

Maybe he doesn't need to. Ignacio, I get. He's a swollen-headed wanker. But what is it with Arlo, anyway? And how come, whatever it is, I get the feeling there's more to come?

After standing the cracked weapons rack back on its feet, Brohn barks at the rest of us to stay focused and line up again at the firing range. He doesn't say another word about what happened between Ignacio and Arlo.

With the chaotic moment behind us, we get back to our training, which goes on for hour after hour with Brohn bombarding us with a relentless barrage of tips, criticism, feedback, and promises that "failure in here means death out there."

How does he expect me to load, aim, and fire when my shoulders and arms are burning, and I can't feel my fingers?

After a few hours of crossbow training, we switch over to the longbow.

That's harder, but more fun.

Once again, Ignacio is the best at it. He doesn't hit any

bullseyes, but he does strike the edges of the target a few times. The rest of us ninnies couldn't hit the ground if we fell out of a fracking tree.

Toward the end of class, Brohn stops us and leads us over to one of the racks of weapons against the wall.

He draws out a dozen of the weapons, one at a time, teaching us about their origins, uses, plusses and minuses.

"You already know about me. What about your other teachers? What do they use?"

I thrust my arm into the air, eager to show off my knowledge and possibly to be useful as something other than a crappy archer or a human punching bag.

Brohn smiles. "Branwynne?"

"You use an arbalest. Kress has Talons. Those are special gloves with retractable blades. Rain has Dart-Drivers that fire little silver arrows. Terk uses a flail." I swing around to face the other members of my Cohort who weren't with us five years ago on our cross-country adventures. "That's a giant spiked ball on a chain. And Kella...I guess she just uses a regular gun?"

"A sniper rifle," Brohn clarifies. "But it doesn't matter with her. She has perfect accuracy with any weapon. It's part of her enhanced abilities as an Emergent."

Libra's eyes go wide. "Is it true she can really hit anything?"

Brohn suppresses a smile. "I have yet to see her miss."

Libra mumbles, "Marvie."

Hanging his arbalest onto two massive iron hooks on the wall, Brohn returns his attention to the long table and the row of racks in front of us.

"Now...it's time to meet *your* weapons."

13

INTRODUCTIONS

"THESE ARE ALL NON-PROJECTILES," Brohn explains, taking down the various knives, razor-edged disks, axes, slingshots, long-handled clubs, and bladed weapons and showing them to us again, only in more detail this time and with a whirlwind of quick, introductory demonstrations.

He slips his hands into the handles of a pair of steel-black claws.

"These are called Bear Claws. But they have other names: Barbecue Claws. Pork Shredders. They're supposed to be used for shredding meat."

Sara fires off a sarcastic roll of her eyes. "Perfect...if we ever get attacked by a giant ham."

I expect Brohn to get mad, but he chuckles. "Don't forget, Sara. People are meat, too."

Next, he introduces us to a pair of S-shaped, sharp-edged throwing weapons, each with a steel handle at the center and a curved, retractable blade, sharp and hooked as a raven's beak, extending out from either side.

Brohn grips the central handle in his fist, leaving the two silver blades to extend from the front and the heel of his hand.

"These are Serpent Blades. Think of them as kind of like fris-bees. They can be used for close-quarters or distant combat situations. In some of the upcoming classes, I'll be teaching you how to throw them with distance and accuracy."

Libra's hand goes up. "What's a frisbee?"

"It's a flying plastic disk kids play with," I tell her with an impatient groan. But then I feel bad. After all, it's not Libra's fault she spent most of her life as a test subject in a Processor.

Of course, with her bouncy, perpetual perkiness, she's bound to get on *somebody's* nerves, so who knows? Maybe it *is* her fault after all.

After a brief description of a frisbee and a quick story about how he once caught one on the bridge of the nose when he was a little boy growing up in the Valta, Brohn moves on to the next weapon. "These are cricket bats with razor strips running along the edges of the blades. They're homemade right here in the basement of the Academy. You can thank Terk for them."

Brohn starts passing the weapons around for me and my Cohort to inspect.

"This is a three-pronged grappling hook. And here are a pair of Irish *shillelaghs*."

He pronounces the name of the glossy black clubs with the thick knob at the top as *Sha-LAY-lees*. "It has a strap here to keep it secured to your wrist during battle. Great combination of lightness and strength. There's an old book that talks about Shil-lelagh Law."

"Shillelagh Law?" Ignacio repeats.

"Basically, it means your standard fist-fight just got a lot more interesting."

Next, Brohn shows us what he calls a Masai *rungu*. "It's a wooden throwing club. Often ceremonial but deadly if used properly on the battlefield."

"These are Scottish *sgian-dubh*." He pronounces the name of the stocky, two-edged blade as *skee-en-DOO*. "They're originally ceremonial knives. According to Granden, one of the gen-techs on the team that started the Academy had a fondness for them and left a whole crate of them in one of the storage lockers downstairs."

Sara giggles when Brohn shows us the next weapons: a cluster of miniature, needle-like swords he holds in the open palm of his hand.

"These are throwing darts. Kind of like what you would have found in a London pub. When there *were* London pubs. These darts are innocent-looking but handy, easy to conceal, and highly effective, especially when aimed at the eyes."

Sara frowns and barks out a derisive laugh. She tells Brohn they look more like toothpicks for hors d'oeuvres. "I don't suppose you have any cocktail wieners to go along with those little things?"

My Cohort laughs...right up until the split-second when Brohn—in an impossible blur of speed—flings the darts at Sara with two of them lodging into each of her shoulders.

She screeches and whips her head side to side.

What the—? I can't believe he just did that!

As if he's magically read my mind, Brohn says, "Believe it. By themselves, these little guys can distract or disable." He draws a small vial of glowing purplish liquid from his pocket and bounces it in the palm of his hand. "Add a little bit of this home-made neurotoxin, and you can paralyze. Add a little more, and you can kill."

Walking over to Sara to pluck the darts from her shoulders, Brohn invites her to boot down to the Infirmary to get herself looked at, but she declines and apologizes.

"Nothing to be sorry for," Brohn assures her with a gentle laugh. "But thanks for helping with the lesson."

As Sara crosses her arms in front of her, one palm on each

shoulder to stop the small trickles of blood soaking into her shirt, Brohn returns his attention to the introductions.

"These uniquely curved steel daggers are called *kirpan*. Traditionally, they were carried by Sikhs as part of what was known as the Five Articles of the Faith. Like you, the Sikhs were dedicated to ferocity on the battlefield but also empathy for the enemy. They were sometimes known as 'Warrior Saints.'"

He calls the next weapon a *mambele*. It's a ferocious looking two-foot-long throwing knife of flattened iron with an oddly-angled blade and a separate, smaller blade branching out from its middle. It's like someone turned the letter "F" into a deadly weapon.

"The smaller blade is designed to ensure that the mambele stays stuck in the body of your enemy. The weapon originally comes from East and Central Africa."

Brohn whips the multi-bladed dagger across the room, and we watch as it lodges in the black center of one of the thick, round wooden targets on the wall.

From under his hood, Arlo whispers, "Marvie."

Brohn scoops up a set of *Kunai* knives. There are five of the arrow-shaped weapons, each with foot-long razor-edged blades, an iron ring at the base of each handle, and leather thread wrapped around the hilt.

"They look like throwing knives," Brohn says, fanning the five knives out in his hand. "But they're best used for stabbing or..."

Brohn sets four of the knives back down. With the remaining one in hand, he slips a length of thin white rope through the eye of the handle, ties it off with a flick of his fingers, and whips the slender knife across the room. The needle-sharp point plunks into the center of the same target as the mambele. Brohn tugs on his end of the rope and explains how the weapon, when attached like this, can be used as a climbing spike.

"Finally," Brohn says, sliding open a panel in the wall to reveal a whole new set of tools and weapons on a board of hooks and shelves, "because of where we are, the Academy also comes with a whole supply of climbing and mining equipment. Some, we've set aside for actual, you know, climbing and mining. But these others here..." Brohn waves a hand at the rack and back down to the long table full of tools, "we've set aside as potential weapons."

With rapid-fire explanations, he introduces us to pickaxes, sledgehammers, rope and carabiners, a whole family of serrated hunting knives, and a set of Ninja Weapons, including two *katana* swords, a sickle shaped tool called a *kama*, one with a chain called a *kusarigama*, and a *manrikigusari*, which is basically a chain with two heavy, plum-sized balls of steel on either end.

"Okay," Brohn says with a soft smile, "time for you to learn, practice, master, and choose."

14

SELECTION

AFTER OVER A WEEK OF RELENTLESS, non-stop (and often ragingly painful) training, the day comes when we make our final selections.

Brohn has the entire buffet of weapons, gadgets, and tools laid out for us.

Ignacio nudges me with his elbow. "About time, eh?"

"You're drooling."

He drags the back of his hand across his mouth and smiles. "Can you blame me?"

We've come to know these weapons pretty well by now. We know which ones work for us and which ones don't. More important, like Brohn's been teaching us, it's more than knowing which one feels right. We need to know which one make *us* feel right.

"After all," he constantly reminds us, "Emergent or not... other than each other, your weapon will often be about all you have out there."

And Haida, I remind myself. *I'll always have Haida. And she'll always have me.*

Brohn steps to the side, giving us a half-bow and a grand

sweep of his arm in the direction of the stockpile of weapons we've been getting to know so well.

We accept his invitation and prepare to make our final selection.

Libra fondles the various knives, clubs, and cudgels. She drags the back of her hand over some of the farming tools and offers up exaggerated "Hmmmm" noises like she's arriving at the single most important decision any human being has ever made.

To my surprise, she stops at the last weapon in the world I'd have expected her to pick.

She lifts up the sixteen-pound, hickory-handled sledge-hammer in both hands and asks Brohn what he thinks.

He taps various parts of the hammer with his finger, calling out their names as he goes. "Well, as you know, this particular tool has a face, a head, a cheek, and an eye." He pats the end of the handle with his open palm. "And a pretty nice butt."

Libra laughs, and Brohn adds, "I'd say that's one handsome partner you have there."

Libra beams at the silver-headed hammer and says she agrees.

Brohn says, "Here," and hands her a leather shoulder harness with a holster to hold the hammer. Libra slips it over her head and rotates it around, with the hefty hammer slung guitar-style against her back.

She grins again, pats the leather strap across her body, and says, "Marvie!"

Sara, looking unusually mousy for her, slinks over to the table and makes a beeline for the throwing darts.

Without saying a word to Brohn or to any of us, she slots the two dozen or so silver spikes with their stiff tail flights into their bandolier and buckles it across her chest.

It's an odd choice, considering a week ago, she had one of them lodged in each shoulder.

Or who knows? Maybe it makes perfect sense. The other day, when I told Kress about my time as a little girl sneaking in and out of the Tower so I could witness the death and destruction of my city, she didn't seem surprised. Instead, her voice got soft, and she said, "We're often attracted to the things that hurt us" and then went back to teaching me how to use my Emergent abilities to walk through walls.

(I still can't do it very well, and I can't do it all without Kress, but with her help, I've been getting better.)

As Sara steps to the side, Mattea slips her hands into the handles of the pair of Bear Claws. The pointed tips of the slightly hooked talons glitter glossy silver, practically begging for something—or someone—to tear into.

Ignacio picks up a pair of the *shillelaghs,* bounces one in each hand, and twirls them baton-style until he looks like a twin-propeller airplane.

"Perfect," he beams, giving Brohn a cocky wink. "In case we need to invoke Shillelagh Law."

Brohn's lips twitch into a grin, and he tells him, "Good choice."

Libra nudges me with her elbow. "What about you, Branwynne?"

I love hand-to-hand combat. But I don't mind having a gun on me when one is available. A bladed weapon like the Talons Kress uses is tempting.

But I also want to add distance to my arsenal.

There was one weapon we worked with—a pair actually—that felt...*right* in my hands. During our target practices, I felt like I couldn't miss with them. When we sparred, they worked just as well for defense as they did for offense. They're perfect for close-quarters combat. They fold up for easy carrying. Plus, I can throw them. And if I miss, which I don't intend to do, they come back to me, boomerang style. (It's a good way to get my hand cut off, which Mattea nearly did when she tried them out a few days ago, but my enhanced reflexes enable me to pluck them out of the air as easy-peasy as pulling petals off a daisy.) They're light, practical, versatile, and strong.

Plus, they look totally bad-ass.

"These," I say, picking up the pair of Serpent Blades.

I feel the weight and balance of the weapons. The curved blades glint frosty silver in the room's crisp white light. The handgrip in the middle feels like it was made for my palms.

Brohn hands me a thin leather belt with sheaths on each side to hold the weapons.

I tell him, "Thanks." He calls me "Miss Deadly" and asks me if I want him to set me up for some private lessons with Kella, our resident, deadeye sharpshooter.

I tell him, "Frack yeah!" and slip my new holster over my hips.

Meanwhile, Arlo drags his fingers along the rest of the weapons and tools in the rack and then along the bigger ones hanging on the wall. He stops at a long-handled scythe, which he takes down gingerly with both hands. With the weapon in hand, his hood up, and his face encased in shadow, he looks like a seventeen-year-old Grim Reaper.

Sara points this out, and Mattea slings her arm around Arlo and agrees. "Cutest specter of death I've ever seen!" she laughs.

I expect Arlo to grumble or get mad, but he smiles, his glistening white teeth and a few loops of his curly, wheat-colored hair visible in the shadows under his hood.

Even Brohn gets in on the fun and gives Arlo an approving, corner-mouthed grin. "Not every day we get a smile out of Death."

Ignacio chuckles and heaves a melodramatic sigh of relief. "I'm just glad you're on *our* side!"

After their dust-up in class a while back, I figured there'd be bad blood. But apparently Ignacio has a short memory, and I'm not sure Arlo even remembers that it ever happened.

With our weapons selected, we stand around chatting with Brohn for a few minutes during some very rare downtime. He compliments us on our choices and tells us he thinks they're spot-on.

When Brohn dismisses us, we trundle up to the Lounge to rest and recover until it's time for Puzzles, Codes, and Game Theory with Rain—the brilliant mathematician, logician, and chess prodigy from Kress's original Conspiracy. Switching places in the schedule, Cohort B has the same Alternate Weapons Training we just had.

After the Afternoon Module, our two Cohorts gather upstairs again in the Lounge. This time, we're all newly armed.

I have to admit, it's fun comparing notes on the various weapons everyone selected.

(I spent the last few days guessing which weapons my classmates would pick based on their personalities and what I know of them. I got every one of them wrong.)

Sitting casually on the couch, Arlo leans his scythe against the wall next to him. Glinting in the light, the long, curved blade hovers over his head.

Mattea walks over and pivots the weapon so the blade faces the other way. "We can't have this thing falling on your head," she tells Arlo with a goofy grin.

Lucid and Reverie proudly show off their *katana*. It's an odd choice for such docile, mysterious (and frankly sort of unathletic kids), but the twins are beaming and seem bolder with the lethal weapons in hand.

Chace shows off her loops of rope and carabiners. "Not much of a weapon," she confesses with a blush. "But I figure, we go to school on top of a mountain, so who knows when some good climbing gear might come in handy?"

Sara tells her it was a smart choice.

"Thanks!" Chace beams.

"Especially if you plan on getting attacked by a steep cliff."

"Leave her alone," Libra snaps, her hand on Chace's shoulder. "At least she's thinking ahead."

Sara plops down on the deep purple love seat and swings her legs up onto one of its arms. She flicks three of her throwing darts across the room and says, "Whatever," as the needle-like swords lodge—*plink, plink, plink*—into the wall just above Chace's head.

Chace shrieks, ducks, and then glares over at Sara, who offers up a gaping yawn in return.

Trax sees the attack against his sister and frowns, but since nothing comes of it, he turns back to his own weapons.

He lays his holster of hunting knives out on the table and starts polishing them one by one with the bottom part of his shirt.

I swing around to face Roxane and ask, "What about you?"

She looks up from where she's busily gnawing on the cuticle around her pinky finger. "No."

"No, what?"

"No weapon."

"What's she mean?" I ask Trax.

He doesn't look up from his shiny collection of new toys when he mumbles, "She didn't pick one."

"Why not?"

"I don't know."

Sitting in the small armchair across from me, Roxane hangs her head. "Regret."

"You regret not picking a weapon?" I ask. "You can always pick one tomorrow."

Looking up from her wet, chewed-up fingernail, Roxane shakes her head. "Remorse."

"Remorse?" Libra asks. "Like, you feel bad about something? Remorse for what?"

But Roxane doesn't answer. Instead, she gets up, draws her swan-white hair into a short, messy ponytail, and plods off to bed.

15

WORRIED

THE NEXT DAY, Cohort B is already in the Lunchroom when we file in after Morning Module.

We're all sweaty.

With a morning class, an afternoon class, Apprenticeship training, and with just a few hours of sleep each night, these days, it seems like we're *always* sweaty.

Libra slips into the seat next to mine and manages to knock against my shoulder even though there's more than enough room on the long bench seat. I shift to the side, so now I'm sitting with half my arse hanging off the edge. But it's better than being shoulder-to-shoulder with Miss Human Chatterbox.

True to form, she's babbling on about our weeks of training sessions with Brohn.

Ugh. I guess she's harmless enough. But does she really have to always be such a pleasant little chuffer?

"At first, I couldn't even hold that arbalest of his," she giggles. "And now, I have my own sledgehammer!" And then, she launches into a five-minute soliloquy about what a good teacher Brohn is and how much she's looking forward to carrying her new toy into battle.

Then she asks us about all the weapons we selected and if we're set up for private lessons yet.

"*I* am," she boasts with a thumb pressed to her chest and before anyone has a chance to answer. "War's going to work with me in one of the Combat Skills and Training rooms. We're going to work on strength training, balance, combat simulations..."

I swear, I don't know how anyone can have lungs big enough to hold the amount of air needed to keep their mouth moving non-stop like this.

As if her unending prattling isn't enough to annoy me, she has the lovely habit of nudging against me or squeezing my arm every time she makes a point or thinks she's being clever. Like I'm going to encourage her or something.

When I try to shrug her away, she acts like I'm kidding around and rambles on.

It's Roxane who cuts her off, which is ironic since Roxane has spent most of her life mostly mute. When she *does* talk, it's almost always just a word or two or a cluster of random words the rest of us have to try to assemble, jigsaw puzzle-style, if we want any hope of figuring out what she's on about.

As far as I know Trax and Mattea are the best at deciphering her monosyllabic gibberish.

This time, she says, "Worried," before sweeping her hair behind her ear and nibbling on the tip of her pinky finger.

Libra rolls her eyes, apparently annoyed at having her monologue interrupted. "Who's worried, Rox?"

When Roxane doesn't look up, I ask her if she's worried about something. She shakes her head but doesn't answer.

I look over to Trax and Mattea for help, but they both offer up flustered, apologetic shrugs.

Roxane lifts her eyes and stares at Libra, but I don't think she really sees her. There's a weird, distant blankness to her face. Roxane blinks hard, points at Libra and asks, "Meaning?"

"What do *I* mean?" Libra laughs. "You're the one who said someone's worried."

Roxane's head doesn't move, but her pale blue eyes scan the rest of us sitting at the table. "Worried."

"What?"

"Kress."

"Kress is worried?" I ask, leaning forward now. "Or you're worried about Kress?"

If this barmy nutter even thinks about doing anything to Kress...

Roxane scrunches up her forehead and blinks hard like she's staring into the sun.

Sara rolls her eyes and tilts her head toward Roxane. "I swear," she says to Ignacio who's sitting on her other side. "Sometimes, I just don't understand this girl."

Ignacio grins through a mouthful of food. "Well, you don't have to live in a tree to be a nut."

Roxane scowls at the insult and stamps her foot under the table. "Danger."

Ignacio scowls back, and I don't blame him. Roxane's already picked one fight with him for no reason. Now, it looks like she's coming back for seconds.

The next three words tumble out of her mouth faster than she can control them. "Leaving. Planning. Capture."

Normally, I wouldn't pay much attention to Roxane. But since this is pretty much the most I've ever heard come out of her mouth at a time, I'm curious. Besides, if it has something to do with Kress, my mentor, I have a right to know about it.

I put my hand on Ignacio's arm to stop him in case he's planning on lunging at her again. I lean in, my elbows on the table, and ask her—with as much patience as I can manage—to explain what she means.

Roxane shrugs and drops her eyes. But I'm not letting her off that easy. Reaching across the table, I clamp my hand onto her wrist. "What is it, Rox?"

The tendons in her neck strain like she's trying hard to swallow or to hold back tears. "Overheard."

I take a deep breath.

Stay in control, Branwynne. No need to lash out. Yet.

I take one more breath and ask, "What exactly did you overhear?"

But Roxane bites her lip and shakes her head, her eyes distant and glossy.

Chace takes a rare moment to look up from her holo-pad. "I think...I think maybe I know what she's talking about," she says under her breath.

Ignacio crosses his arms hard across his chest. "Great. Care to share with the class?"

"I was there," she says. "On the stairs. Right near the Techno-Genetic Research Lab. The door had glitched open, and Terk was trying to fix it. Roxane was sitting on the stairs, and I stopped to make sure she was okay."

"And...?" I ask.

"Kress and Brohn were talking about some threat to the Academy."

"What threat?" Mattea snaps.

"I don't know. They mentioned the Devoted. The Unsettled. Civillains. Plaguers. The Cysters. They were talking about a *lot* of stuff."

Ignacio rolls his eyes and shoos Chace away with his hand. "And you happened to overhear them without being noticed?"

Chace holds up her holo-pad. "I'm the Chronicler. It's my job."

"Cysters?" Reverie asks.

"A band of women survivors of the Cyst Plague," Trax clarifies on behalf of his twin sister as he picks at a spot of dry skin on the back of his hand. "We learned about them from Granden back in D.C. They're crazy, and they hate men."

"Doesn't sound so crazy to me," Sara grumbles. "Have you *met* some of the men out there?"

Chace shakes her head. "I don't think that's who Kress was worried about."

"Who then?"

"I don't know. But I think…"

"Spit it out, Miss Chronicler," I hiss.

"I think maybe someone knows we're here."

"Impossible," Ignacio boasts. "This place is locked up and secure at the top of a mountain, and it has a Veiled Refractor. No one can see it from the outside, and Kress and the others would kill anyone who tried to get in, anyway."

"They don't kill for no reason," Lucid says quietly.

Ignacio responds with a condescending grunt. "Protecting this place—and us—wouldn't be for 'no reason.' Let's not forget, our teachers have killed before."

"But only when it's been necessary," Mattea chimes in.

We all jump when Roxane smashes her fist onto the table, and our plates, glasses, and silverware rattle and bounce into the air. "Danger!" she hisses.

Ignacio leans toward me. "I don't know what the frack she's talking about, but the real danger is me bashing her face in."

"That won't stop her from being right," I tell him.

He points a stabbing finger at Roxane, who doesn't react as his voice peaks with a cocktail of fury, impatience, and disbelief. "Don't tell me you're buying this garbage?"

"Maybe not 'buying,'" I concede. "But I'm willing to rent it for a minute."

Reverie nods her agreement, which makes Ignacio back down. He's a tough guy, and I don't think there's a lot he's afraid of. But the twins—especially Reverie—seem to set him a bit on edge.

Her voice soothing and low, Reverie turns to Roxane and asks what she thinks we should do about this "danger."

Every one of us around the table leans forward, anxious for the big revelation.

But Roxane blinks at us and frowns like she's waking up from a dream.

"See!" Ignacio exclaims with triumph. "There's no danger. She's dumb as a soup sandwich. And you're all just as bat-barf crazy for listening to her, and I don't want to be late for Propaganda."

He scoops up his silver tray, drops it into the cleaning chute, and storms out of the Tavern.

16

PROPAGANDA

A FEW DAYS LATER, I'm just finishing washing up in the Dorms following a fast but intense workout in the gym.

After a very pleasant sonic shower, I gather up my books and am just getting ready to head downstairs for Afternoon Module when Libra pops out of nowhere and hooks her arm into mine.

"It's been quite a few exciting days, hasn't it?"

I slip my arm out of hers and give her a death-glare she doesn't seem to notice.

"Come on," she pleads. "Weapons. Drama. Secret Meetings. Some unknown threat to the Academy. You can't tell me you're not worried."

"That's *exactly* what I can tell you. What do I have to be worried about?"

"Well, for starters what's with the weird power outages?"

"What? The lights? They're just glitches."

"And the doors and lifts not working?"

"Glitches."

"And the way Kress and the others have been walking around looking worried and having secret meetings all the time? And *don't* say, 'Glitches.'"

"It's nothing."

With the straps of her sagging blue Academy shoulder bag slung over her shoulders, Libra folds her arms hard across her chest as we walk. "Then what about the stuff about War being afraid? Lucid and Reverie being so weird about it...? Roxane...?"

Not wanting to be late for Granden's class, I pick up my pace and wait for her to finish. When she doesn't say anything and just sort of stares at me as we get to the top of the stairs, I ask her why she's making such a big deal out of it. "Lucid and Reverie have always been weird. Trust me. I've seen them in action. Roxane is...*Roxane*. And War...maybe Mattea was just reading him wrong."

Libra frowns and mutters, "Maybe," but I can tell she still thinks there's more going on than some nervous teachers, a couple of weirdos, and a few glitches in the Academy's power.

We've been in classes together and living in the same dorm room for months now. I've rarely seen Libra worried or without her signature smile for more than about three seconds at a time.

But now...

Oh, wait. There it is. The smile has returned.

Libra grins and pokes me in the arm. "I thought you were going to punch Sara the other day. Seriously, who died and made her leader of our Cohort?"

I just shrug and keep walking, but Libra's more than happy to fill the dead air. "And you have to admit, Ignacio's pretty cute when he's pretending to be brave."

"Ugh. He's a self-involved wanker."

I feel dumb for letting Libra draw me into whatever teenage girl drama she's trying to stir up, so I clamp my lips tight as we get to the classroom where Granden is standing next to his slender teaching console with the other four members of our Cohort sitting in front of him in a semi-circle at their glass-topped desks.

He's already started the class, and Libra and I offer meek apologies as we slide into our seats next to the others.

"Welcome, ladies," he says before turning back to the holographic projection hovering next to him. As he touches the image, it morphs and shifts into a scroll of text and pictures.

"As we talked about last week, when it comes to propaganda, what you see is definitely *not* what you get. That's the point of propaganda. It's a trick. A manipulation. A way for someone to get you to do what *they* want." Granden taps a finger to his temple and scans the class, his eyes stopping for a full second on Sara, although I'm not sure why. "Only, the *real* trick is how the 'someone' gets you to think it's what you wanted all along."

Libra launches her hand into the air. "And how are we supposed to fight against that?"

"First, by understanding that it's happening. Second, by having enough personal pride to get offended when you know someone is trying to manipulate you. Third, you need to be educated, which is part of why you're here. People who aren't exposed to other ways of thinking and to other ways of *being* are the ones most likely to fall for propaganda. That's because they need something to follow. We all need someone or something to follow. That's human nature. We begin life as a connected entity. But sometimes, laziness and the temptation of taking the easy route convinces some people to let others do the thinking for them."

Mattea raises her hand and asks a question about the homework from the night before.

We were supposed to read a sixty-page article posted to our holo-pads about the historical role of repetition in advertising and propaganda.

I got through nearly all of the first page before I got restless. Instead of focusing like Kress has been teaching me, I jogged up to the roof to visit Haida Gwaii, and then jogged back downstairs to the third floor for a workout in the Fitness Center. (I lifted weights, ran on the treadmill, and practiced with my Serpent Blades until I got bleary eyed and headed back up to bed.)

Granden asks Mattea what *she* thinks about the article, and she replies in that measured, even way of hers—as if she's afraid the person she's talking to is judging every syllable. "The power of propaganda is in its repetition. If you say anything enough times, almost anyone will start to believe it."

"But why?" Granden asks with a smile and a rolling, "tell me more" motion of his hand.

Mattea shrugs and looks over at me like I'm somehow going to magically know the answer. After last night's workout, I'm too tired to remember my own name.

Granden surveys us all. "What is it about repetition that winds up being so seductive?"

Sara has her elbow on her desk and her face scrunched up in the palm of her hand. "We're stupid," she grumbles.

Granden gives what I think is an annoyed sigh and asks her to elaborate.

"We're stupid. We're instinctive and lazy by nature. We're not born to be critical thinkers. So we take the easy path, the one we've heard about or tried before, and we know it works."

"That's a good way to wind up with your head buried in the sand," Ignacio objects.

"Sometimes 'buried in the sand' is the safest place to be," Sara replies.

"It may be safe," Mattea says, "but it's also a sure way to stay ignorant."

Granden crosses his arms and says, "Hm. Interesting point."

Without raising his hand or even looking up, Arlo suggests that it all has to do with fear. "Scared people do bad things and are the most easily manipulated by bad people."

Nodding his partial agreement, Granden says, "Part of the power of propaganda comes from its reliance on fear. I think Arlo makes a strong point. Fearful people are always more likely to fall for propaganda, buy into conspiracy theories, and see existential threats everywhere around them." He taps the pad on the podium next to him, and the hologram of a familiar face—wrinkled mouth, beady eyes, weathered skin, oily-black hair—springs to life just over his shoulder.

Libra and Sara are the only ones from our Cohort who were born in the U.S., although they were taken overseas to Europe when they were only about six years old, so I know they don't remember or know much about our adopted country. Still, we all moan and boo at the image of former and long-dead President Krug.

After all, his reach extended well beyond the borders of America. According to Granden—and he should know—a few million people around the world wound up rich because of him. But a few *billion* more wound up dead.

Granden pumps his hands in front of him to calm us down. "So, to start, let's talk about Krug. I'm assuming you know who he was?"

We all nod that we most definitely do.

Although we arrived here months after Krug was thankfully tossed off a roof by Kress and her Conspiracy, we've all heard stories, and we've all suffered through the violence and cruelty he so casually and *globally* spawned.

For the rest of class, Granden leads us through a whole history of slogans, deception, and rhetoric—all the things that brought Krug to power and enabled him to embark on his greedy, ego-driven campaign of global terror.

Granden's a good teacher. He's not as intense as Brohn, as demanding as Kress, or as scary as War. But he knows a lot.

Except for War and Mayla, he's the only one of our teachers who's old enough to really know what life was like before and after the wars.

And he's definitely the resident expert on Krug.

After all, Krug was his father.

17

BRAINWASHING

OVER THE NEXT couple of weeks, Granden been introducing us to a bunch of old movies, most of which we watch for homework.

Sometimes, our entire Cohort reserves the Movie Room just off of the Lounge.

One day, Granden tells us about the long tradition of eating popcorn at the movies.

We don't have popcorn, but thanks to Mayla and her class on Hunting and Foraging, we have an ample supply of pine nuts from a part of the woods on the south side of the mountain. The woods on one part of the mountain have only recently recovered from a long history of drone strikes and toxic, radioactive fallout that Mayla thought might keep the land barren forever.

So when we're not in classes or engaged in apprenticeship training with our personal mentors, my Cohort and I sit around watching old movies and munching on pine nuts out of a collection of small ceramic bowls.

Back in class, Granden grills us about the reading he's assigned, and we take tests every couple of days to see how well we're keeping up, how much we're retaining, and whether or not we're ready to move on.

Most of our readings come from holo-texts, but Granden boasts that he's "old school" and has decided to also give us supplemental assignments from the shelves of musty paper books in the Academy's sprawling, second floor library.

I must be "old school," too, because I prefer the paper books to the holo-texts, which make my eyes hurt and bore me with their flat, soulless, uniformity.

Like most birds, ravens use their heightened sense of touch to adjust to changes in air pressure, temperature, and wind speed. They also have tiny, sensitive whiskers called rictal bristles on their beaks, which gives them extra tactile sensitivity. So maybe I'm channelling that from Haida Gwaii as I run my finger along the grainy paper pages.

The stack of books on my nightstand keeps getting higher and higher, and Libra jokes about how she's afraid one day it's going to topple over and crush me in my sleep.

Like me, Sara does most of the assignments, but sometimes she bins off.

"Grades are just another form of brainwashing and propaganda," she tells Granden one day in class.

"That's an interesting point," he answers and then gives her an "F" for not handing in her work and then tells her she has to go do it anyway.

She grumbles, but I know she'll do it. The only thing she hates more than being told what to do is being told that she didn't do it very well.

In class, Mattea gets decent scores, but she doesn't stress about it one way or another. She does enough to fly under Granden's radar and seems happy being out of the spotlight.

Arlo and I are toward the bottom of the class.

Although I *do* like reading a lot, I'm usually too distracted to bother with most of the written assignments and too focused on my apprenticeship lessons with Kress to keep up properly in Granden's class.

He holds me after class sometimes and lectures me about the need to be disciplined. I promise I'll try harder, and I usually manage to keep up...for the next couple of days, anyway. And then, I get distracted by one thing or another and wind up falling behind again.

Unlike me, Libra is hyper-competitive about the assignments and isn't shy about announcing her marks to the rest of us every night in the Dorms.

When Ignacio finally cracks and tells her nobody cares, she gets pouty.

"Granden cares."

"Well, I don't," Ignacio snaps.

Except for the faint orange glow from the security panel, the room is dark. Still, I can see Libra's gleaming white teeth when she smiles at me from her bed. "He's just jealous," she whispers with a head tilt toward Ignacio.

"I'm sure that's it."

I mean, it's true. Ignacio *can* be a bore and a bully. Maybe Libra's right. Maybe he's been so snarky lately because he's mad about her being so much smarter than him and how she keeps exposing him as a total thicko.

The next day, we're all surprised when Granden congratulates Ignacio for having the highest marks in the class at the mid-term break.

Ignacio mumbles, "Thanks," but he doesn't seem too happy about being outed as a proper, upstanding intellectual.

Wow! From meat-head to egg-head right before my eyes. What else is this guy hiding?

After we've settled down and Libra has uncrossed her arms

and unclenched her teeth, Granden turns our attention back to the day's lesson.

Mattea raises her hand and says something's been bothering her.

Libra reaches over and squeezes Ignacio's upper arm. "You mean besides Mr. Grumpy here being such a secret genius this whole time?"

Ignacio rips his arm from her grasp and grumbles that he's *not* a genius.

"Fine," Libra says with pretend offense. "Then just grumpy."

"What's your question?" Granden asks Mattea.

"Well...I've been wondering. Is there such a thing as *good* propaganda?"

"How do you mean?"

"Well, for homework, we read *The Jungle* by Upton Sinclair. Last week, we read *Silent Spring* by Rachel Carson."

"Go on."

"Well, aren't they all just forms of propaganda? Aren't they all just doing what Krug did? What I mean is, isn't *everything* just designed to make people do or think or feel what the designer wants them to?"

Libra stabs a hand into the air like she's trying to poke a hole in the ceiling. Without waiting to be called on, she belts out her opinion.

"Krug's propaganda tried to scare people into being afraid and hurting other people. Krug was motivated by greed, selfishness, and personal insecurity. The movies and books Mattea is talking about are trying to scare people into being nicer to animals and to be better human beings."

Sara shakes her head. "But fear is still the key ingredient, isn't it?"

Like a leaking balloon, Libra's hand sinks down out of the air. "Um...I guess."

Granden lets us talk a little while longer before guiding us in a series of lessons about free will and something he calls, "Priming."

"Priming," he explains, "is based on repetition but also on visual or verbal cues that take advantage of our ability and our desire, conscious or unconscious, to connect one thing with another."

With my entire relationship with Haida Gwaii in mind, I ask, "Aren't connections a *good* thing?"

"Very often," Granden concedes. "But they have a downside too, since connections made in haste or out of ignorance are what lead to simplistic thinking patterns and stereotyping."

From there, Granden gives us some more of the historical story of Krug's rise to power, this time with an emphasis on the subconscious power of priming.

When I ask if he can tell us what it was like to have Krug as a father and to see (and help!) him get killed, Granden shifts on his feet and tells us those are all stories for another time.

So instead of hearing the super interesting stuff about how Granden managed to aid in the overthrow and assassination of his own father, we hear more about how Krug drew on events, fears, and insecurities of the past to promote ignorance and fear in the present.

As tough as classes like Unarmed Combat are on my body, this class is just as tough on my brain.

I'm surprised when Sara raises her hand. She's confident in an I-don't-care-what-you-think sort of way. But she's more inclined to mock someone—usually me—for participating than to be a participant, herself.

She doesn't blink when she addresses Granden. "We've spent the past few days talking about how easy it is to brainwash someone. How do we know that's not what you're doing to us?"

I expect Granden to get offended or maybe even laugh. But

he does neither. Instead, he nods and eases down onto his mag-chair next to his teaching console.

"What makes you ask that, Sara?"

"Well, if propaganda is based on fear, what you're telling us seems designed to make us afraid."

I'm looking back and forth between Granden and Sara. I can't believe he's even treating this like a serious question, and I keep thinking he's going to cut her off or something.

"It's true," he says. "I'm trying to teach you about fear. But I think that's different than trying to make you afraid."

Sara squints at him and doesn't seem satisfied.

"*Are* you afraid?" he asks.

"Of what?"

"Of the world outside of this Academy."

"I was," Sara admits.

"When?"

Sara bites her lip, and I think she's going to start crying, but her voice is solid and strong. "In the Processor."

"The one in Spain?"

Sara nods. "But only at first. When I was little."

"You were in there for a long time, right?"

"From the time I was six." Sara's eyes dart around the room. "We all were. Except for Branwynne."

For some reason, I feel offended at being left out. Which is stupid, right? The five other members of my Cohort spent six years as the En-Gene-eers' lab rats until Kress and her Conspiracy got them out. Why would I want to be part of that?

"Well, I can tell you this much at least," Granden promises. "I don't want you to be afraid *or* ignorant."

Sara slides her fingers through her short blond hair and then leans back and crosses her arms across her chest. "But isn't *all* teaching just a form of propaganda?"

Arlo shakes his head under his hood. "Sara, I think teaching is the *opposite* of propaganda."

Ignacio leans forward, a deep crease forming between his eyes. "How do you figure? I'm with Sara on this one. I'm sure you remember what they did to us in the Valencia Processor, right?"

Arlo hangs his head, and when no one answers, Ignacio answers for himself. "They said they were 'teaching' us to use our abilities as Emergents." Under the blanket of silence that follows, Ignacio continues on, his voice in a quiver of restrained anger. "They hooked us up to diagnostic equipment. They ran us through impossible puzzles and VR-sims designed to weed us out. They manipulated us, monitored our every move, pretended we were being prepared to help in a global war, and they kept us in cages the entire time. *They* called it teaching. We called it *torture*."

I'm watching my Cohort and expecting Granden to lead the discussion one way or the other, but instead, he sits back and lets us talk.

I wag a finger at Ignacio. "Propaganda is a tool to get others to do what you want. *Teaching* is a tool to help others figure out what they want for themselves."

Sara laughs. "Sounds like the same thing."

"It's not," I insist. My head hurts all of a sudden, and I sort of see her point and almost want to agree with her. But no—I'm not going to give her the satisfaction.

Shaking her head, Sara flicks her thumb toward Mattea. "Mattea said it, herself. Propaganda and teaching...they're both tools one person uses to manipulate someone else. Is it really anyone's place to stop someone from believing what they want to believe?"

"It *is*," I say, my words crisp and deliberate, "when what they believe in is murder and getting rich and powerful while everyone else suffers and dies."

Sara swings around to fix her eyes on mine. "Is it really *our* responsibility to stop people from suffering and dying?"

I roll my eyes. "Um...*yeah*. That's why we're here."

"Not me," Sara says with a vigorous shake of her head. "Not any of us. We're here because we're different...No—we're here because we're *better* than the Typics, and they want to use us as weapons against each other."

"Bollocks!" I shout, rising to my feet, my palms planted firmly on the glass top of my desk. "We're here because Kress saved us. We're here because Wisp really thinks we have a chance to save the world. We're here because we'd be dead if we weren't."

I feel myself starting to cry, and now I feel like a total tosser.

Libra raises her hand.

Great. The last thing I need is Miss Full-of-Beans over here coming to my rescue.

"I agree with Sara," Libra says.

Wait. What?

Libra waits for someone to object, but no one does, so she soldiers on.

"Sara's right. Teaching is just another form of brainwashing." She swings her eyes around the room, taking in all of us, the rows of glass-topped desks, the holo-displays behind Granden, and the glass wall looking out into the empty, wood-paneled corridor. "Maybe all of this is just another Processor. Maybe it's all just another trap to weaponize us for someone else's war."

I frown and offer up a long, "Ummmm" of objection, but Libra ignores me and locks her eyes on Granden's instead.

"From what we've heard and from what you've been telling us, Krug tricked people into thinking everyone else was out to get them. Then, he convinced them that they were superior to everyone else. *Then*, he got everyone fighting and killing each other while he gathered up more and more wealth and power for himself. How is that any different from what's happening here?"

"Good question," Granden says, a glint in his eye. "Now, answer it."

Libra stares but doesn't answer, so I give it a shot, my voice struggling through an angry quiver.

"There's a difference between tricking someone and teaching them. There's a difference between trying to get what you want and helping others to get what *they* want. Krug was all about fear. You knew him better than anyone, right? He was afraid of his own flaws. He was afraid of being laughed at or ignored or forgotten. He was afraid of being vulnerable or wrong. He was afraid to listen and afraid he might not be God. The Academy is the opposite. It's like you said. You're teaching us the opposite. You're teaching us how *not* to be afraid."

Sara rolls her eyes at me. The other members of my Cohort are also glaring at me like I've somehow betrayed them, like *I'm* the daft cow of the bunch, ready to let myself get brainwashed and sucked into some villainous propaganda machine.

Granden must notice because he stands up and tells us this is probably a good place to stop for the day.

Standing and hoisting our bags onto our backs, my Cohort and I file out and head down to the Tavern for lunch.

Trudging a few steps behind, I stop on the first floor and hold up my arm with the blue-gel cast on my wrist. "I need to stop at the Infirmary to see if Mayla can fix the crack in this thing."

"I'll keep you company!" Libra beams.

"Not me," Ignacio says. "I'm hungry."

Mattea and Arlo heartily agree with Ignacio, and they all follow Sara downstairs to the Tavern while Libra skips along next to me on my way to the Infirmary.

Finally, I can't take it anymore, and I swing around to face her, my hands clamped to her shoulders. "Where the bloody hell did *that* come from?"

Libra's eyes go wide, and her lips quiver under a stammer of surprise. "W-w-where did *what* come from?"

"That bloody rubbish back there in class...about this being just another Processor."

"I don't..."

"Don't give me that crap. Sara was being a gormless, grade-A twat-waffle, and you and the others were right there, mucking along with her."

"But I wasn't..." Her lower jaw hanging open, Libra shakes her head as her eyes go wet and glossy.

"Since when did you get so chummy with Sara, anyway?" I ask through clenched teeth.

Libra blinks hard and curls her fingers around my wrists. She tugs my hands from her shoulders. "Branwynne, I wasn't agreeing with Sara."

Her voice sounds weird, and it occurs to me that she's asking a question more than making a statement.

"Sure sounded like it," I sigh, letting my tight jaw relax again. "Sounded like *all* of you had gone completely off your trolley."

Libra offers up a weak, forced smile and starts to tug me along toward the Infirmary. "I guess a lot of things sound like a lot of things. Come on, now. Let's go get you fixed up."

Mayla greets us as we enter the Infirmary, and I hop up onto the mag-table so she can work her healing magic.

Standing next to me, Libra is all smiles again.

She laughs and says, "What?" when she catches me staring at her.

But I just shrug and tell her it's nothing.

Only, I'm not so sure it *is* nothing. Something strange is going on, and I'm not convinced I'm the only one around here who needs healing.

18

RECRUITING

A FEW DAYS LATER, we all roll out of bed with a chorus of groans and with our bones creaking loud enough to hear across the room.

Alternative Weapons training and our Propaganda classes have been especially intense. Brohn's been in an unforgiving mood lately, and I'm pretty sure Granden is trying to make our heads explode with this new unit he's teaching us about rhetoric.

At least the weird squiffiness from the other day seems to have faded away, and we're pretty much back to our normal routine of struggling to keep up in Granden's class and to stay alive in Brohn's.

Cohort B isn't faring much better. Bleary-eyed, they meet us in the hallway, and the eleven of us trudge downstairs for breakfast where we eat in dreary, hypnotized silence.

Back upstairs, the Assembly Hall is dimly lit when we enter.

The normal banks of holo-lights running in long strips along the tops of the walls are smoky gray. The room is bathed in long shadows from the orange-hued backup emergency lights above the doors and by the faint-white reflective plasma lenses above the stage.

The curved stage of polished oak glows weirdly hot under the reddish-white light. I think it looks a little hellish, but Wisp and our teachers are all smiles and don't seem to notice.

As they always do for Morning Address, Kress and the others are sitting in their semi-circle of low-backed silver mag-chairs. The chairs are designed to handle pretty much any weight, but Terk's chair always hovers a little lower than everyone else's.

As a Modified who's had much of the left side of his body integrated with a network of circuit boards, cables, and synth steel pistons, he's a lot heavier than he looks. And he already looks huge, with shoulders as wide across as I am tall.

Wisp and Granden are standing together—like they do most mornings—behind the thin podium of glass and chrome at the front of the stage.

Clearing her throat, Wisp says she has an important announcement. "Kress, Brohn, Rain, Terk, and Kella—the five members of the original Conspiracy—will be leaving for a while. War and Mayla, too."

"Leaving?" The word is past the lump in my throat and out of my mouth before I realize I've said it.

"Not forever," Wisp laughs. "They're going on a mission."

We all squirm in our seats, and I raise my hand and ask, "What kind of mission?"

Wisp slides a lock of hair behind her ear and grips the edges of the podium. I'm expecting some sort of apocalyptic revelation:

Maybe the warring factions down below have made their way up the mountain. Maybe the Veiled Refractor has gone to all to pot, and we're about to be invaded. Maybe a massive drone strike is on its way...

Instead, Wisp scans us back and forth and tells us not to worry. "We still have allies out there."

"And ravens," Kress adds.

"Right. All helpful in gathering information. And there are reports—some have turned out to be myths, rumors, and false leads, but there've been some confirmed reports as well—of more Emergents, kids like you."

Ignacio leans forward in his seat far enough so I think he might face-plant himself to the floor. "Emergents...with abilities?"

"Possibly."

"Where?" Mattea asks, leaning nearly as far forward.

"Multiple places throughout the country, actually."

"And the world," Granden adds for emphasis. "Here. But also in Ghana. Sardinia. Greece. Turkey."

Wisp nods her thanks to Granden before turning her attention back to us. "Our intel is sketchy, but we're fairly sure some of the Emergents are scattered, imprisoned, or on the run. As you know, communication is a problem in the best of times. We're working on that. In the meantime, we need to use the resources we have."

"We think there may be a Processor west of here," Granden tells us, his eyes shifting nervously between us and the ceiling. "Not all that far away, actually."

Kress leans forward in her mag-chair, her arms draped over her knees. "A while back...after we escaped from our own Processor, we ran into a military outpost on our way to San Francisco. I had some...visions there."

Libra thrusts her hand into the air. "Visions? What kind of visions?"

"Dead soldiers, right?" I ask. I've heard this story from Kress during some of our one-on-one, rooftop training sessions.

"That's right," she confirms for the rest of our two Cohorts.

"Dead soldiers. A dead girl. It's when my connection to Render started to jump into an evolutionary high-gear."

Granden rubs his jaw. "Getting good information is challenging, to say the least. But between the tinkering Rain, Terk, and the Auditor have been doing upstairs with the rooftop Sensor Array and Kress's surveillance with Render, we've gotten some pretty reliable intel that something big may be about to happen. We don't know if it's the facility itself, its location, or the people involved. But there's a mystery out there, and it could have to do with all of you."

"And possibly with why we are what we are," Rain adds, looking practically microscopic in her seat between the giants, Terk and War.

Granden gives us a few more details, but there's something off about him. Like he's nervous or unsure.

And I don't think I've ever seen Granden nervous or unsure.

"We have word about the possibility of a new coalition of True Blues—the East Coast faction of the Devoted—who could be working with the Deenays and the En-Gene-eers," he explains. "The military base Kress and the others are going back to out here could be one of the ones being resurrected and repurposed as a home base for the next phase of a techno-genetic program designed to pick up where Krug's experiments left off."

"But Krug's gone," I remind him.

"True. But you aren't."

Brohn nods his agreement with Granden and sighs. "As long as there are potential Emergents out there, there are going to be groups like the True Blues, the Devoted, the Unsettled—you name it—who see them...who see us...who see *you* as something they can weaponize for their own ends. We need to find out what they're up to. If they're building a new Processor, if they're trying to gather up kids like they did with us..."

Chace looks up from her holo-pad. "You really think there are kids out there?"

Kress nods. "According to Render, there may be as many as twenty or thirty. Only..."

Chace looks worried when she asks, "Only...what?"

Kress and Brohn exchange an uneasy look of their own. When Brohn gives her the slightest nod, Kress reveals a horrifying element of their intel. "Some of the kids are most likely already dead." Her eyes glisten and glaze over as she reports that Render has seen bodies in the desert near the military installation.

In the graveyard stillness hovering in the air, our two Cohorts sit for several seconds in stunned silence.

Libra repeats the word, "Dead." I think she means it as a question, but it falls from her mouth like a stone.

"It's possible that they were subjects. Like all of you were at one time or another."

Not me, I think with pride. *I've never been captured by anyone.*

I almost raise my hand to remind her of that fact, but then I think better of it.

Instead, I *do* raise my hand, but it's to ask if I can go with them. "I fought against the Unsettled with you. I helped half the people in this room escape from a Processor. I was there when we escaped from the Devoted down in New Harleck."

I can tell Kress is suppressing an amused grin when she tells me, "Not this time, Branwynne."

Everyone in her semi-circle is quick to agree.

"It's too risky," Kella says.

"And more dangerous and probably more vital than any other mission we've gone on before," Brohn adds. "This could be the start of something very exciting and important..."

"Or it could wind up being the end of the road for a lot of innocents out there," Rain finishes.

Wisp pushes up the sleeves of her oversized military jacket. "We're not exaggerating when we tell you your mission is to save the world. There are some dangerous people building some big armies out there. Unless we want to work for them or else get killed *by* them, we need to continue to build one of our own."

Crossing my arms and feeling sorry for myself for getting left behind, I lock eyes with Kress, but it's Sara who asks with a snarly drawl, "So...you're going to be recruiters?"

I'm sure she means it as an accusation, but Kress chuckles. "Ironic, right?"

Chace is back to being hunched over her holo-pad, tapping out text and taking her job of Chronicler *way* too seriously. She doesn't even look up when she raises her hand. "Excuse me. But who's going to teach us while you're gone?"

"Wisp and Granden are going to stay behind."

"Don't worry," Granden announces. "Tomorrow, we have some challenging activities for you and maybe a nice VR simulation after that."

"Lots of fun and supremely dangerous challenges and combat situations," Wisp adds. "A good chance to test what you've learned so far and to explore your limits."

Next to me, Ignacio doesn't look happy as his eyes drift over to Kress and her Conspiracy. "When do you leave?"

Brohn stands up, and the rest of the Conspiracy follows suit. "About now, actually."

My eyes and mouth are competing over which can be wider open in shock. "*Now?*"

"We can't afford to waste time. If the intel is accurate, we might already be too late."

"For some of those kids," Terk growls as he heaves himself to his feet, "it sounds like we already are."

19

LEAVING

WE ALL FOLLOW Kress and the rest of our teachers downstairs to the Sub-Basement garage where Terk releases the Terminus from its mag-pad. The huge truck floats down, landing lightly on its thick, studded wheels.

The holo-lanterns hanging high overhead beam down shafts of warm, particle-filled light.

Silvery reflections glisten from the crisscross of steel support beams in the cavernous hangar where the Terminus and the Academy's other transports—treadchairs, wide-wheeled grip bikes, motorized tri-blades, modified Skid Steers, snowmobiles, and grav-charged wing-gliders—hover on their own mag-pads in their individual glass-walled storage stalls.

Although it's a strange and sad moment—after all, it's not every day a girl gets abandoned by her mentor—I can't wait to learn how to ride, drive, and fly all of those amazing vehicles!

As we look on, Kress and her Conspiracy cluster around a row of silver lockers and assemble their weapons, piling them up neatly in a hard-shell carrying case with multiple compartments.

"Is that all you're taking?" I ask when I see the meager supply of weapons in the suitcase-sized tote.

"We need to ration our ammo," War explains.

Slinging his arbalest onto his back, Brohn reminds us that weapons are getting harder and harder to come by. "Like I told you...the Wealthies have barricaded themselves in their Arcologies and have hoarded most of the firepower. That's why it's important for you all to continue your training with Wisp and Granden. It won't be long before it's just us and our Emergent abilities out there against a bunch of armies with homemade weapons and whatever guns are left."

"What about rations?" Trax asks.

Kella gives his shoulder a light pat and tells him, "Already packed."

Already packed? How long have they been planning this mission, anyway? And how come they're only telling us about it now?

I feel my cheeks go hot. I've known Kress for over five years, and I've been working one-on-one with her practically every other day for most of it. She's taught me more about how my abilities work. She's taught me how to make better connections with Haida Gwaii and how to be a proper Ravenmaster for Render and Haida's six offspring.

So how come in all of our talks and with all of our training, she kept something so big from me?

Wisp and Granden confer with Kress and the others for a minute or two while our two Cohorts mill around trying not to look scared.

Off to the side, Lucid and Reverie, their foreheads nearly touching, seem to be having their own mini-conference.

Next to me, Ignacio jabs his elbow into my side and points to the vehicles lined up in their stalls. "Can't wait to try those, eh?"

"I was just thinking the same thing." (If my brain had hands, right now, it'd be rubbing them together with glee.) "As soon as Kress and the others get back, I'm going to ask if we can get special training."

From over my shoulder, Libra says she wants in, too. "War's been teaching me how to fix them up, but he says he's not ready to teach me how to ride them yet."

Sara suggests we sneak down here sometime after Kress and the others are gone and take one or two of the specialized mountain vehicles for a spin. I laugh, but Mattea—probably the most strait-laced and play-by-the-rules conservative of us—says she's in, too.

Even Arlo nods. "After Kress and the others leave, it'll just be Wisp and Granden with us. We could be gone and back before they know we've left."

I scowl at Sara and tell her what a terrible idea this is.

What is it with this girl, lately? Is her Emergent ability the skill to stir up trouble wherever she goes? If so, she's getting jolly good at it.

Roxane nudges me as she slips past.

Barely loud enough for me to hear, she says, "Watch out."

"Um...*You* bumped into *me*, Rox."

Roxane's eyes glisten, and she shakes her head. "Misunderstand."

Already annoyed, I'm about to ask her what she's on about this time, but Granden waves his hand and calls us over.

With their pre-departure discussion completed, our teachers climb into the Terminus with Kress and Render as the last ones aboard.

Like adoring fans clamoring around the tour bus of our favorite band, we all say our goodbyes, and Chace promises to keep chronicling everything that happens in the Academy.

Kella, her mentor, thanks her and tells her not to worry. Patting the long, black sniper rifle case in her hand, Kella says,

"I'll personally make sure we stay alive so your story will have a happy ending."

Chace beams up at her and waves.

As everyone else from the two Cohorts cheers out their last goodbyes and backs away, I linger by the side door of the Terminus.

"Take care of Haida and her brood," Kress calls down to me from the open doorway where she's standing with her hand on the grab bar next to the door. Render gives me a stern glare from her shoulder.

"I will," I promise.

"And take care of yourself."

"I will."

"Most important, though, take care of the ones who can't take care of themselves."

I try to say, "I will" again, but the words lodge in my throat, and I wind up puckering my mouth open and closed like a dying fish.

Smiling, Kress retreats into the Terminus and slides the door shut behind her.

The massive truck grumbles to life. The front floodlights blast on, and the power and charging indicator lights along the back and sides of the giant vehicle flash red and white.

The huge, segmented silver panel on the far side of the garage grumbles up to reveal the long, dimly lit tunnel leading to the network of old mining shafts in the mountain.

I take a few big steps back to rejoin my classmates as the Terminus rumbles into the dark open jaws of the tunnel, and the giant silver panel rattles down behind it.

We're all milling around like abandoned puppies when Wisp claps her hands together. "Okay. Go get some rest. All of you. Tomorrow, we'll be throwing you into a series of competitive challenges and then into a VR combat sim after that. We'll promise not to try to kill you if you promise to try not to die."

And with that cheery thought bouncing around in our heads, we file out of the hangar and walk upstairs, anxious about being left alone and uncertain about what's to come.

20

GLITCHES

AT A BIT OF A LOSS, for the rest of the day, the eleven of us lie scattered around in the Lounge.

It's not often we have a day off, although it doesn't really feel like one.

I should be feeling relieved at having a pause in all the training we've been doing for the past months, but the emptiness of the moment is heavier than I expected.

It's only been a couple of hours, and I already miss the combat and weapons training and my one-on-one, Ravenmaster sessions with Kress.

Being a Ravenmaster is a lot harder than my parents made it look. I thought it was just a matter of feeding the birds and keeping them healthy.

It turns out there's a lot more to it. Kress has to know the personality of each bird, its quirks, its strengths and fears, and its place in the "pecking order."

I can't communicate with any of the six young ravens in Render and Haida Gwaii's young Conspiracy, but Kress can. I know I'm supposed to be in awe of her abilities—and I am. It's just hard to be around someone who's so great at everything while I continue to suck.

I'm antsy, and I feel like getting into a fight. Or even picking one.

Over on one of the orange couches, Chace is scrawling away on her holo-pad. I've been sneaking peeks over her shoulder. She's really good. I don't know what she's writing, but her drawings are spot-on.

Her recent collection is a catalogue of all of our weapons. Every few minutes, she uses the projection feature on her holo-pad to show us.

One by one, the images scroll in the air as she flicks them along:

Libra's sledgehammer.

Mattea's bear claws.

Ignacio's shillelaghs.

Sara's throwing darts.

Arlo's scythe.

Chace's rope and carabiners.

Trax's serrated hunting knives.

Lucid and Reverie with their matching katana swords.

And my twin serpent blades.

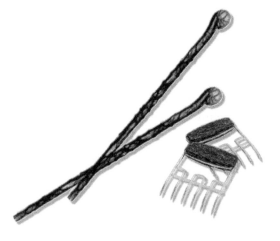

CHACE IS odd because she's so brainy and talented. But in a lot of ways, she's like a little girl. She doesn't crave attention like Libra does, but she seems to enjoy the pats on the back we give her in recognition of her talent.

And she *is* talented.

In addition to our weapons, she also has dozens of pictures of all of us from around the Academy: Our two Cohorts in class, in training, and gathered around in the Lounge to talk, rest, or play competitive games with each other.

"*And*," she beams at us, "there are stories to go along with each picture."

She shakes her head when Mattea asks if we can hear them, but she promises that someday, she'll share them with us.

"After all," she giggles, "technically, the stories are *yours*. They belong to you."

She really is a Chronicler, and there's no doubt that her ability to record stories—through words and pictures—is part of some enhanced Emergent ability.

I especially like how in the pictures, she makes me look taller than I really am.

Still, it's a little weird how obsessed she is with recording everything we do around here.

It's like she expects something terrible to happen, like we're all going to die and she's desperate to make sure something of us survives.

Honestly, it's equal parts impressive, morbid, and creepy.

Libra is lying upside down on the couch with her feet dangling over its back and her hair splayed out on the floor. She pivots her bright eyes over to me. "What do you think?"

"What do I think about what?"

"Kress and her Conspiracy going off like that?"

Arlo mumbles something I don't hear, so I ask him to repeat it.

"What if...?" he begins.

"What if they don't come back?" I ask.

He nods and looks even sadder than usual under the dark shadow cast over his face by the hood of his sweater.

"They'll come back," Reverie promises.

"And you know this, how?" I ask.

"Wait!" Sara chuckles as she waggles her fingers, her voice going comically fortune-teller spooky. "Let me guess. You've seen it in your dreams." Lucid and Reverie exchange one of their cryptic, odd-fish twin glances, and Sara leans forward with a suspicious squint. "Really? You saw it in your dreams?"

Lucid shrugs, and Reverie says, "Kind of."

Fascinated, Sara sits up straight, her eyes wide now. "Branwynne says you know what dreams really are."

"We're learning."

"Well...don't leave us in suspense. 'Cause I had a doozy the other night. See, I was fighting a bunch of naked, inside-out donkey-men who were firing high-caliber bullets from their empty eye sockets."

Ignacio's head snaps up. "Inside out?"

"Yeah. Like, their organs and guts and stuff were on the outside. And their skin and hair and everything was on the inside."

Ignacio stares at her for a full three seconds, before he breaks his gaze and glances down toward his crotch. "What about their...you know..."

"Their private parts?"

"Um...yeah."

"Wait," I interrupt. "Sara had a dream about killer donkey-men, and that's what you want to know? What happened to their twigs and berries?"

Ignacio offers up a bashful grin. "I was just asking."

"Interpreting dreams can be fun," Reverie explains.

"And the science and speculation behind dreams goes back

into pre-history," Lucid adds quietly, his eyes fixed on the ceiling.

"But in our experience," Reverie continues, "dreams are more like microsecond glimpses through distorted lenses into pinprick holes in the universe. What you see is real. But you're bound to misinterpret it since it happens so fast and takes place in a realm beyond the ability of the human mind to process."

"And that's where you come in?" Sara asks.

"What do you mean?"

"Well...you're not exactly human, are you?"

"We're human," Reverie says.

"Hardly. We're all here because we're Emergents."

"Emergents are still human," Lucid protests. "Just enhanced."

"Or *advanced*?" Sara asks, although it's not really a question.

"Or just a next-stage evolution," Mattea offers. "No better. No worse."

Sara scoffs at this. "We need to stop believing that. Kress and the others aren't out there risking their lives to help a bunch of ordinary kids. There's no way they'd have left if that's all that was out there. They're out there to rescue Emergents because Emergents—like us—are all that's stopping the Typics from finishing what they started: blowing up the world."

Libra flips herself upright and draws her hair back into a thick ponytail. "I don't see what any of this has to do with inside-out donkey-men."

Sara points an accusing finger at Lucid and Reverie. "The point is, these two dream-readers know more than they're saying."

"We think we know what dreams are," Lucid explains. "But we don't have any power or control over them."

Reverie blushes. "But we're getting better at it."

I back them up and tell the rest of our Cohorts that it's true.

"And how do you know that?" Sara snaps.

"We have the same mentor," I explain. "Kress and the twins and I...we share a connection."

Libra gives a gleeful smile and a little clap of her hands. "Tell us! What's your connection?"

Still shoulder to shoulder, Lucid and Reverie sit back in unison in their seats, leaving me to try to explain what's frankly unexplainable.

"There's a place called the *Lyfelyte*. It's an access point or staging area where we can see what's known as dreams. Well, Kress and the twins can see it. I can just catch glimpses here and there. But only when Kress is around."

Mumbling to herself, Mattea stands and starts pacing, dragging her fingers along the back of every piece of furniture in the lounge as she goes.

Ignacio turns back and calls out to her over his shoulder. "What's with you?"

"I was just getting good, too."

"At what?"

"My languages. Rain was helping a lot."

"Um. She's not dead," I remind her.

"I know."

"She'll be back. They'll all be back." I give Mattea a dismissive wave of my hand. After all, I've seen Kress and her Conspiracy in action more than anyone in this room. "I still think I should have gone with them," I sigh.

Swinging herself around, Libra gives me a skeptical squint. "We're not ready."

"Speak for yourself. I fought side by side with them in London and all across this country from D.C. to here. I can handle myself. They probably left me here to protect all of you."

"I don't need protection," Ignacio insists, flickers of blue and white electric sparks lighting up his dark eyes.

The bands of holo-lights running along the ceiling blink off for a second and then snap back on.

"Did you do that?" Mattea asks.

Ignacio shakes his head. "Wasn't me."

"Either you're wrong," she says with a flat, unamused smile, "you're lying, or else this place is getting glitchier by the minute."

It's the first morning without our teachers and mentors, but it already feels like they've been gone forever.

Griping and dragging, we get suited up and are ready to head down to the third floor Combat Skills and Training Rooms, but before getting to the door, we go crashing into Libra who's in the lead.

She presses her palms to the door's glossy surface. "Door won't open again."

"Too bad Manthy's not here," I say. "She'd have it fixed in no time."

At the sound of her name, everyone goes quiet. I knew her the best, but the others all met her. They know what she could do, and they know about how she left.

After years of pain caused by her Emergent abilities, she and Cardyn—two members of Kress's original Conspiracy—walked into the *Lyfelyte*.

Ignacio bangs the side of his fist on the doors a couple of times.

"Who do you think you are?" Sara asks with a snide grin. "Terk? You're *not* going to smash it down."

I slip over to try the door leading into one of the communal washrooms, but it's sealed, too.

"Call Wisp on the intercom," I suggest.

Libra presses her thumb to the black intercom button and tries to connect with Wisp, but nothing happens. Not even static.

"Now what?" Arlo asks.

One of the many things Kress has been teaching me is how to use my limited access to the *Lyfelyte* to walk through walls. She calls it "traversion." It's an insanely painful trick that I've only done successfully twice before. And never without her present.

Taking a deep breath and with my palm pressed to the panel of cold steel, I'm just about to give it a shot when the door wiggles a little and then slides fully open.

"Funny," I say, drawing my hand back and secretly happy I didn't have to try my trick. (Kress warned me that failure could mean an agonizing death with my molecules mixed in the with the molecules of whatever I'm trying to pass through.)

Libra asks me, "What's funny?"

"Well, it's just...I've been here since the beginning. I was here when Terk and the Auditor and the others activated all the energy and security systems in the place."

"And?"

"And...everything worked like a charm. No glitches. No stuck doors or inactive mag-lifts. No flickering lights."

"Systems get old," Arlo assures me. "Things get glitchy and break down all the time. Sometimes the systems you put in place to help you wind up working against you."

Sara says, "So do people," and starts heading down the stairs ahead of us.

21

SIX-STATION RACE

WISP MEETS us in the Tavern and even joins us for breakfast, which is weird because I don't think I've ever seen her eat anything.

While the rest of us scarf down our modest meal of pine nuts and protein cubes, Wisp makes small talk with us about how our lessons have been going so far. She asks about any problems we might be having and listens patiently while we go one-by-one around the table, rattling off a list of all the things we're learning, all the physical challenges we've endured so far, and all the hours we've spent being patched up by War and Mayla in the Infirmary.

(There's even an amusing bout of one-upmanship where we take turns holding up our arms, tugging up our shirts, or planting our boots on the table and hiking up our pant legs to show off our assorted, grisly injuries to Wisp.)

Nodding her appreciation, she tells us she's proud of us and that she predicts great things from us in the future.

She doesn't eat, but when the rest of us are finished, she stands, claps her hands together, and says it's time to take the next steps toward that great future of ours.

With Wisp leading the eleven of us up the wide glass and wood staircase, we're escorted to one of the Combat Skills and Training Rooms.

Although we've been in it before, the whole room can be reconfigured to suit the needs of whatever class we're being taught at the time. Which means we never really know what it's going to look like from day to day.

In the past few weeks, it's been a martial arts dojo, a boxing ring, an indoor racetrack, a sand pit, a rock-climbing training course, a simulated junkyard, and a knife-throwing range.

According to Trax, it's even been set up as a mock trauma center for the Field First Aid class his Cohort's been taking as a supplemental seminar for the past couple of weeks.

This time, the doors open to reveal what looks like a long obstacle course running the length of the deep, arena-sized room. A wide walkway of glossy white tiles runs along its entire length as well. Six pairs of glowing pink circles of light are embedded side by side in the floor and spaced at intervals down the length of the laneway.

Altogether, it looks like pictures I've seen in holo-books of street fair midways with stands and activity booths set up along an illuminated promenade.

Now all we need is a carnival barker.

"Welcome to Command Post Exercise Alpha," Wisp announces with an attempt at a grand bellow...Sort of like, well, a slightly tinny-voiced carnival barker.

Perfect. What sort of circus is she going to make us perform in now?

"Today, instead of your regular classes, mentoring sessions, or fitness training, you'll be competing in a series of physical and mental activities in the six stations you see set up before you. Each station presents a unique challenge specifically designed to test your balance, reflexes, mental acuity, and unarmed combat skills. You'll be in two teams based on your Cohort."

Our two Cohorts buzz and chirp back and forth. We don't have many classes as one big group, so we mostly see each other for a few minutes in the Tavern, recuperating in the Lounge, or passing in the halls outside of the Infirmary on days when we need to get bandaged up.

Except for Libra and Ignacio in my Cohort and Trax and Reverie in Cohort B, we're not the most competitive bunch.

Not like Kress and our teachers, anyway.

They compete *non-stop*—in the gym, on the firing range, in the VR Battle Sims, and even over the chess tournaments they play in the Tavern or even on the stairway landings from time to time. And throughout it all, their Conspiracy stays stronger than any people in any relationship I've ever seen or heard about.

Someday, I'll have to ask Kress how they do that.

Pushing her sleeves up above her elbows and slipping a lock of hair behind her ear, Wisp makes a sweeping gesture at the spectacle in front of us, directing our attention to six specific stations running along the white walkway and counting them off on her fingers.

"The six stations you see are loosely based on the five Disciplines that form the core of your education here at the Academy. At Station One, you'll be required to display your long-distance sniper shooting. At Station Two, you'll need to demonstrate what you've learned in Transportation and Mechanics. At Station Three, your balance and coordination will be on full display. Station Four will challenge your reflex skills. And you'll be required to solve a series of puzzles at Station Five."

Wisp doesn't have the ability to command a room with her voice like her older brother Brohn does, but she has a magical way of focusing us and drawing our attention to her all the same.

It's almost hypnotic. Or, who knows? Maybe it *is* hypnotic.

At the moment, though, she looks completely innocent, like she's fighting not to smile when she adds, "The first team to complete all the stations, wins."

Trax steps forward, his thick eyebrows pinching down toward his nose. He toggles his thumb between our two Cohorts. "Um...wait. There are only five of us and six of them."

"That's true. And because your Cohort only has five students, Granden will jump in with you to even out the teams. The members of the Cohort who aren't competing at the time will gather in one of the two pink viewing pads in the walkway at the front of each obstacle."

Chace raises her hand and tilts her head toward the array of labeled stations spread out in front of us. "How come there's *six* stations?"

"Station Six, the one at the far end, is for Tap-Out."

"Tap-Out?"

"Each Cohort will select one member to square off in the pit at the end of the course."

"And do what, exactly?"

"Fight."

We look around.

"Don't worry, though," Wisp adds. "It won't be a fair fight! Whichever team is the first to finish the five stations with the best time and the highest score gets a bonus."

Apparently sensing some sort of injustice on the horizon, Libra frowns. "What kind of bonus?"

"Whichever Cohort loses, their champion will have to fight blindfolded."

Next to me, Libra gulps. She's a decent fighter when she's pressed. But she *hates* getting hit, and I know the thought of playing punching bag to someone from Cohort B is pretty much her nightmare scenario.

Behind us, the door opens, and Granden strides in to take his place with the cluster of Cohort B.

Trax and his Cohort break into a buffet of happy grins and gather around him.

Decked out in his military cargo pants and camouflage t-shirt, Granden looms over the kids in Cohort B like a drill sergeant.

Wisp directs each Cohort to gather at the start of the course. She makes a grand, sweeping gesture in the direction of the five stations, making a special point of drawing our attention to the sixth and final station—the Tap-out pit, recessed into the floor, like the dot above a lowercase "i"—barely visible way down at the end.

"Since this is a relay race," Wisp explains, "the first step is the identification of talent and the allocation of your Cohort's personnel. You have two minutes to decide who will attempt which station."

We gather ourselves into a huddle while Cohort B does the same.

"Not fair," Sara complains from her spot across from me. "Granden's older and has a ton of experience."

Libra's lower lip juts out, and she presses her fists to her hips. "Wisp is going to make one of us fight blindfolded! I think she's made it pretty clear that 'fair' isn't high up on her list of priorities."

Grinning, I rub my hands together, eager to jump into the challenges, fair or not. "No sense training us to fight fair in here when we'll face all kinds of unfair odds out there, right?"

I may not be competitive, but I do enjoy a good punch up.

I've got the different possibilities for my preferred stations rolling around in my head when Arlo asks, "So...who's going to tackle which station?"

I'm waiting for someone to step up, take the lead, and dole

out the responsibilities. When no one says anything, I realize they're all waiting for *me* to take charge. Even Ignacio, usually brimming with willy-waving, alpha masculinity, is staring at me, helpless and wide-eyed.

Is this part of the game? Figure out who's going to lead and who's going to follow? Come on, guys. We've been at this for months now. I'm a soldier, not a captain.

"Fine," I sigh. "Here's the order I think we should go in from Station One to Five: Ignacio's our best sniper. Libra crushed us all in Mechanics. Sara, you've got the best marks in all the balance and coordination drills. Arlo, you've got decent reflexes —when you use them. Mattea's got the best skills for puzzles and problem-solving. That leaves me to take the final fight."

Ignacio gives Sara a light elbow to the arm. "Hey. What do you say we sabotage this thing?"

"Sabotage?"

"Sure. We'll tank a couple of the stations, let Cohort B beat us in the challenges, and make Branwynne here have to jump into the pit blindfolded."

Sara laughs, and she and Ignacio exchange a happy high-five.

"Knock it off," Libra says. "We're *not* going to lose on purpose."

"We're not going to lose at all," Mattea adds through a clamp-jawed scowl.

Ignacio slaps a fist into his open palm. "Mattea's right. Trax is pretty good, but all Chace can do is draw pictures and write stories. Lucid and Reverie are lost in their own little dream world. And Roxane's a psychopathic waste of skin. That means all we really have to worry about is Granden. And he can't participate in *every* event. So this should be a nice smooth ride."

Sara gives us all a slow nod of agreement followed by an

exaggerated sigh. "Still...it'd be kind of fun to watch Branwynne do her best imitation of a human punching bag."

I don't respond. I also don't take my eyes from Sara's as I slide my long, coffee-brown hair into a ponytail.

Too bad I can't face you *in the pit. Now* that *would be fun.*

22

STATION ONE - SNIPER

SINCE THE COURSE runs in a long line, our two groups shuffle forward in the aisle and take up positions—one Cohort per viewing pad—in the two circles of pink light.

"This will be your viewing gallery," Wisp explains. "From here, you can watch your teammates in action and cheer them on."

A giddy buzz runs through our two Cohorts.

"Sooooo...?" Wisp asks with her best carnival barker grandeur, "who will be your champions for the first challenge?"

Trax gives Reverie a nudge with his elbow. She steps forward, shoulders back, head held high, and announces that she'll be the representative from Cohort B.

"And from your Cohort?" Wisp asks, her little brown eyes locked onto mine.

Ignacio practically leaps forward, snatching the sniper rifle from the silver stand in front of the station and twirling it baton-style as his chest swells with macho confidence.

Next to him, Reverie picks up her own sniper rifle and inspects it, bouncing it in her hands and squinting down its scope.

The rest of us stand in a clump in our pink circles, our eyes focused on the long shooting range running perpendicular to the aisle.

We've done all kinds of target practice, but none with ballistic weapons so far. Although we've all been anxious to try out the Academy's arsenal of firearms, Kella's Marksmanship and Sniper Training class doesn't come up for another term.

So we're all a little jealous.

The far end of the range is a churning cluster of bouncing and darting wheels, blinking skeets, and colorful, rotating cube targets ranging in size from tiny to practically microscopic. All of them hover within a special magnetic field that keeps them suspended in midair like a raven riding an updraft.

We know the scoring system from past classes, but Wisp reminds us anyway. When she's done, she calls for the two snipers to begin. In unison, Ignacio and Reverie raise their rifles and begin firing at the distant, dashing targets.

As Reverie fires, the sound of her targets being hit down range pings back to us in little, rapid-fire explosions.

"That's another hit," Reverie exclaims. "And another. And another." She blasts away with deft precision, calling out her successful strikes as she goes. She narrates her shots like a sports announcer commenting on a game she was watching in slow motion. "One skeet. Two skeets. That's another cube down. Large wheel. Medium. Small. See how they fall!" She giggles behind her hand and calls back over her shoulder to her Cohort, "This is way too easy!"

I never knew Reverie was quite so talkative. Or competitive. Or cheeky.

Meanwhile, in the stall next to her, Ignacio is struggling. He's missing badly, and he keeps scowling over at Reverie and then up at her score as it ticks higher and higher on the shimmering holo-display.

I never knew Ignacio to be so flustered. Or off target. Or sweaty.

The projected holo-counter above their heads records their final points: Fifty for Ignacio. One hundred-twenty-five for Reverie.

Wisp calls an end to the sniper-rifle challenge and directs Ignacio and Reverie to the two crossbows sitting on the tables next to them.

"It's not over yet," she says, her attention focused mostly on Ignacio. "Let's see if you've learned anything from Brohn."

Setting down their sniper rifles, Ignacio and Reverie take the new weapons and prepare for the second stage of the competition while the rest of us cheer them on.

Down range, a cluster of round wooden targets—each about the size of a tea-cup saucer—descends from a series of open ports in the ceiling.

Floating on mag-currents, the disks bob and shimmy in the air.

After the first round with the sniper rifles, Reverie's way ahead on points. To hear her tell it, the competition's already over.

"Let's face it, Igs," she taunts with a side-eyed glance over her crossbow, "you gave it your best shot. Nothing wrong with losing."

"It's not over yet," he growls back. "And don't call me 'Igs.'"

Reverie plants her palm on her chest. "Oh. I'm sorry, *Iggy*."

I half-expect him to lean over and hammer her in the temple with the butt of his crossbow. Instead, he squints back down his sight and fires off his first volley of shots.

His bolts whistle one by one down the range and thunk into several of the wooden targets. The holo-counter hovering above the range flashes his new score.

"Beat that," he crows.

"Okay."

Reverie doesn't squint down the sight of her crossbow. In fact, she holds it sort of casually at her side with one hand while she gives Ignacio an annoyed stare. I figure she's preparing herself before she fires. But then she whips her weapon up and blasts away, almost before she's even turned away from Ignacio.

In a flash, she reloads the crossbow, over and over, firing quickly and casually as she goes.

Above the range, the holo-counter ticks off her score: seventy-five points better than Ignacio's.

We're all standing there open-mouthed. Well, my Cohort is, anyway. Reverie's Cohort turns to us as one, as if they were a four-headed unit with Granden standing cross-armed and pleased behind them.

"What can we say?" Lucid grins, tilting his head toward his sister, who has her crossbow raised and resting on her shoulder. "Wisp says she could be the next Kella."

"Well," Granden drawls through a cool grin, "I don't know about that. On the other hand, if you're playing second fiddle to Kella, you play a pretty good fiddle."

Wisp says she's impressed with both scores, which is clearly a lie, and announces Reverie as the winner.

Ignacio sulks back to our Cohort, his face a jigsaw puzzle of surprise, anger, and embarrassment.

"Sorry. I had no idea she could shoot like that."

"Don't worry," I tell him with a firm pat to his shoulder. "I had no idea *anyone* could shoot like that."

As the rest of our Cohort offers condolences and support to Ignacio, Cohort B keeps cheering for their champion until Wisp announces that it's time for the next station.

Hustling along, she leads us to the next pink circles where our Cohorts congregate while Wisp announces the beginning of the second challenge.

23

STATION TWO - GENERATOR

"PLEASE HAVE your champions for Station Two step forward."

Libra and Trax step out of the pink circles and walk up to the silver work bench where Wisp explains the challenge.

"You each have an inactive magnetic pulse-converter in front of you. Using nothing but the tools and materials on the bench, your job is to register an energy signature powerful enough to activate the propulsion energy generator on this monitor."

A tall gauge—sort of a holographic thermometer with unlit, gray bands rising from the bottom to the top—sits at each end of the workbench.

"This will measure your generated energy. The higher the band you can light up, the higher your score."

I laugh when Libra cracks her knuckles, steps forward, and says, "Easy-peasy."

That's my line!

Trax snaps his fingers, flicks her a "get out of here" thumb, and tells her she doesn't stand a chance.

You're the one who doesn't stand a chance, I think, smiling to myself about how nice it is to see that he's got a cute, sweet side *and* a studly, saucy side.

I'm definitely glad I gave this assignment to Libra. The workbench is a hodgepodge of useless stuff—from radish-sized stones and a tangle of dried tree roots to an old wine-bottle opener and what looks to be part of a rusted hubcap. And that's just for starters.

There's an entire assortment of random junk—cracked bolts, glass shards, chips of some sort of glossy black ore, bent silverware, clumps of yellow dirt, thread-thin coils of rubber casing, splintered animal bones, and two headless plastic dolls—crammed up into mini jagged-topped mountain ranges.

Basically, Libra and Trax will have to use a pile of discarded scraps in order to activate one of the most sophisticated pieces of digital technology we have in the Academy. The thought of it alone is enough to send my brain into a nosedive.

The *sight* of it is enough to send my nosediving brain crashing to the floor in a splattery mess of gray-matter goo. (I don't handle disorganization well.)

Libra may not be my favorite person in the world, but I've seen her do a similar assignment in War's class before. It wasn't as complex, and War gave her plenty of guidance, but it was still a task no one else in our Cohort was able to complete.

There's no way she'll lose this race.

Wisp calls out, "Go!"

Trax dives into his pile of supplies, and next to him, Libra's fingers, in a burst of seamless motion, fly over her own workbench.

As if she's done this a million times before, she strips casings off of a dozen wires, ratchets toggle bolts, reconfigures the slender chambers of a manifold, and solders leads to a cluster of tiny, burned out circuit boards.

She plucks from the pile of junk like it's a neatly organized medicine cabinet.

Discarding some pieces but inspecting some of the others

under an angled holo-light attached to the workbench, Libra weighs her options like a pastry chef measuring out ingredients for a Victoria sponge cake.

Finally, with a flick of her wrist, she wraps a thin copper wire around a finger-sized plug of iron to create a small electromagnet.

Flipping over the clunky transistor array next to her, she slaps together a Frankenstein monster of a machine. With micro-tools in hand, she dances around the thing in a blurry ballet of motion, a big smile spread across her face the entire time.

When she's finished sealing the ends of a field coupling, she slaps her palm to a magnetic grav-pad and thrusts her hands into the air.

The highest band on the tall gauge at her end of the workbench flashes blue, and Wisp declares Libra the winner.

Trax, his own gauge showing a very weak yellow band toward the bottom, hangs his head and sulks back to his Cohort while Libra—her face and eyes lit up—charges at us, launching herself into my arms.

Thankfully, Ignacio peels her off of me and joins Mattea, Arlo, and even Sara in a rowdy, bouncing fit of hugs, back slaps, and hearty squeals of congratulations.

From his circle, Trax catches my eye and gives me a polite nod and a thumbs up. He tilts his head toward Libra and mouths the words, "Nice job" before turning back to apologize to his Cohort for his defeat and to receive their words of consolation.

In our pink circle, gushing and with the words tumbling out of her mouth in an unstoppable avalanche, Libra tells us about how she was able to re-route a micro-current and harness molecular energy from the decay she found in some of the synthetic materials she was able to patch together. She goes on and on like that for what feels like an hour, but I don't understand half of it.

Machines are Libra's thing. She's tuned in to them like I'm tuned into Haida. She gets systems the way I get telempathy—the psychic bond Haida and I share—and she enjoys the challenge of fixing stuff as much as I enjoy the thrill of combat.

And she does it all with pure pleasure and genuine modesty.

Wait a bloody minute. Am I actually impressed *by Libra—the annoying girl who talks non-stop and smiles her bubble-headed way through this nightmarish cock-up of a world?*

No. I'm just happy for my team's success and for the chance to beat Cohort B and have bragging rights when Kress and her Conspiracy return.

Yeah. That's got to be it.

With her hands cupped to either side of her mouth, Wisp calls out to remind us that the competition isn't over yet.

24

STATION THREE - JUGGLE

Wisp draws our attention to the next station, which consists of two side-by-side labyrinths of elevated wooden beams running along the tops of a series of thin silver posts.

The beams range in height from a few inches off the floor to at least ten feet high. They zigzag, double back, and wind around to form what look like two giant, steeply-angled mutant pretzels.

There are two indicator lights—one green, one red—at the beginning of each track.

"For this challenge," Wisp announces, "all you need to do is navigate this agility course. As you can see, it will require great concentration and coordination on the part of our two participants. When I give the signal, first, hit the green button. That starts your timer. Run along the beams. Return to the starting point and hit the red button. That sets your finishing time. Whoever completes the course and hits the red button first, wins."

Sara rubs her palms together and nods. "Sounds straightforward enough."

"It's not," Wisp assures her. "You'll be given a three-second penalty for every fall."

"No problem," Sara grins. "I don't plan on falling."

Wisp taps the input-panel on the thin podium between the two starter buttons.

"One other thing..." she says as sections of some of the beams start rotating, while retractable, silver six-inch blades start popping out of others, "...the beams that will assist you are also obstacles."

"Let me guess," Ignacio says with a snide grunt, his eyes locked onto the menacing silver blades snapping open all over the course. "This is a metaphor for life outside the Academy."

Wisp points at him, laughs, and says, "Exactly!"

"Only, metaphors usually don't end in minced skin and trips to the Infirmary," I say, but not loud enough for Wisp to hear.

In front of us, Wisp turns to Roxane, who has stepped forward as the Station Three champion for Cohort B. "Do you understand the challenge?"

Foggy-eyed, Roxane doesn't so much as smile, nod, or indicate she's heard her at all, but Wisp grins pleasantly and says, "Marvie."

Then, she pulls three chrome-colored balls out of each of the side pockets of her oversized military jacket. "Oh, and you have to do it while juggling these."

Sara does a double-take that makes us laugh and says, "Wait! What?"

"Juggle," Wisp says, the hint of an amused giggle behind her otherwise serious expression. "You do know how to juggle, right?"

Sara squints her eyes and bites her lip. Roxane stares.

"Like this," Wisp illustrates. She slips three of the balls back into her bulky jacket pocket. With the other three, she launches into a blurry-handed vortex of motion with the mirrored balls flashing high into the air, slapping down into her palms, and then flying up again in a dizzying silver arc.

"See," she beams, plopping one set of the three juggling balls into Sara's hand and the other set into Roxane's. "Nothing to it."

Sara turns her eyes from Wisp's and says, "No problem," through clenched teeth.

Roxane stares down at the juggling balls in her palm like they're venomous spiders that'll bite her if she makes any sudden moves.

Now, I'm wishing I had selected *myself* for this challenge. Thanks to lessons from my weirdly coordinated mother—who also for some reason knows how to make balloon animals—I've known how to juggle since I was about five years old.

Of course, I didn't know when I was assigning my fellow students to the various stations that Wisp was going to throw us such a deadly curve ball.

At Wisp's instruction, Sara and Roxane take their positions at the starting point of each course.

Wisp taps a pad on the glass-topped podium, and a holo-display appears in the air with an indicator for each girl's time and a red column for any penalty points they get slapped with.

Our two Cohorts are standing inside of the next set of glimmering pink holo-circles embedded in the floor as we start to cheer on our champions.

"Too bad we can't bet on this thing," Trax says to me out of the side of his mouth.

"Who says we can't?" I whisper back across the few feet of space between our two viewing circles.

"Stakes?"

"If Sara wins, you stop hogging that good sonic-shower at the end of the row every morning."

"But it's the best one," he whines. Then he huffs out an annoyed, "Fine. And if Roxane wins..."

"Yeah?"

"You go on a date with me."

"A date?" I laugh. And then I realize, I've never been on an actual date before.

"A date," he repeats.

"And where are we supposed to go, exactly? It's not like we can just waltz out of the Academy."

"Well...I don't know how to waltz. But I think there are places we can go to find a little alone time. Maybe have a chat. Get to know each other outside of the daily routine of being trained as world-saving superheroes."

"You're pissing around."

"I don't know what that means. But no, I don't think I am."

I don't know why he's looking so smug. I'm not sure Roxane knows her own name. I do know, however, that Sara—despite being a total trouble-maker—is super coordinated, a quick-study, and wickedly skilled at stuff like this.

"Okay, you cheeky nutbar. I'll have you on. It's a bet."

Trax gives me a wink and folds his arms across his chest as our two heroes—Sara and Roxane—take their positions at the starting line for their last round of instructions.

After going over the rules one more time, Wisp calls out, "Go!" and the two girls—juggling balls whirring in front of them —take off like a shot.

Apparently, Sara's never juggled before, but you wouldn't know it to look at her. She shimmies and skips along the winding matrix of elevated planks, juggling the three balls with circus-level expertise.

She pauses as the beam in front of her goes into a slow deathroll, and then she bolts across, leaping over the series of snapping blades in the section after that.

I take a break from cheering her on to turn to the side and stick my tongue out at Trax.

He smiles and redirects my attention back to the course where Sara is still straggling and stumbling along...but Roxane is...*sprinting*?

In a full-on wind sprint and somehow juggling all three balls in one hand, Roxane speeds across the beams. Her hand and the three juggling balls are a glittering blur of motion.

As if she knows which way each beam will spin and when the blades will strike, she glides over the obstacle course with cheetah speed and Billy goat dexterity.

Sara's jaw drops, and she stops right in the middle of the course.

Meanwhile, Roxane slides to a stop at the end, catches all three balls in one hand, hits the red buzzer, and takes a mute mini-bow before hopping over to the cheers and back-slaps of her adoring Cohort.

What the hell?

Sara dashes her three juggling balls to the floor, leaps down from the beam she's on, and grumbles her way over to our surprised, sulking Cohort.

Stepping out of his own Cohort's pink viewing circle, Trax slips up behind me and whispers in my ear. "For our little date, shall we say...tonight after everyone's asleep?"

I've never wanted to punch someone this cute so hard in the face.

But a bet's a bet.

Besides, tonight's a long way away. And who knows what might happen between now and then?

Maybe luck will be on my side, and I'll get killed in the final fight.

25

STATION FOUR - SCARS

"STATION FOUR MIGHT BE A BIT TRICKIER," Wisp announces.

From the middle of her Cohort, Chace raises her hand. "Can you define 'trickier'?"

"Sure," Wisp smiles. "*Deadlier.*"

We all wait for Wisp to laugh and tell us she's joking. But she doesn't say a word through her amused grin.

Sara claps Arlo hard on the back. "Looks like you're up, Mr. Reaper. Try not to get *yourself* killed."

"You're not being helpful," Libra scowls.

"*Good*," Sara growls. "I wasn't trying to be."

Wisp asks Granden to do the honors, and he obliges with a crisp, military-style salute.

"The last challenge with the juggling on the 'killer beams' tested your balance and coordination. This one will test your instincts, anticipation skills, and reflexes. And also, how much pain you can endure."

From the center of Cohort B's viewing circle, I hear Lucid say, "What did he just say?" followed by Reverie telling him not to worry.

Personally, though, based on what we've seen so far, I'd say a good dose of worry couldn't hurt.

Granden calls out for Arlo and Lucid to step forward.

Lucid slides his hand out of his sister's and makes his way to the starting line at the beginning of the course.

Arlo tugs his hood even farther up onto his head and ambles to his own starting line.

"As you can see," Granden says, his hands directing our attention to the walls. "There are ports—small openings—in the two side walls, in the floor, and in the wall at the end." He points off to the far wall, past the holes in the floor and the dozen spinning, corkscrew-shaped posts with the light glinting off of their razor-sharp edges. "This will be a straightforward, there-and-back race. You'll notice a baton at the end of each course. Your job is simple: Get from the start of the course to the end, grab the baton, bring it back. First one who places the baton in my hand, wins."

Mm-hmm. Why do I think there's going to be waaaay more to it than that?

"And in case you're wondering why it sounds so easy," Granden announces, "it's because it's not. Behind those walls is an arsenal of darts, arrows, steel pellets, and other assorted projectiles. They'll fire randomly at the two competitors along the way."

Standing shoulder to shoulder with Granden, Wisp gives us the rest of the bleak news:

"Of course, our goal isn't to *kill* Arlo and Lucid. But their best instincts and their Emergent abilities need to be challenged to make them as effective as possible."

"So the darts and things won't kill them?" Reverie asks, her lip in a twitchy quiver.

"Probably not," Wisp shrugs.

"*Probably* not?"

Wisp and Granden exchange a look I can't read, but it seems far too serious and scary considering this is just a little in-school challenge to pass the time while our other teachers are out on their little field trip.

Libra grabs my arm. "Branwynne, maybe you should stop Arlo from competing in this one."

"Are you suggesting you want to take his place?"

"Um. No."

"Arlo? Are you up for it?"

Arlo gives me a half-turn and a "don't-ask-me-dumb-questions" look of disdain.

"I think he's going to go through with it," I tell Libra.

"I think maybe I won't look."

Mattea and Ignacio agree, but Sara grins. "If you don't look, you'll miss all the carnage and fun."

"I've got this," Arlo says evenly, without turning around.

Great. We've got probably the quietest and most harmless member of our Cohort about to jump into a fun game of certain injury and probable death.

And *I* assigned it to him.

Good going, Branwynne. It's not enough you almost get killed in class, yourself. Now you've gone and tossed this poor sot into Wisp and Granden's sadistic line of fire.

"Okay," I say to Libra. "Maybe you're right." I wave my hand to get Wisp's attention. "Maybe I should do this one?"

After all, if I concentrate hard enough and focus just right, I can channel Haida's instincts and reflexes to get through the race without getting turned into a bloody, plug-ugly carcass.

"It's your choice," Wisp tells me.

But, whipping fully around this time, Arlo glares at me from under his hood. "You trusted me with this challenge. Take that trust back now, and maybe I won't trust *you* next time."

Ugh. He's right. It's hard enough being responsible for your own life. Being responsible for someone else's is way worse. This is why being in charge is a piss-poor muck all.

"Okay," I concede. "Just do me a favor and don't get killed."

Arlo smiles and tugs his hood up higher on his head. "Never."

"All settled then?" Wisp asks.

I assure her we are.

"Okay," she says, swinging around to face Arlo and Lucid, who are standing side by side at their marks. "Ready? Set? Go!"

Lucid sprints into the minefield, darting left, right, and doubling back as a hail of thorn-sized spikes blasts at him from the ports in the wall.

He's lithe and quick, with almost predictive instincts about what's coming and when.

The first volley misses, but a second one isn't far behind.

He shrieks and drops to a knee as one of the sharp barbs pierces the side of his thigh.

Snatching it out, he rolls deftly to one side and ducks as another hail of darts whizzes over his head.

I hate to admit it, but his reflexes are really good. I've never seen him in action like this before. It's impressive, but I can't get distracted by the graceful ballet of evasive maneuvers he's doing. I've got my own champion to root for.

Unlike Lucid, who's pirouetting, weaving, backtracking, and then advancing his way through the course, Arlo walks in a straight line—past the posts of spinning blades, ignoring them like they're not even there—and we all scream at him to look out.

But he doesn't hear us, or else he isn't listening.

One of the corkscrew blades shears angled gashes in his shoulder and down his arm. A swarm of darts lodges in his chest. A steel-tipped crossbow bolt pierces his calf. From just underneath him, a surge of electric-blue fire bursts up and consumes him.

Stepping through on the other side, he pats his hips and both shoulders to put out the bits of flame and embers still lingering as he walks on.

Seemingly oblivious to it all, Arlo reaches the end of the room, plucks the baton from its holder, and walks—casual as a weekend sightseer—back to the finish line.

Along the way, he gets shot, pelted, and scorched all over again as Lucid—scrambling around in the course next to him—shrieks and squeals and looks more and more like a singed, human pincushion.

Slapping the baton into Granden's palm, Arlo joins us in our circle of pink light where we stand, stunned in open-mouthed shock.

"How—?" is all Libra can say, and I know we're witnessing something truly special. And not just the fact that Arlo walked out of the course alive. The fact that he's left Libra speechless... *that's* the real miracle.

Still in the course, Lucid's skill, stamina, or luck runs out.

A spray of silver pellets ripples the skin on his neck and arms. A finger-sized dart pierces his side just below the rib cage. He screams in agony and begs Wisp to end the game.

With a tap of a button on the glass-topped control stand, she does. And then she and Granden jog onto the shut-down course to lift Lucid up and drag him back to his Cohort where the two of them—apparently without a trace of panic or worry—pop open a med kit and begin tending to his wounds.

With everyone fussing over Lucid, I think I'm the only one who notices what's happening to Arlo.

I catch a glimpse of his face under his hood.

His skin is an even worse patchwork of scars than it was before.

I put a hand on his shoulder, but he lurches away.

"Are you okay?"

"It doesn't hurt," he murmurs. "It never hurts."

He sounds almost disappointed by that fact.

Looking over at us from next to Lucid where she's applying an aerosol healing spray out of a small yellow can, Wisp snaps at us for staring, but Arlo says it's okay.

"Are you sure?" Wisp asks.

"Yes."

"Do you want me to tell them?"

"No. I will."

"Tell us what?"

Arlo opens his mouth but doesn't say anything.

Libra whips around to Wisp. "What's going on with him?"

"It's not for me to say."

Arlo gulps and clears his throat. "I've been working with Mayla." He swallows hard and runs a finger along one of the many raised, crisscrossed red marks running across his face and down his neck. "This is part of my ability as an Emergent."

I don't see how getting covered with brutal looking scars counts as an "ability," but I'm hardly about to say anything.

"I heal quickly," Arlo explains. "Just not well."

"And he doesn't feel pain like the rest of you," Granden adds.

"That's not entirely true," Arlo corrects him. "I feel pain. It just doesn't last very long." I catch a glimpse of his face under his hood before he disappears into its shadow. Walking over to make sure Lucid is okay, he tells us, his voice barely above a whisper, "My scars are *all* that lasts."

26

STATION FIVE - RIDDLES

With Arlo retreating to the back of our Cohort and with Lucid grimacing in pain but looking very happy to be alive, we all shuffle along to the next pair of pink viewing pads.

Wisp calls our attention to Station Five, which, thankfully, looks harmless enough. It's just two tables with a gun-metal gray safe sitting in the middle of each one. Each safe is pretty plain except for the long, bright green input panel running along its front surface.

"For this challenge, the two champions will race to open the safe on the table. It requires an eleven-digit combination. You'll need to decipher a series of puzzles and get the code to punch into the safe's input panel."

Mattea lets out a cocky chortle. "Puzzles?" she mutters. "No problem."

"As long as the puzzles don't involve you getting your body shredded to pieces," I mutter back.

Wisp taps her bracelet, and a scrolling, yellow-framed holo-display appears in the air over the two tables behind her.

"There are six puzzles. The first player to solve them all and open the digital combination lock with the eleven-digit code wins."

Mattea slides forward, her hand half-raised in the air. "I'm the rep for Cohort A," she tells Wisp, who nods and directs her to go stand by her table.

"And I'll be the champion for Cohort B," Chace says without a hint of excitement or confidence.

"Pay attention, now," Wisp instructs. "The riddles will come at you fast. You need to focus your energy and attention, calm your nerves, and solve each puzzle before moving on to the next."

Ignacio thrusts his meaty arm into the air. "And what happens if they get a puzzle answer wrong?"

"Nothing," Wisp assures him.

Ignacio's eyebrows pinch together. "Really? Nothing?"

"Nothing," Wisp repeats and then, after a dramatic pause, adds, "Just a mild shock."

Even from fifteen feet away, I can see Chace's eyes go wide as a blue whale's bum.

"Shock?" she stammers.

"Yes," Wisp sighs. "I'm sorry, but yes—you may experience a shock if you input an incorrect answer."

"A *mild* shock?" Trax asks on behalf of his sister.

"Sure," Wisp agrees. "Mild. It won't kill the competitors if that's what you're worried about."

"But it'll hurt, right?"

"Naturally."

"A lot?"

"Naturally."

Mattea slaps her palms together and rubs her hands up and down with enough friction to start a fire. Figuratively speaking, of course.

Chace doesn't look nearly as eager, but her brother nudges her forward as the rest of their Cohort cheers her on.

From his spot behind me, Ignacio gripes into my ear about how it won't be fair.

"How do you figure? Mattea's got a gift for this stuff. Why do you think I picked her for this assignment?"

"Sure. But have you talked to Chace lately?"

"No."

"Of course you haven't. That's because she's always got her face buried in her holo-pad. Reading and writing fast is her thing."

"Don't underestimate Mattea," Arlo says.

From where she's standing next to me, Sara gives the tiniest of nods. "Mattea *is* good."

Wisp starts the contest with a tap on her bracelet and a wave of her hand. Blinking on and then off again, one at a time, seven riddles flash in a scrolling holo-text above the tables.

They come at our two competitors with the relentlessness of the spikes and fire that just consumed Arlo and took down Lucid.

I can barely read the seven riddles, let alone solve them.

RIDDLE #1:

A girl was asked her age. She answered, "In two years, I will be twice as old as I was five years ago." How old is she?

RIDDLE #2:

A married couple has five daughters. Each daughter has one brother. What is the total number of people in their immediate family?

. . .

RIDDLE #3:

What number comes next in the pattern?

2, 3, 5, 9, 17, _____

RIDDLE #4:

A man is fifty-four-years-old. His mother is eighty. How many years has it been since the mother was three times as old as her son?

RIDDLE #5:

A bird is given nine seeds to eat for breakfast.

A spider is given thirty-six flies to eat for lunch.

An ant is given twenty-seven drops of nectar to eat for dinner.

How many mice would be given for a mountain lion to eat for its midnight snack?

RIDDLE #6:

A girl goes into battle and brings home eleven severed heads of her enemies as trophies. On her way back to her village, all but four of the severed heads get carried off and eaten by wild dogs. How many of the severed heads are left for the girl to show off to her family as spoils of war?"

RIDDLE #7:

If two is company and three's a crowd, what are four and five?

AS THE LAST of the seven riddles fades, Chace hums to herself and taps in a number on the input panel in front of her. Mattea does the same. No shocks yet.

Turning back over her shoulder to look at us, Mattea gives a wink of assurance as both girls continue to input numbers.

Mattea is good. She's got a quick mind and way more confidence than I do when it comes to stuff like this.

Chace—mousy and usually hunched over her holo-pad—is somehow even better.

As our two Cohorts cheer the two girls on, it's Chace who punches in the final combination, calling out the answers to the riddles as she does:

"For riddle number one, two times five is ten, plus the two years yet to come. So the answer is 'twelve.'"

She taps in "12," and the number appears on the safe's input panel and also in bright white light on the overhead holo-display for the rest of us to see.

"For riddle number two, the married couple is two people. They have five daughters for a total of seven. Each daughter has one brother, who is the same brother to each daughter. So the answer is 'eight.'"

She taps in her answer as Mattea, working feverishly next to her does the same.

"For riddle number three, each number is double the number that comes before it, minus one. So the answer is 'thirty-three.'"

Chace inputs her answer and moves on.

"For riddle number four, there's a thirty-six-year difference between mother and son. Thirty-six divided by three is thirteen. The answer is the man's age of fifty-four minus thirteen. So the answer is 'forty-one.'"

Tapping in her response, Chace turns over her shoulder to offer up a happy nod of assurance to her Cohort.

"For riddle number five, the pattern is four-and-a-half units per number of legs on the animal. So the answer is eighteen."

Chace's fingers are flying, and I can tell Mattea is getting flustered.

"For riddle number six, it doesn't matter how many heads she severed. All but four of them get stolen. So, she has four."

Mattea nods, but it's Chace who inputs the answer.

"For riddle number seven, four and five are nine. So the answer is nine."

Chace does a little bounce, inputs her answer, and steps back to check her work.

"So the final combination," she announces, first to herself and then, louder for the rest of us to hear from our viewing circles, has to be..."

Her voice drops off as she inputs the numbers: 12, 8, 33, 41, 18, 4, 9.

After punching in the last of her numbers, the safe on the table in front of her clacks open, and Chace steps back from the display, her arms thrust into the air in triumph.

While she's beaming, Mattea slaps an angry palm to the top of her own safe and hangs her head.

Libra says she can't believe it, but the results speak for themselves.

Chace bounces back to her cheering Cohort as the scores for our two teams update on the holo-screen.

"Well," Ignacio says, consoling Mattea, "at least you didn't get shocked."

"Unfortunately," Sara points out, "we kind of needed that win."

It's true. The final tally appears on the holo-display above Wisp's head.

Over the course of the first five stations, Cohort B outscored us by six points.

...which means I have to fight Granden.

Blindfolded.

27

STATION SIX - TAP OUT

INSTEAD OF CONGREGATING in the pink holding circles, this time, our two Cohorts gather around the recessed fighting pit way down at the far end of the high-ceilinged arena.

"This is the Battle Bowl," Wisp announces, pointing down into the shallow, obstacle-filled ring.

Set three steps down from the room's main floor, the bottom of the large round space is lined with gravel and small chunks of brick. Rising up like cacti in a desert, five wooden posts, each about six feet high and each with a starfish array of steel spikes splaying out, are planted randomly in the middle of the ring.

Just for fun, there are also three sofa-sized concrete blocks in the pit, coiled loops of razor wire around the perimeter, and the low walls are lined with shards of glass and more of those lovely steel spikes.

And if that wasn't enough, the floor is tilted on a weird angle, and I think it's moving.

Forget about fighting. I could die just stepping down into this thing!

"This will simulate the dangerous conditions you'll face out in the world," Wisp announces. "Where you'll have to fight your environment as well as your opponent."

If only I had Brohn's impenetrable skin. Or even Arlo's healing ability.

Shut it, Branwynne. No sense whinging on about what you don't have. Focus on what you do have: a very low chance of survival and a very high chance of getting your head beaten to a pasty dough.

With the stations we've already completed literally behind us, I'm feeling more than a little trapped.

Of course, I'm the one who doled out the assignments for my Cohort, so I also sort of trapped myself.

Why didn't I pick Sara for this challenge? I would've *loved* to see Granden sling her around by her snarky little face. Or Libra. Although I don't think even a broken jaw could stop her jabbering. Or Ignacio. He really needs to have some of the hot air let out of that swollen head of his.

As for Mattea and Arlo...well, I don't really have a problem with them, so I guess I'm glad I didn't give them this particular assignment.

Either way, I've got to start being more careful about making decisions on behalf of an entire group.

Focus, Branwynne. You're in it now, and that's a lesson for another time.

A flurry of motion from behind us causes all of us to jump and spin around.

I laugh as Haida Gwaii flaps and then glides down the length of the obstacle course, leaving a cloud of dust and tiny white feathers in her wake as she settles on my extended forearm.

"I think she wants to help you," Libra giggles.

"Or else stop you from going down into that pit and getting beaten to a pulp," Ignacio jokes.

I stare for a second into Haida's blue eyes. The truth is, a lot of times, including now, I have no idea what she wants. Sometimes we communicate pretty well. But most of the time, she's still a mystery to me.

As I run my first two fingers over the white feathers of her smooth, round head, I reach out to her with my mind like Kress taught me:

What is it? Are you here to help?

I feel her trying to connect with me from her side of our bond, but then things fizzle, and we're just a girl and a raven again.

She unfurls her wings, and flaps off to land on Trax's shoulder.

When did you two get so chummy?

"Come on!" Granden urges through a steely, taunting grin. "Time to show you what a good old fashioned Typic can do in a very unfair fight."

With Wisp nudging me forward, I step down the three stairs and into the deadly, slanted Battle Bowl where Granden is waiting, his fingers curled into loose fists at his sides.

Walking up behind me, Wisp holds up a strip of thick black fabric and tells me it's time.

Gulping, I say one last telempathic goodbye to Haida Gwaii...just in case.

It was nice knowing you.

~ It was nice being known.

With a mental chuckle, I start to ask her when she got so cheeky, but our connection fades out again as Wisp starts to slip the blindfold on me.

"You'll...um...go easy on her, right?" Libra calls down from where she's standing between Ignacio and Arlo.

The last thing I see before Wisp finishes securing the blindfold over my eyes is Granden swinging around in the pit and looking up to face Libra. He gives her a big thumbs up and says, "Nope."

And then the world goes black.

From Ignacio's shoulder, Haida gargle-clacks what I hope is her encouragement as Wisp ties a tight knot into the blindfold, pats my shoulder, and wishes me luck.

I've lived in some pretty raw conditions. And I have a lot of experience finding my way around in the dark.

So that part doesn't bother me.

Besides, Kress says my senses are evolving. She always says being an Emergent isn't like having a super power. She says it's more like having a third arm or an extra eye...something that can be a handicap instead of an advantage if you don't learn how to use it right.

Funny, she didn't say anything about being blindfolded and forced to fight a grown man in an angled and spike-filled pit of death.

I do a quick review of my mental map of the pit. In my mind, I mark off where Granden is and where the obstacles are. I shift my weight over my feet as the floor tilts one way and then the other. Finally, I orient myself and note how much space I have to work with in every direction.

And then Haida Gwaii's fragmented voice nudges itself quietly into my head.

~ *More than eyes.*

Haida?

~ *More than eyes.*

More what than eyes?

~ *Vision helps. Sight hurts.*

I appreciate the advice, Haida. But can you just tell me how to not get killed in here?

~ *No.*

Great. Thanks.

Whens he doesn't respond, I ask her, *Wait. What do you mean? Can you help me here or not?*

But anything Haida might be trying to say to me after that

disappears in a fading pulse that ripples through my head and dissolves somewhere down the back of my neck.

So, with that bit of completely useless conversation rattling around in my head, Wisp calls out, "Hajime!"—the Japanese word for "Begin!"

Any hope any of us had of Granden taking it easy on me flies out the window faster than the air leaves my lungs as he drives his thick-knuckled fist into my ribcage.

I slam back into one of the spiked obstacles, and one of its thin iron skewers pierces the side of my calf.

I let out an involuntary cry of pain and leap away...

...right into what feels like Granden's flying elbow.

I see a flash of light, my head slams to the ground, and my brain does a roller-coaster drop into darkness.

In all her stories about what school was like in her time, I don't remember Mayla telling us about teachers beating the snot out of their students.

And yet, for me, it seems like it's becoming a way of life.

Or death?

No. I'm not giving up. Haida's right. I've got more going for me than just a pair of eyes.

I scamper back, my hand finding the surface of one of the concrete blocks. I vault over it and plant myself behind it, making sure to keep the thick barrier between me and Granden.

I hear his boots scuffle against the pit's gravelly surface. He's trying to stay quiet, trying to stalk me.

His strategy is clear: He'll advance carefully and circle around.

Above us, the two Cohorts cheer and shout.

Cries of "Get her!" and "Look out!" mix in with a muddled chorus of random hoots and hollers.

A scrunch of gravel comes from my right. But there's a displacement of air from my left.

Uh oh!

The crinkle of fabric alerts me to the hammer-fist swinging toward my head.

I lean away but not quite fast enough, and the blow catches me on the collar bone.

I feel myself starting to black out. Granden may not be trying to kill me, but he's not exactly pulling his punches, either. And he's definitely not feeling sorry for me for my little disadvantage of being completely sightless.

In my fuzzy and rapidly fading mind, I remember Kress's lessons about how to stay focused in the face of fear.

In that second, I sense Haida giving me her fragmented, cryptic wisdom about vision. I hear Sara giggling a few feet above me over the sight of me staggering around, getting done up, and potentially having my teeth kicked in by Granden. I hear Cohort B cheering Granden on, and I hear my own Cohort shouting at me to get up.

Come on, Branwynne—get it together! That's too many bloody voices!

I take a breath and recenter myself, but it's too late. Granden isn't as light on his feet as Kress is. Not even close. But he's muffled his steps just enough to make me think he's taking up a flanking position when really, he's slipped around behind me.

I feel the air from his leg sweep before I feel the impact of his shin smashing into the back of my knee.

My leg buckles.

Some opponents would gloat right now. But I know Granden well enough to know he'll try to press his advantage. He's not going to let a little thing like me being a hundred and twenty pound, blindfolded teenage girl stop him from teaching me a *very* painful lesson.

Re-centering myself, I take my own advantage of being down on one knee and launch into an evasive shoulder-roll before springing back up into a crouch, my head tilted just enough for a phase variance in ambient sound waves to reach my ears.

Now that I'm able to judge the distance between us, I let Granden stalk me in a slow, boot shuffling circle around the ring.

For a second, the clamor of the two Cohorts slips into my head, but I concentrate and block it all out—even Haida's gurgle-croaks of encouragement.

Now that I've filtered out all the extraneous noise, all the sounds in the pit—Granden's breathing, his footsteps, the rustle of material from his cargo pants...even the rasp of his hair against his collar—all get weirdly crystal clear.

He lunges again with a quick jab. I dodge but not quite fast enough. His punch doesn't fully connect, but it's enough to feel like his knuckles just pounded a row of dents into my upper arm.

I spin away, lashing out with a back-fist as I do. He ducks, but I smile. His lungs tightened while his heart just shifted into high gear.

I can read you. You're surprised. So close to being afraid. Let me help you get there.

Like all birds, ravens have an exceptional sense of direction and a keen sense of where they are in space.

Their specialized trigeminal nerve enables them to create a type of olfactory map. Coupled with their ability to align themselves with the Earth's magnetic poles, they have what could be considered a sixth—and even a seventh sense.

For humans, Kress once called the ability "proprioception."

As she explained it to me, "It's a kinesthetic, automatic neuro-response that enables balance and, in your case, enhances flexibility, reflexes, and spatial awareness."

"Yeah," I asked. "But will it help me kick somebody's arse?"

Kress assured me it would.

Taking her at her word, I channel that ability now. Plus a few more.

Granden dodges.

Or, at least he *thinks* he does.

My jab was just a set-up, a way to get him to look for an attack in one place when, really, it's coming from somewhere else.

Just a little trick I picked up from Rain when she introduced me to Game Theory a couple of years back.

By the time Granden figures out where I am, he's got my sharp elbow cracking into his lower back.

But that's not the real attack, either. It's just a second set-up for the flurry of Krav Maga strikes I unleash.

And it's not out of desperation. And it's not anger.

This is slow-motion and clinical. I'm in total control, not of him or of the fight but of *myself*.

The collage of the five senses of a Typic—binocular vision, sound, touch, smell, taste—paints a detailed mental map in my head.

But that's just the beginning of what's whipping through my brain.

Other senses—infrared, echolocation, neural mediating reflexes, magnetic wave identification—flow around me and turn the 3D images into an almost overwhelming mass of detail.

It's not just me in the pit anymore. I don't know how, but Haida's here, too, fluttering around inside my head and turning me from an isolated individual into a connected, dual unit.

It's two against one, and Granden doesn't stand a chance.

I see currents in the air, magnetic pulses in the objects around us, temperature fluctuations in and around Granden's body, and I see every move he makes before he makes it.

As we circle each other, both of us wary of the sharp shards and stinging barbs in the arena, I hear and can easily differentiate every voice of the two Cohorts howling above us. Not only that. I can smell their sweat.

But it's not distracting in the slightest. In fact, a wave of hyper focus washes over me, and it's like I'm suddenly able to pay full attention to every touch, taste, sight, sound, and smell all at once.

The heel of Granden's left boot shifts a fraction of an inch to the right and presses into the gravel. He's bracing himself for a lunge and probably gearing up for another desperate leg sweep.

He doesn't get a chance to start his next attack, though.

I dig the toe of my own boot into the gravel. In a flash, I kick a spray of it up into Granden's face. He barely has time to register or react before I'm on him.

A sharp uppercut to the solar plexus knocks the wind out of him, and a side-fist hammer strike disorients him for a split second. Which is longer than I need to finish my attack with a side kick to the back of his knee.

I'm behind him now and have him in a chokehold before his knee hits the ground.

With my forearm locked in place by my other arm and pressed against his trachea, his body goes limp under me.

I barely feel his tap-out pat on my shoulder, but Wisp's top-of-the-lungs cry for us to stop clangs in my ears like church bells.

My vision returns to normal. Too bad. I was getting a kick out of seeing the world through eyes and a buffet of other senses *way* more advanced than my own.

Huffing for breath and with his hands clamped to his knees, Granden tells me, "Nice job" and reaches out to grab my wrist.

At first, I think it's some new, underhanded attack, and I tense up. But he raises my arm in the air as I slip the blindfold from my eyes.

"Cohort A," he announces grandly, "that is one very superior warrior you have there!"

Except for Sara—who I think was really banking on me getting my arse shredded—everyone from my Cohort bursts into a refrain of fist-pumping cheers.

Even Cohort B offers up a round of tepid applause.

Haida Gwaii bursts up from her perch on Trax's shoulder and flutters over to land on the railing circling the pit. She cackles out a phlegmy screech, spreads her white wings , and clenches and releases her grip on the rail.

Like slow-moving water in an icy river, her voice crawls into my head.

~ *Did you think there was only one way to see?*

I did. But now I know there's more.

~ *Then you really did win.*

"So...wait," I say out loud, blinking against the arena's starchy white light and catching Wisp's eye. "I won?"

Wisp assures me I did. "And in style," she adds. "I've never seen anyone move like that."

And then she says the three most beautiful, flattering words ever spoken:

"Except for Kress."

I really wish Kress had been here!

As if she's read my mind, Chace bounds up, her holo-stylus in hand.

"Don't worry," she beams. "I'll make a whole illustrated story to show her!"

"Show who?" I ask.

Chace looks confused for a second, and then the wrinkles in her forehead smooth out. "Kress. I'll make sure Kress knows about the competitions and about your final fight against Granden. After all, I'm the Chronicler, right?"

"Um...sure?"

Grinning, Chance bounds off to rejoin her Cohort.

Now, how did she know what I was thinking?

Before I have a chance to wonder any further, Libra and Ignacio flank me and get to gushing over how fast I moved.

"It wasn't fast," Reverie announces from behind us as we make our way out of the arena and start heading back down the aisle, past the obstacle challenges, and toward the door.

"What are you talking about?" Mattea laughs. "Branwynne made Granden look like he was a sick tortoise in cement shoes!"

"It wasn't *fast*," Reverie corrects her, her voice even and firm as if she was stating the simplest, most obvious thing in the world. "It was *interdimensional*."

28

DATE

It's in the deepest, quietest part of the middle of the night when I slip out of bed.

After hours of revelry in the Lounge—with our two Cohorts laughing, bickering, and trading embellished stories about the competition we were all just a part of—exhaustion hit everyone hard. We were practically asleep before our heads hit our pillows.

Now, with everyone else purring, prone, and dozing, I snap awake and tiptoe out of the Dorm and into the hallway where Trax is already waiting for me. He's leaning against the wall by the stairs, his arms folded across his chest.

Instead of our usual training kit, he's in blue pajama bottoms and a form-fitting white tank top with the Academy crest, the same outfit most of us wear at night.

Because he's not in my Cohort, I haven't seen him looking quite this casual in a long time.

Great. All he needs now is a pipe and a leather chair, and he could be a seventeen-year-old version of my father.

Although he's not quite as frail-looking as he used to be,

Trax is still on the thin side. His forearm muscles are long and ropey, and his teeth are nearly as white as Libra's.

His thick brown hair glistens in the dim light of the corridor. He must have wet it before coming out here.

Nice of you to make the effort.

With his combination of lanky limbs, lean muscles, pajamas, and military boots, he looks half-boy and half man as he grins a tight-lipped greeting to me.

He waits until I'm standing right in front of him before his small grin breaks into a big, dorky, cheek-crinkling smile.

"So," he whispers, "you showed up."

"A promise is a promise," I whisper back.

"You look very nice," he says. "Nightwear suits you."

"About that date..." I make an exaggerated show of looking down both ends of the long corridor leading to all of the bedrooms and shower rooms in the Dorm. "I don't see many pubs around here...."

Trax chuckles and asks, "Are you up for some fresh air?" He whips out a pair of jackets stashed behind his back and holds them up by their collars like they're the puffy pelts of two dead, polyester animals.

"I was thinking maybe a stroll downstairs to hang out in the Tavern?" I tell him.

"How unadventurous of you. We spend every day down there." He holds up three fingers and waggles them in front of me. "Breakfast. Lunch. Dinner."

"We'll trip a dozen alarms if we try to leave the Academy."

Trax flicks his thumb toward the ceiling. "True. But not if we go up."

"The roof?"

"Sure."

"Which one?"

Trax smiles. He knows as well as I do that the Academy is huge. It's got flat roofs, gabled roofs, parapets with stone balustrades, and even a set of dormers jutting up from the angled roofs around the fifth floor.

"The top," he says with a wink. "Only one alarm, and I know for a fact you know how to deactivate it."

He's right. I do. Because I've been training with Kress for so long, she and Wisp gave me special access to the Academy's highest flat rooftop where Render and Haida Gwaii roost with their six offspring. As a result, I'm the only member of either Cohort who gets to come and go as she pleases.

Not that anyone else really has any reason or desire to get out onto the roof. Other than the roost, there's really not much there.

And, because our school overlooks the remains of the Valta, we have an unfortunately unobstructed view of the bombed-out town far below and the scorched woods around it.

"Wisp won't be happy if she finds out," I warn Trax, even as I slip into the hooded thermal jacket he holds out for me.

"And I won't be happy if we don't give it a shot. So I guess the question is, what'll make *you* happy?"

"Fine," I smile. "Let's go."

His hand brushes mine as he slides his arms into his own jacket. At first, I think maybe he's trying to get me to hold hands, which isn't going to happen.

But he winds up walking ahead of me, so maybe it was just an accident.

After climbing the narrowing staircase to the Academy's top level, I punch in the access code on the input panel, and the big steel latch clicks open. I push the heavy wooden door outward, and it creaks against the layers of snow and ice on the other side.

The sky is black and bleak, but the reflected light from a

blood-red crescent moon is casting a hazy pink glow over the top of the Academy.

The wind is kicking up a fog of dry snow and a swirling vortex of stinging ice crystals.

"Hard to believe it gets so cold up here when it's so hot down there," Trax calls out over the whipping wind.

I wrap my arms around myself. "I know. It's like the world doesn't know what to do with itself."

"Well, I guess that's our fault, not the world's."

"I'm going to check on Haida," I tell Trax as I make my way over to the makeshift enclosure Kress and Brohn built along a natural ledge running along the length of the rock face.

After the competition, I brought her back up here. I tried to connect with her, to thank for her advice and for cheering me on. But she was tired, and all I got out of her was an overwhelming desire to go to sleep.

Like all ravens, Render, Haida Gwaii, and their brood like to sleep in a group.

I poke my head over the stone wall designed to keep the powerful wind at bay.

Under the overhanging, rocky crag and tucked into the shallow roost, Haida and her six offspring are huddled against the cold and are deeply and quietly asleep.

Normally, Render would be with them, joining in and watching over his family. But he's off on his adventure with Kress, and none of us who are left in the Academy have any idea when they'll be back.

Sighing, I take a second to marvel at Haida and her six-raven brood. I've gotten to know the newest ravens really well over the years.

We named the biggest one "War Jr." after our tank-sized teacher. Like our own War, this onyx-black is no gentle giant. He established his place in the pecking order right away, nudging his brothers and sisters to the sides of their nest and claiming the largest middle part as his own.

Cheyenne is our resident nuzzler. She loves human companionship, and Kress says she thinks Cheyenne is secretly a tender little human being under all those oily-black feathers.

The two smallest of the brood—the female Apache and the male Comanche—are mottled in an unusual black-and-white cheetah pattern. They're also the only ones who'll occasionally stand up to War Jr. when he's being bossy. Alone, they're easily intimidated. Together, they seem to think they're indestructible.

Arapaho, one of the two white ravens, is probably the most independent of the bunch. He'll disappear for days at a time, and no one knows where he goes off to, not even Kress.

Shoshone, the second of the two white ravens, is the largest of the females, bigger even than Haida Gwaii and nearly as big as Render. Kress and her friends named Shoshone in honor of the bombed-out shell of a high school they lived in during the drone strikes.

"It's a strange feeling," Kress once explained to me as she paused to look out over the Valta during one of our earliest training sessions, "to be terrified in the one place you rely on to feel safe."

Right now, gazing over the sleeping brood, I wish I could crawl in and join them in their peaceful, unified slumber. Sure, I've always preferred solitude. But looking at Haida and her offspring makes me long for something else, a connection even beyond the telempathic Emergent bond Haida and I share.

I'm tempted to reach out with my mind and connect with Haida like Kress has been teaching me, but I know Haida way too well by now. Being woken up, even if it's just to say a middle-of-the-night "Hello," would make her as bonkers as a bag of ferrets, and she likely wouldn't let me connect with her again for at least a week.

To my surprise, she must sense my presence because she shakes herself awake and greets me with a cheerful cackle.

~ Awake?

Yes. I'm on a date...sort of...with Trax.

~ Happy?

Am I happy? Sure. I guess so.

~ Let yourself be.

I'm trying harder. I really am.

~ Try softer.

Are you okay?

~ Missing Render.

I know. Join me?

~ Yes.

Her consciousness slips back out of mine as smooth and easy as a yolk from an egg, and I'm left as just myself again.

Haida lets me scoop her up and slip her onto my shoulder. I turn back to join Trax, who seems mesmerized by the way the angled rooftops of the Academy and its twin turrets rise skyward, melting into the jagged rocks leading up to the highest parts of the mountain.

He does a little double-take when he sees we'll be joined by my blue-eyed, white-feathered raven companion, but, other than a nod of approval, he doesn't comment on her.

Side by side, he and I walk across the flat part of the roof, past the exact same spot where we watched Kress, Lucid, and Reverie open a portal five years ago. We saw with our own eyes how Cardyn and Manthy walked into it and disappeared.

"This way," I say to Trax, leading him over to the stone ledge where Kress and I often sit and talk during our Apprenticeship lessons.

I hop up onto the cold stone wall, swing around, and dangle

my legs over the steep side of the Academy. From my shoulder, Haida bobs her head and stares at Trax for a second before hunching down and pressing her head against mine.

"Come on up," I say, offering him a hand.

He peers over the ledge and down into the dark abyss below. "I think I'll stand. Sitting's for the birds."

"Don't let Haida hear you say that."

"Oh, right. Is that an insult?"

"To someone who can fly, yeah."

"My apologies," Trax grins, reaching out with two fingers to pat Haida's head.

"Come on," I say again, offering him a hand this time.

Gingerly, like he thinks the stone blocks might crumble to dust under him, Trax eases his way up onto the wall next to me, only with his legs hanging over the flat roof and with his back to the valley.

"What do you think happened to them?" he asks, pointing to the roof. "Cardyn and Manthy, I mean."

"I don't know."

"Do you think they...?"

"Died?"

"Well, they went *somewhere*. And they're not here."

"That's not the same thing as being dead," I tell him.

"It's close enough."

Haida adjusts herself, digging her talons into my shoulder, which makes me twitch at the sudden twinge of pain. Taking care not to hurt or startle her, I slip my hand under her cottony-white body and bring her down to rest in the crook of my arm.

"There," I whisper to her. "Isn't that better?"

"You're like Kress with that raven," Trax says with an impressed smile.

"There's a lot about what Kress can do that I still don't understand."

"Tell me about it." Trax bumps his shoulder against mine and directs my attention back to the rooftop. "What she and Lucid and Reverie did over there was insane. And for Kress to say goodbye to two of her best friends like that..."

"I didn't really know Cardyn or Manthy all that well..."

"But?"

"But there's two things I *do* know."

"What's that?"

"They left *together*. And they were happy."

Trax takes a long look at the flat stretch of roof. "They really were happy, weren't they?"

"You were there. Did they look sad to you?"

"Well," Trax chuckles, "Cardyn seemed a little nervous, but I know what you mean. There was something...quiet about it."

"Quiet?"

"Not like 'dead' quiet. More like the kind of quiet that has the potential to become sound. Does that make sense?"

"No," I laugh.

Trax nudges my shoulder again and reminds me what War always taught us. "Things can leave or fade or disappear, but nothing's ever really dead—not how we've been conditioned to think of death, anyway."

I tilt my chin toward the mountain range and the deep valleys and the vast expanses of dark forests below us. "Do you think Kress and her Conspiracy are okay out there?"

"I don't think there's much they can't handle. If anything, it's everyone else who should be scared of *them*."

"I wish I was with them."

"I know."

"It's a little frustrating, though."

"What's that?"

"I don't know. I guess not being able to really control my Emergent abilities like Kress does."

Trax says, "Ha!" and reminds me that I've walked through walls before.

"True," I admit. "But only twice. And I can't do it without Kress."

"Really?"

"I'll be able to on my own one day. That's what Kress says, anyway."

"You did great against Granden. It's like you could see better blindfolded than most people see normally."

"In a way that's sort of true," I confess.

"Does it have to do with your eyes?"

"My eyes?"

Trax locks his eyes onto mine. "They're so...unusual. Black with tiny white flecks. It makes it hard to read you."

"Good!" I laugh. "I'm not interested in being read. As for how I see the world, I don't know how it works. And it doesn't always work. There are plenty of times when I can't do what Kress and our other teachers think I should be able to do."

Trax blows into his hands and then plants them under his legs.

He leans over and kisses me lightly on the corner of my mouth.

I turn toward him and squint into his birch-brown eyes. "Why'd you do that?"

"I thought maybe it'd make you happy."

I give him a huffy snort. "I think you thought it'd make *you* happy."

"You're so different from the rest of us."

"Oh, yeah?" I ask as I pet Haida with long, soothing strokes. "How's that?"

"Well, for starters, except for Roxane kind of, you're the only other one of us in the Academy who's never been a prisoner."

"And I never will be," I snap back.

Trax raises his hands, palms out. "It wasn't an accusation. I'm just impressed."

"Nothing to be impressed about." I'm about to tell him how there's no way in hell I'd let myself end up as someone's guinea pig or as a puppet in a Processor, but I take a breath and decide on the truth:

"I was lucky." I wave my free hand in the general direction of the bleak landscape below. "You all lived out there in that cock-up of a world. I lived safe and sound in the Tower of London. I had my mum and dad with me. And the ravens."

"I have to admit, I'm a little jealous."

"Because I lived in the Tower?"

"No. Because of the ravens."

"What's to be jealous about?"

Trax is quiet, and at first I think he didn't hear me. But then he sighs and leans back, his hands pressed again to the cold flat stone. "You have a connection the rest of us don't. What I mean by that is we're all struggling to figure out our place, who we are, how we're supposed to be with each other."

"I'm trying to figure that out, too."

"I know. But you already have an...intimacy. You have Haida. I think it makes you more complete somehow. Like you've got a head start and an automatic soul mate."

"I wouldn't go that far," I laugh. "Yes, we're connected. Yes, our telempathic bond makes our relationship...unique. But trust me, I don't feel any more complete than any of you. Besides, you daft bugger," I remind him with a playful elbow to his arm, "you've got a twin sister."

"And she's my best friend. But..."

"But what?"

"Well, lately she's been so into her writing and drawing. She's consumed with the idea that we're going to split up, go our separate ways."

"You and her?"

"No. All of us here at the Academy. She says she senses death and separation. She says chronicling our lives is the only way to keep us safe and together. So...she writes and draws. Obsessively. It's like it's all she needs these days."

"Could be worse. She could be Libra and just want to smile and hug everyone all the time."

Chuckling, Trax tells me that's a fair point. He looks up at the sliver of the moon visible through the dark red haze of the polluted night sky. "Well, I think maybe we should be getting back."

"Really?"

"Yeah. Chace is a light sleeper, and she'll lose her mind if she gets up and I'm not there."

"Okay. Let me put Haida back in her roost with the others."

Trax hops down onto the roof with a light grunt.

I swing my legs around, drop down to the rooftop next to him, and start walking back to the roost as Haida compresses herself into the crook of my arm to keep out the cold.

As gently as I can, I slip her back into the shallow fissure under the craggy overhang where she settles down on a bed of sticks and dry grass in the corner.

Thanks for joining me.

~ We join each other.

Haida's voice fades from my mind as she drifts back to sleep.

"Okay," I whisper, turning back to Trax, "Let's go."

Trax makes a gentlemanly show of opening the big door for me and letting me walk inside ahead of him.

Together, we slip back into the Academy and head down the stairs toward our Dorm.

Outside of my door, Trax extends his hand to me. I pause for a second, but then I accept his handshake and tell him, "Goodnight."

"How was that for a first date?" he asks.

"It was actually really nice," I tell him. "Cold. But nice."

He heads to his dorm, and I head to mine.

Once inside, I slide into my bed, fully prepared to spend the rest of the night staring in quiet solitude at the ceiling.

But Libra's voice, barely a whisper, flutters to me out of the darkness.

"So...how was it?"

"He's nice," I whisper back.

"Are you going to go on another date with him?"

"I don't think so."

Our beds are set up on a semi-circle, and we usually sleep head to foot. But Libra pushes herself up and turns around so her head is close to mine.

"Did he kiss you?"

"Kind of. Not really."

"Did you want him to?"

"Maybe."

"He's cute, don't you think?"

"Can I tell you a secret?"

"Of course."

"I haven't talked to anyone about this. Not even Kress."

Libra pushes herself up onto her elbows, her chin resting in her cupped hands. "Yeah?"

"I met a boy. A long time ago." I wait for Libra to interrupt, but she's uncharacteristically quiet. "With Trax just now, up on the roof, I felt good. But with this boy from a long time ago..."

"Yeah?"

"I felt *right*."

"Who was he—the boy from a long time ago?"

I don't answer at first. Partly because I'm really tired, and I feel myself drifting off. Partly because I feel like if I say too much, I'll lose the memory, and it won't be real anymore.

With my eyelids fluttering shut, I feel myself mumble, "There's something missing from inside me. I don't know what it is. But I'm pretty sure it's not Trax."

Libra asks, "Who then?" The answer is on my lips, but I lose the battle with sleep and drift off into a hazy mist of dreams.

29

BREAKFAST

It can't be more than an hour later when the morning wake-up lights flash in the room.

Libra is the first one up. I'm the last.

"Come on!" she laughs, her hand on my shoulder.

I bare my teeth and growl at both her *and* her intrusive hand. "You're about to draw back a bloody stump. I had a long night. Leave me alone."

"We've got work to do and fun to have!"

"Hey!" I call over to Arlo. "Does this girl have an off switch?"

Arlo tugs his hoodie over his head and smiles at me from across the room, the raised, rubbery scars on his cheeks tugging back toward his ears. "I'm not about to check."

"What do you suppose they'll have for us today?" Mattea asks.

"Knowing Wisp," Sara answers with a morning yawn, "it'll be inappropriately deadly."

Wearing just his blue and white checkered boxer shorts and his white Academy tank top, Ignacio plops down next to me on my bed and gives my knee a squeeze. "You *destroyed* Granden, yesterday," he beams.

"Speaking of 'inappropriate…'" I say, slapping his hand off of my leg.

Ignacio blushes and says, "Sorry." He smacks the back of his own hand, waggles his fingers, and shrugs. "Sometimes this thing has a mind of its own."

"Now, if only *you* did," Libra snaps, pinching Ignacio's ear in her fingers and hauling him to his feet.

"Ow!"

"That's for being a handsy turd-burglar," she scolds, swatting him on the rear-end with a loud "thwack!" "Don't worry, Branwynne," she says, turning to me with a wink. "I'll protect you."

I'm about to grumble at her that I don't need her protection, but I catch myself smiling, instead. I tell her, "Thanks," as I hop up and prepare to fight Sara for one of the better sonic showers in the bathroom.

Once we're all dressed, we head downstairs to the Tavern where Cohort B is already nearly finished with their breakfast.

In unison, they stand when we enter, clap their hands, and bow.

Lucid, his hand on his sister's shoulder, tips his head and says, "Nice job."

Even quiet, mostly-monosyllabic Roxane—her sugary white hair practically glowing under the Tavern's holo-lights—offers up a goofy grin and claps along, although completely out of synch with the others.

"Seriously! Well done!" Trax calls out, raising his glass in a dramatic toast as my Cohort and I take our seats on either side of the long table.

I smile my thanks to Trax. I expect him to say something about our little rendezvous last night, but he's thankfully discreet. His eyes linger on mine but just for a split-second longer than normal.

It's not that I'm sorry I went up to the roof with him. That part was actually really pleasant.

It's just that with all the competitions going on, I don't want my Cohort to know I've been fraternizing with the enemy. And I especially don't want them to know that this particular member of "the enemy" is actually a pretty cute and unexpectedly easy guy to chat up.

Her jacket slung over her shoulder, Wisp comes into the Tavern with Granden walking along just behind her, wincing and doing an amusingly piss-poor job of trying to hide his limp.

We all stop talking and snap to attention as Wisp addresses us. "Both of the Cohorts did a very nice job yesterday. And, although we don't believe in taking breaks from your training, just this once, we're going to go against our own rules and give you the day off."

"Kind of," Granden cuts in.

"Right," Wisp agrees. "Kind of."

"What are we going to do then?" Reverie asks from down at the far end of the bench seat.

"You're going to get to use the Virtual Reality Simulator," Wisp announces.

There's a moment of stunned silence while we gauge her for signs of deceit or possibly brain damage. When Granden nods his confirmation, everyone from our two Cohorts—minus myself—bursts into a simultaneous, unified whoop of cheery-eyed glee.

Kress and the other teachers use the VR-sims for their own training all the time. It's a top-of-the-line system that Terk and the Auditor call a "triumph of engineering." It's designed to run participants through complex, ultra-realistic battle and problem-solving simulations, the kind that can't be replicated in the real world without causing serious injury or, what's even more serious, *death*.

My fellow Academy students have been begging Wisp to let them have a go at it for weeks now, but she always refuses.

During one of my Ravenmaster training sessions about a month ago, Kress told me why:

"The technology in the VR-sims—in this entire Academy, actually—comes from Krug."

"What?"

"Well, not Krug, personally. But from his techno-geneticists."

"The Deenays?"

"And the En-gene-eers. Yes."

"So...are they dangerous?"

"The VR-sims? No. Well, yes. Potentially."

From there, Kress went on to tell me about her experiences in the sims in the Processor where she and her Conspiracy were first trained. She told me about endless battle-simulation loops that were enough to drive her and her friends completely off their trolley.

"It's not a game," she explained as we stood outside of the ravens' roost on the roof. "You're not just an avatar of yourself. You're still you. All the feelings, emotions, and physical consequences of your actions—it's all in the sim. At our core, we're nothing more than electrical impulses. The VR-sim takes advantage of that fact and replicates you with neurochromatic precision."

I guess she saw the stunned look on my face because she laughed and threw her arm around me.

"Don't worry about it," she said. "We have the Auditor now. She oversees all the tech in the Academy. As long as she's around, we don't need to worry."

I know Kress meant it to be comforting, but honestly, the Auditor has always given me a mild case of the creeps. As the disembodied female voice "living" in a collection of circuit boards and micro plasma panels in a black glassy disk on Terk's back, the Auditor looks like a machine but sounds like a living, thinking human being.

But I have to admit, on our way here five years ago, she *did* get us away from some deadly people and through some dangerous places.

The Auditor saved me, Kress, and Kress's entire Conspiracy a dozen times over.

She's able to tap into what's left of the nation's network, which makes her a great asset to have around.

But, since she's attached to Terk, and because Terk is off with the rest of our teachers on their recruiting mission, she's *not* around now. And, unfortunately, her consciousness—including her personal ability to monitor and defend the Academy's network—goes where she goes.

That leaves us without her protective oversight and very much in the hands of the VR-sim.

Having my life in *anyone's* hands is enough to give me a serious eye twitch. Having my life in the hands of a disembodied techno-consciousness...well, that's enough to make me think twice about the whole idea of turning myself over to a VR-sim, especially one based on a design that's evidently caused so many life-or-death problems in the past.

On this fine morning, Ignacio apparently doesn't share my reservations. He bounces up and comes around to my side of the table, wedging himself between me and Libra.

Snarling through a mouthful of one of the plump strawberries Mayla left us from our greenhouse, I plant my hand on his chest and push him away.

"What's with everyone touching me today? Am I wearing a sign?"

"Come on!" Ignacio urges. "The VR-sim. *Finally!*"

"Are you ready?" Wisp asks. "I mean, I know breakfast is the most important meal of the day..."

"We're ready!" Trax shouts, rising to his feet and pumping both fists in the air.

Wisp laughs and says she hopes we all share Trax's enthusiasm. "Follow me. The program is fun, deadly, and ready for you."

30

VR-SIM

EVEN THOUGH THEY'RE on the same floor as the Combat Skills and Training Rooms, the Weapons Lab, and the Fitness Center (where I've been spending way too much of my time these days), this will be our first time stepping into one of the actual VR-sim rooms.

When Wisp and Granden lead us in, though, I'm profoundly disappointed. It's got to be the most boring room in the entire Academy.

It's just one big empty space with a tube-shaped console suspended from the ceiling. About a dozen thin black cables hang down from the mirrored cylinder and drape over each other on the floor in a maze of lazy tangles.

If Wisp and Granden wanted to replicate the look of a droopy, octopus-shaped chandelier, this would be it.

"Not much of a room," Trax mutters, reflecting my own disappointment.

"The room doesn't matter," Granden explains. He presses a fingertip to his temple. "It's what's in *here* that makes all the difference."

"We're not plugging you into a machine, "Wisp explains.

"The sim is designed to let you work cooperatively with some of the neglected parts of your own brains."

Libra elbows me and flicks her eyes toward Ignacio. Under her breath, she says, "Some of our brains are more neglected than others," and I put a hand to my mouth so no one will see me laugh.

Granden has us form a circle under the hanging octopus arms and takes notes on a holo-pad while Wisp gathers up the dangling black tentacles and, one by one, loops the ends of them around our heads.

Once on, they constrict a little, not enough to hurt but snug enough to stay fixed in place.

"I thought there'd be seats or chairs or something," Trax says to me from his side of our eleven-person circle.

"You know what they say," I tell him with a wink. "Sitting's for the birds."

Trax laughs loud enough to startle Roxane, who is standing next to him, her arctic blue eyes flashing as they dance nervously around the room.

Wisp tells us to brace ourselves, and Trax turns to Granden. "Aren't you joining us?"

"Not this time."

"But the teams won't be even. Cohort A will have a numbers advantage."

"You won't be competing against each other this time."

"We won't?" I ask.

"You know about the Unsettled, right?"

"Up close and personal," I boast.

Is it weird that I wear the deadliest moments of my life as a badge of honor?

"Okay then," Granden continues, his eyes on mine, "once you're in the sim, I'll count on you to introduce your classmates to their army."

At the word, "army," Libra gulps, and Roxane giggles.

"What's so funny?" Sara asks her.

Roxane's grin drops, and her pale cheeks flush pink. "Army. Personality. Illusion."

With no idea what she's on about and getting eager for combat, I ask Wisp if we can start the program now.

With an impish grin, she tells us, "Absolutely" and hits a series of pads on her input panel.

I hold my breath and feel a surge of electric warmth flow through my head as the room around me pixilates away.

WHEN THE WORLD OF COLOR, depth, and definition returns, I'm standing in a simulated desert-scape with both Cohorts.

Our normal clothes are gone. Instead, we're all dressed head-to-toe in matching slate-blue body suits with white trim and long white lines running down our sleeves and pant legs. White military vests and ankle-high patrol boots complete the kit.

Wisp's voice is soft and warm and seems to bubble up from the air all around us.

"This will be nice and simple. There's an army coming toward you. The Army of the Unsettled. They want a war with you. They're not programmed with weapons. Neither are you. This will be a hand-to-hand combat scenario against superior numbers of an unpredictable opponent. All you need to do is not die."

"Great," Mattea mumbles. "Is that all?"

Ignacio stops in the middle of rubbing his hands together and looks down at them like he's seeing them for the first time. "Marvie!"

"What is?" I ask, looking down at my own hands.

"It's me. I mean, it looks like me. And feels like me. But there's something missing."

Sara claps her own hands a bunch of times in front of her and then stares down at her palms. "I know what you mean. I can feel my skin, the air, even. But it feels..."

"Fake?" I ask. "That's because it is."

Libra reaches over to tug at the tight compression sleeve of my body suit. When she does, I get a better sense of what Ignacio and Sara are talking about. I can feel the pull from Libra's hand, but the fabric feels odd. Like it's too distant or the wrong material, as if someone painted it on me, and now the paint is slowly drying against my skin.

Libra points out into empty the wind-swept desert. "There's nothing here. The sim...is it running?"

I pivot around to where a few dozen of the Unsettled are sprinting right toward us at top speed, their bare feet kicking up clouds of swirling red dust as they charge. "I don't know if the sim is running...but *they* sure the frack are!"

We know from Kress and the other teachers how sophisticated the VR-sims are. We can't die or even really get seriously hurt. But, as Wisp likes to remind us, getting *really* hurt and getting *simulated* hurt aren't that far off.

"Pain," she always says, "whether it's in our nerve endings or in a complex computer code, is just a matter of electrical impulses. And we have plenty of those."

The Unsettled—simulations or not—are insane, ruthless fighters. I know that from personal experience. Whoever programmed this thing knows it, too.

"They're programmed to be as realistic as possible," I shout out to the others. "Right down to their bad breath and the long, sharp fingernails."

I know my body is standing in a room, plugged into a sophisticated computer program, but there's nothing I can do to will myself back there.

With no weapons, we have to rely on our training from Unarmed Combat. We put up a good fight. Only it's not quite good enough.

The Unsettled are a horrifying, snaggle-toothed bunch of desperate, hazy-eyed scavengers. The mass of dusty rags bearing down on us splits up into dozens of individual fighters, who move with a blinding speed way too fast to be real.

Practically falling over each other, they launch themselves at us with a ferocity I wasn't expecting.

The simulated battlefield is open and empty with nowhere to hide and with nothing to use as a weapon.

I don't think the Army of the Unsettled care.

They take Lucid and Reverie out first. The twins are amazing when it comes to their ability to access other dimensions.

In hand-to-hand combat, they leave a whole new dimension to be desired.

Their virtual bodies slam to the hard-packed desert floor with a very real, very loud smash.

Before they've even hit the ground, the other twins—Trax and Chace—disappear under a swarm of the Unsettled fighters.

We're definitely going to need more training.

Mattea and Ignacio jump into a defensive, back-to-back position and square off against four of our attackers.

Sara lunges at another one of our enemies—a stocky boy who must be her height and War's weight. Bare-chested and coated in hair and sweat, he swats away her attack, latches onto her arm, and slings her, Olympic discus-style, right into Arlo.

Sara and Arlo crash together and reel backwards, falling to a stop in a tangle of twisted limbs.

As a half dozen of the Unsettled descend on Libra, two of their horde—a thick girl and a thin boy—splinter off and advance on me from opposite sides. They may not be real, but the pain sure as frack is.

I last longer than my classmates, but in the end, I wind up on one knee, waiting for the girl's clenched fist hovering over my head to come smashing down.

Only it doesn't. In fact, the leathery, scabby-skinned fist of my female attacker freezes exactly where it is.

I look up into her crusty eyes. The pause doesn't last more than a half-second, and the fist jumps back to its wrecking-ball path toward my face. Only, this time, I'm able to roll to the side, dodging the strike before launching one of my own.

Feeling like I'm moving at high speed, I leg sweep the Unsettled off her feet and drop a ferocious elbow to the bridge of her nose while she's on the ground. Before her partner can react, I've got my hands latched around his head and my thumbs pressed hard into his eyes.

Squealing, he staggers back, blood gushing down his face and all the way down his neck and through his tufts of mangy chest hair.

Around me, my classmates have also regrouped and are having equal success dispatching their own attackers.

I'm not connected to Haida Gwaii or anything, but it feels like I'm moving at lightning speed.

"They don't stand a chance against us!" Ignacio boasts as he side-kicks a tall Unsettled in the midsection and hip-flips him to the ground. "It's like they're moving in slow motion!"

Swinging around in front of me, her voice thin behind her mischievous, knowing grin, Roxane says, "They are."

Their chests heaving, the two sets of twins are standing over a pile of the Unsettled. Libra and Mattea are high-fiving over a small pile of their own opponents.

Rising to his feet, Ignacio claps his hands together and then slings his arms around me and Libra, pulling us in tight. "We kicked their virtual ass!"

Libra and I push his arms from around our shoulders. I'm annoyed, but I can't help smiling. Ignacio might not be my favorite person in the world, but I do appreciate someone who appreciates a good fight.

"Did you do this?" I ask Roxane.

She stares at me through those ghostly, pale blue eyes but doesn't answer.

In fact, she looks like she's just seen a ghost of her own—a ghost that just stomped on a kitten.

"What's wrong?" I laugh, my hand on her shoulder. "Ignacio's right. We just beat the hell out of this sim. If you had something to do with it somehow..."

Roxane grips my wrist with both hands. "Trapped."

"Trapped? What do you mean?"

Libra calls our attention to the bodies of the Unsettled, which are now nearly pixilated away—along with the desert, the sand, and the sky, leaving us standing in a vacuum of white space. "Um. If we beat the sim, how come we're still in it?"

"I'm sure it's just a computer glitch," Trax says, scanning what has now dissolved into...nothing.

We mill around for a while, waiting for something to happen. Nothing does.

So we wait a little longer.

Still, nothing.

We try to walk, but it doesn't make any sense. There's nowhere to walk *to*. And, since we're basically neurochomatic representations of ourselves created by a quantum computer program and without any external point of reference, there's nowhere to walk *from*.

After a while—there's no way to tell how long—our moods

drop from idle curiosity to mild worry, and then, to the brink of pure terror.

Sara gives an unamused laugh. "I'm waiting for one of you to tell us we're trapped inside a VR-sim."

Trax wrings his hands and bites his lower lip. "Um...I think we're trapped in a VR-sim."

DOUBLED-OVER, her breath coming out in hacking spasms, Chace goes into a full-blown panic attack.

Trax leans over her and tries to assure her that everything's going to be okay.

Through her gasps, Chace stammers something about how she knew this was going to happen. "Who'll...tell...our...stories... now?" she manages to choke out in between raspy coughs.

Roxane steps over and practically shoves Trax aside. Before he can react one way or another, Roxane is running her fingers through Chace's dark hair and petting her like she was a feeble kitten.

"You."

Chace manages to look up at Roxane. "Me?"

"You. Chronicle. We. Live."

I don't know how or why, but that seems to do the trick, and Chace stands up, takes a breath, and apologizes for freaking out.

With the rest of us gathered around her, Roxane turns in a slow circle, her eyes meeting ours as she does.

"Home."

And then my head explodes.

Not literally, fortunately. But it sure feels like it.

Before I black out, I catch a glimpse of the rest of our two Cohorts, also doubled over in agony, their hands pressed tight to the sides of their heads as we all scream in pain.

And then, just like that, it's gone. The excruciating lightning strike melts into a comforting hum inside my head.

When I open my eyes, I'm back in the VR-sim room, standing in the circle under the octopus console with everyone else.

Mattea pats her hips and breathes a puffed-cheek sigh of relief.

Dressed in our normal Academy gear, we slip the black octopus tentacles off of our heads and let them slump to the floor.

Her face in a knot, Sara strides over to Roxane. "What the hell did you do to us?"

"Hey!" I call out. "She just saved us. Twice."

Arlo looks confused as he pulls his hood up.

"She's the one who slowed down the Unsettled," I explain. "And the one who got us out of there."

"Speaking of which," Mattea says, looking around the room, "why were we stuck in there like that?"

And then it occurs to me: We're alone in the room. "Wisp? Granden?"

"Maybe they went into the Control Room? Or down to the Sub-Basement to check on the Mag-Generators," Lucid suggests.

Sounding nervous, Arlo asks, "Why would both of them go? And why would they leave us here?"

Trax shrugs. "I'm sure they've got things under control."

"I'd feel a lot better hearing that from them, directly," I tell him. "Come on."

The others follow me out into the hallway. The weirdly *quiet* hallway. Where are Wisp and Granden? And if there's a major problem, shouldn't there be alarms going off or something?

"At least the door works," Sara snickers.

"It's about time something worked around—"

I'm cut off by a gasp from Libra. She's pointing down the hall to where a lone figure is lying deadly still on the floor.

We bolt over and slide to a stop over the body of Granden.

"What the hell happened to him?" Sara cries, sliding to her knees next to him. It's more emotion than I'm used to hearing from her, and the quiver in her voice gives me the chills.

"Is he...?" I start to ask.

"He's alive," Sara sighs. "But barely."

"We need to get him downstairs to the Infirmary."

"And we need to find Wisp."

"Don't bother," Chace says, her voice shaking hard and trailing off as she points down the stairwell to the small figure lying half on the landing. "That's her."

31

INTRUDER

A noise from the far end of the hall catches our attention.

The blur of brown and black causes us to go into a simultaneous, eleven-person jump.

"Did you see that?" Libra stammers.

"Yes!" Ignacio tells her. "But who—?"

"I don't know," I say. "We're all accounted for."

Chace takes two huge steps back. "Someone got into the Academy."

I shake my head. "Not possible."

Mattea tugs on my sleeve but doesn't make eye contact when she mutters, "I think Granden and our unconscious dean lying over there on the floor would suggest otherwise."

With everyone from both Cohorts looking to me for guidance, I step over to Trax. "You go check out whatever that was! We'll take Wisp and Granden to the Infirmary. Meet us there!"

Led by Trax, the members of Cohort B go bolting down the hall in one direction while my Cohort and I lug Wisp and Granden down the two flights of stairs to the Infirmary.

Although I always think of Ignacio as the strongest of our

group, Arlo surprises me—and probably all of us—by scooping Granden up as easily as Libra and I gather up Wisp.

We've done a lot of physical training, but carrying a pair of grown people down two flights of stairs is harder than I thought it would be.

Holding them by their legs and under their shoulders, we get Wisp and Granden into the Infirmary and up onto two of the white examination mag-tables hovering in the center of the brightly lit room.

"What now?" Libra asks, her eyes ping-ponging between me and the door.

"Does anyone know how to work the diagnostic equipment?"

Arlo raises his hand halfway.

"You do?"

"Oh, right," Mattea exclaims. "Mayla's his mentor."

Arlo nods. "I've been working with her in here for the past couple of weeks. It's part of my apprenticeship."

"And you know how to work this stuff?" I ask.

"Kind of."

"Well, it's not ideal, but 'kind of' has to be good enough. For now, at least."

We step back as Arlo, looking a little flustered, rummages around in a supply cabinet next to the floating mag-tables.

Returning with a shallow tray of medical equipment, he attaches thin silver leads to Wisp's and Granden's wrists and presses diamond-shaped contact pads to their temples, to the backs of their hands, and along the base of their necks.

Squinting into the yellow holo-display in the air at the foot of the two tables, Arlo shakes his head. "I don't get it."

"Don't get what?" I ask.

"They're registering as fully conscious and alert. I don't think there's anything wrong with them."

"Based on the fact that they're not conscious," Sara sneers, "I'd say there's plenty wrong with them."

Mattea shoulders her way in front of me to stand in front of Arlo. "Are you sure you're reading that thing right?"

"I think so."

"This isn't complicated," I snap. "Were they beaten up? Knocked out? Drugged? What the hell happened to them?"

Arlo looks almost teary-eyed under his hood when he takes a step back and insists he doesn't know. "It's like...it's like..."

"Like what?" I bark, clutching the material on the shoulder of his gray hoodie in my clenched fists.

"Like they've been hypnotized."

I'm just processing that—and all of its implications and impossibilities—when the Infirmary door slides open with a grainy groan.

Red faced and out of breath, Trax and his Cohort come barreling into the room. "Whoever it was got away," he pants.

Whipping around, I ask if he actually saw anyone.

"It was definitely a person," Reverie insists.

"Clothes, hair color...anything?"

"Tall. Skinny. Maybe? Kind of messed up clothes. We couldn't really tell."

"Where?" I ask.

"We heard something up on the fourth floor."

"The Bio-Tech research labs?"

"We went in there. We tried the Techno-Genetics labs..."

"And?"

"Someone's been in there. Looking for something. We think maybe they tried to access the quantum computers."

"But by the time we got there, whoever it was was gone," Reverie says, her eyes red and brimming wet. "We saw something...someone running down that long hallway toward the

East Tower. We tried to follow them, but they disappeared. We were just going to try the Sub-Basement, but Trax thought we should stop here first and check on you guys and Wisp and Granden."

I fix my eyes on Reverie's and ask her as evenly as possible, "Who? Who did you see?"

From next to his sister, Lucid shakes his head, his eyes darting back and forth. "It was a man, I think."

"You think?"

"He had a beard."

"You're sure?"

"I'm not going to bet my life on it, but yes, I think so."

"Great. So we have a skinny bearded intruder in the Academy and the only two properly trained people are unconscious and plugged into machines."

"There's something else," Reverie adds.

"What?"

"He was carrying something. A case of some kind...under his arm."

I'm not sure why that makes my heart jump and causes a lump to form in my throat, but right now, we have more pressing matters to attend to. Namely, our dean and vice-dean lying side by side and mysteriously unconscious on the lab tables in front of us.

Libra squints into the holo-display hovering in front of one of the primary diagnostic input panels. "At least their vital signs seem okay."

Chace jabs her finger at the glowing diagram. "What about here? What's this?"

"That's brainwave activity," Arlo tells her.

Standing next to Chase, I tap the glowing graph, myself. "How come it's moving around like that?"

"I don't know. But I think it means signals are having trouble getting from their brains to their bodies."

"That doesn't sound good."

"It's not."

Libra puts up a hand. "If there's really someone in the Academy, then they did this. Which means they'll know how to fix it."

Pushing up my sleeves, I stride to the door. "You're right. We need to know what's going on."

"So we're just going to leave them here?" Libra calls out to me.

"What choice do we have? Whoever did this to them is in here with us. Which means we could wind up like them."

"Unless we find the intruder first," Ignacio growls.

"My thoughts exactly."

Libra dashes over and grabs my wrist. "Branwynne. Aren't you forgetting something?"

"Like what?"

"Like if there is someone in here, it means they knew the Academy was here, they knew how to get in, they knew how to take out Wisp and Granden...and they know we're alone."

"I didn't forget. And I didn't forget that there's eleven of us and only one of them."

"That we know of."

"We could always lock ourselves in here," Chace suggests, her eyes scanning the room and the open doorway. "Try to contact Kress on the outside."

"That's a great idea," I sneer. "You stay here. Along with anyone else who thinks cornering ourselves and getting picked off is a good plan. Me? I'm going out there, and I'm going to find whoever it is."

"Then what?" Libra asks.

"Then I'm going to make them pay."

Without waiting for anyone else to try to stop me, I dart out into the dark corridor. I stride along, poking my head into each of the glass-walled classrooms as I go. By the time I get to the far staircase, the others have caught up with me.

With all eleven of us gathered at the top of the stairs, Trax puts a gentle hand on the crook of my arm. "Are you planning to search the entire Academy by yourself?"

When I don't answer right away, Chace adds, "It's huge. There are too many places for someone to hide."

"Fine. Then we'll split up. Cohort A can come with me. Cohort B, you stay with Wisp and Granden this time. Just in case. You said the intruder was heading toward the East Tower?"

Reverie nods.

"Then he's either going up to the gardens or down the back way toward the Sub-Basement exits. I'm guessing he's not here to investigate the hydroponics lab. We'll head downstairs. Start there."

"I wish we had more eyes between us," Ignacio says.

"What?" I ask.

"More eyes. That would make our search go so much faster."

"Maybe we *can* have more eyes," I tell him with a cheeky grin. "I know a white raven who's really good at spy work." I concentrate and reach out with my mind to connect with Haida Gwaii.

Nothing happens.

I reach out again. If Haida can lend me some of those same skills she lent me in my blindfolded fight with Granden, there's no way any intruder to the Academy will stand a chance of staying hidden or escaping.

Haida?

Nothing.

I try again.

Haida?

This time, we connect, but only for a split-second. Unfortunately, a split-second is all the time I need to sense, hear, and feel her response. It's an easy emotion to interpret, and it's only one word. The problem is that it's the one word I never wanted to hear:

~ *Help!*

32

TUNNEL

"HAIDA'S IN TROUBLE!" I cry.

"Your bird?" Trax asks. But then he blushes and seems to realize how dumb that sounds and quickly apologizes. "I mean, yes, of course. Your bird. Haida. How is she in trouble?"

"She's in trouble because she's not here!" My throat goes so tight I can barely squeak the words out.

"Not here?" Libra repeats.

"In the Academy."

Chace says, "Whoever is in here—"

"Isn't anymore! And they took Haida with them!" I finish, my eyes heavy with the deluge of tears I'm trying desperately to hold back.

I'm half-expecting to get laughed at. Or maybe have my fellow students roll their eyes, question my instincts, or tell me I'm over-reacting.

None of that happens, though.

Instead, Arlo pushes his hood back from his head, exposing the maze of rubbery scars and deep blue bruises on his face and neck. "We need our weapons."

"Right!" Libra agrees. "And then let's go rescue Haida and find whoever took her."

Ignacio slaps a fist into his palm. "And make them pay!"

Together, we bolt upstairs to the Weapons Lab.

Fully armed now and feeling confident but also angry, confused, and scared, I lead my small squad of classmates back down to the Infirmary.

"We'll split up here," I tell Trax. "My Cohort will track down the intruder and find Haida. You and your Cohort stay here and take care of Wisp and Granden. And make sure no one else is in the Academy."

"What about Arlo?" Sara asks. "He's the only one who knows how to work the med-lab. Shouldn't he stay and watch over Wisp and Granden?"

"It's okay," Reverie assures us. "Lucid and I can take care of them."

I ask them if they're sure, and they tell me they are.

Trax says, "Okay" and calls his Cohort together to strategize their next moves.

Wait. Did I just bark out a slew of orders? And did everyone just listen to me like I know what I'm talking about?

There are lots of good leaders in the world. I'm not one of them. I was meant to be a rogue fighter, not the one in charge.

And yet...here I am.

"Come on!" I shout to my Cohort as I sprint out of the Infirmary toward the stairs leading down into the Sub-Basement.

Slipping out of the Academy is relatively easy.

It helps that I was one of the first ones in here. Five years ago, I helped set this place up. So I know its ins and outs better than pretty much anyone.

We head down one of the sets of back stairs—the ones branching off to the lift access and maintenance ports.

Most of the stairways in the Academy's main buildings and

its two turrets are made up of bright chrome and glass with wide, curving steps and light oak handrails. Very clean. Very pretty.

The stairway we're on now is ugly, cold concrete with crumbling sides. It's narrow enough to scrape our shoulders as we edge our way down into the darkness.

At the bottom, we run into a door with a blank input panel in the wall next to it.

Our reflections are distorted on its wavy face of glistening black glass.

"What now?" Libra asks.

"It's got a handle," Ignacio points out.

"So?"

"So...most of the doors in the Academy operate on sliding mag-tracks."

"I don't—"

Libra slides her sledgehammer from its holster and strap like she's a Medieval knight drawing out a broadsword.

Without consulting us or taking an extra second to assess the situation, she swings the steel head of the powerful weapon onto the top of the pewter-gray lock.

The impact of metal on metal fills the tight space with a deafening ring. Arlo clamps his hands to his ears until the echo fades.

Sheathing her intimidating, long-handled hammer, Libra leads us through the narrow doorway. We follow her past a bank of generators and over to a line of input panels.

"Look," Mattea points out. "The indicator light's off."

"Could be another glitch," Sara tells her.

"Yeah. Or it could be that someone disabled it, came in, and then left again."

"Why come in just to knock out Wisp and Granden, steal a bird, and then leave?" Ignacio asks.

"You can ask them when we find them," Libra says.

"I don't think the intruder was here looking for Wisp and Granden," I tell my Cohort. "I think maybe they just got in the way."

"You could be right," Mattea says. "The VR-sim room is secure. They wouldn't have known we were in there."

"So you think someone broke in looking for us?"

"Yes," I confirm. "Someone who knew Kress and the others wouldn't be here."

"And since they couldn't find us...," Ignacio begins.

"They got the drop on Wisp and Granden and took Haida?" Sara asks. "That doesn't make sense."

Arlo peers down the tunnel into the darkness, but he doesn't step forward. "I think maybe Wisp and Granden knew there was danger."

"And you think they put us in the VR-sim room...," I ask.

"To protect us. Possibly. I heard War and Mayla talking to Wisp about it."

"When?"

"I don't know. A few days ago. Maybe a week."

"And you didn't tell us?"

"What's to tell? They didn't sound so sure about anything, themselves."

"Did you say anything to them?"

"I tried. Mayla's my mentor. I asked what was going on."

"And?"

"And...they said it was nothing."

"Maybe it *is* nothing."

"Maybe."

"You don't sound sure."

"Wisp doesn't worry. Not like that. If you saw her, you wouldn't be sure, either."

"Whatever it was...*is*...they sure as hell couldn't handle it."

Libra latches her hand onto my upper arm. "Branwynne..."

"What?"

"We can't leave the Academy."

"Why not? Has this tunnel magically shut down or something?"

"You know what I mean. Wisp'll kill you."

I point at the ceiling. "She's not exactly in killing shape at the moment."

"What about the security protocols? The Perimeter Pylons?"

"They're for keeping people from getting in, not to stop us from getting out."

Libra takes a step back from the mouth of the narrow tunnel. "I think this is a really bad idea."

"I agree," I tell her. "That's why you should stay here."

"I'm *not* going with you."

"Good. Stay upstairs with Cohort B. Help them take care of Wisp and Granden. Go look around the Academy for the intruder who I guarantee isn't there anymore. You'll just slow us down, anyway."

"Fine. I'll go with you," Libra sighs.

And with that settled, the six of us plunge into the darkness.

We all know about the tunnels, but none of us has ever been in them before.

Thanks to one of the Auditor's many informal history lessons when I first got here, I know how in the 19th century, this part of the mountain was center to a whole hub of mining operations. Mostly silver. Most of the primary mines and tunnels are long gone—either destroyed on purpose or else the victims of the countless cave-ins.

Not long after we first arrived at the Academy, Terk led a crew on a major discovery and excavation mission down here. I wasn't part of it, but I got to hear all about it.

Kress told me about the network of tunnels, the sealed up

mines, and the assorted access ports scattered all around this part of the mountain.

Now, it's not just theory. The black maw of the tunnel—in all of its dark, creepy glory—is right here in front of me.

"Do you think this is how they got in?" Libra asks me.

"It's hard to tell. They didn't set off any of the motion sensors."

"Then how—"

"Speculating won't do us any good," I remind her, directing everyone's attention to the gravel and ice-crusted ground. "I don't know how they got *in*. But look. These are boot prints. And they're facing *down* the tunnel, away from the Academy. Someone got in. I don't know how. But that someone definitely got out this way. Forget about *how*. We need to find out *who* and *why*."

Ignacio points into the tunnel. "And you want us to go in there, chase them down, and ask?"

"I don't think they'll be sending out a holo-blog to explain their methods and intentions, so yeah...that's exactly what I want us to do."

Sara peers into the darkness. "Isn't there an old saying or a fable or something about chasing a dangerous animal into its den?"

"What's your point?" I ask, my voice laced with acid.

She points down into the deep, steep, unlit tunnel. "I think this might just be a terrible idea."

"What about flashlights?" Mattea asks.

Libra beams her big stupid smile and shouts that she knows where they are.

She scampers back the way we came about a hundred feet to a wall cabinet and comes running back with three club-sized flashlights cradled in her arms like firewood.

She passes them to me, Mattea, and Ignacio, and we all click them on at the same time.

Nothing happens.

"Great," Mattea sighs. "Glad to see it's not just the main power supply that's gone glitchy."

"There are light ports in the ceiling," Mattea points out before offering up a pathetic sigh. "Too bad they're not on."

I swing around to face Ignacio. "You've got some sort of bond with electrical energy, right? Can you...you know...light the way?"

"It doesn't work like that. The electro-magnetic pulse I produce just kind of overrides other sources of electrical power. Small ones. Brohn's been coaching me, but I'm not able to generate any light of my own, if that's what you're asking."

"Great. So we've got what could be miles of dark tunnels to walk through?"

"I'll go first," Mattea says, slipping her hands into the handles of her ebony-steel Bear Claws.

Using his long-handled scythe as a walking stick, Arlo strides along after her with me and Libra following him and Sara and Ignacio bringing up the rear.

Hiking our way downhill through the dark like this is a strange, dream-like experience. The walls are rough, but at least the path beneath our feet is mostly paved.

Going as fast as we can without falling or running into any of the walls, we keep our hands on the tunnel's rough, rocky sides or else on the shoulders of the person in front of us.

Without stopping to rest, we hike along like this until, at last, we arrive at a very welcome sliver of light up ahead.

Relieved, we jog up to find one of the access ports.

"It's open," I tell the others, nudging it with my elbow.

"Um...why is it open?" Arlo asks.

"I'll give you three guesses. And the first two don't count."

Libra approaches the portal but doesn't stick her head out. "Branwynne, are you sure about this?"

"I'm sure someone got in here and did something to Wisp and Granden. I'm sure this is where they got out. I'm sure they've got Haida Gwaii." My voice rises as I start through the portal. "And I'm sure I'm not going to give up until I'm holding their still-beating heart in the palm of my hand."

Behind me, I hear Ignacio tell the others, "I think she's sure."

And then the five of them follow me out of the dark tunnel and into the light of the steep and open mountainside.

33

BRAWL

WITH ALL OF us out on the mountain now, we step forward into a steeply slanted swamp of snow and mud.

Ignacio looks back up the sharply angled precipice above us. "How far down the mountain are we?"

"Far enough for it to be easier to go down than back up," Arlo says, taking the lead this time.

We hike for another two hours, hoping not to slip and fall as we hop from rocks to tree roots and into dry ravines as we descend.

When we get to an area where the ground levels out, the mud, the jagged rocks, and the exposed root systems of a million toppled trees give way to a crusted-dry plateau. Another hour of hiking after that, and we step through a small area of woods to arrive at the edge of what seems to be an endless expanse of desert.

Mattea drags her hand across her forehead. "Why's it so hot?"

Up in the Academy, we've gotten used to climate-controlled conditions inside and to the raging storms of snow and ice outside.

Down here, it's like we've dropped into the depths of Hell.

And it just keeps getting hotter as we go.

We're walking across a wide, cracked desert of flat, dried tree stumps and crests of red sand when Ignacio stops fast enough to leave trenches in the thick layer of pebbles and dust with the heels of his boots. He latches his hand onto my arm. "What *is* that?"

"What's what?" Sara asks from the back of our procession.

"Those vibrations."

Everyone stops and listens for a full three seconds before Mattea asks, "What is it, Branwynne?"

I don't answer right away even though I know exactly what it is.

For the others, this is all new. Well, the *reality* of it is.

For me, there's no mistaking the rumble in the ground or the massive cloud of dust and sand rolling toward us from up ahead.

I've seen them before. I've fought them before. There were fourteen of us before—fifteen if I count the Auditor—and we barely escaped with our lives.

I turn to Libra and feel my voice catch in my throat.

"It's the Army of the Unsettled. The *real* one!"

"What do we do?"

"Run!"

No one needs convincing. Without another word, we bolt like hell across the expansive patch of land, back toward what we hope will be the safety of the woods.

The Unsettled have little training and crappy aim. But they make up for it with wild-eyed relentlessness and sheer numbers.

Kress once called them a moving city. It's true. Their entire population drives around endlessly in a miles-long caravan of old RVs, buses, campers, and fleets of construction vehicles.

Most threats out here consist of small pockets of desperate

people struggling to survive. I've seen it all first-hand, and it was terrifying.

Being chased down by the Unsettled...that's another brand of terror entirely.

Their moving city is molasses slow. But it doesn't matter how fast we run. Their fleet of chase-down vehicles—at least a dozen modified, two-person Skid Steers—are way faster.

We can't get back to the woods and the foothills fast enough, so we make a break for a cluster of dunes and boulders in the distance. Maybe we can lose them in there.

But it's too far, and the Unsettled are too fast.

In seconds, the Skid Steers grind to a stop and surround us, kicking up pebbles and sand, and cutting off any hope we might've had of escape. We shield our faces and cough as the dust cloud sweeps over us.

The advanced recon hunters—all teenagers—hop down from their vehicles, and we tighten our defensive circle in preparation for their attack.

There are at least twenty of them, all dressed in an array of patchy rags, similar to what we saw in the VR-sim. They're armed with a variety of knives, machetes, spiked gloves, and long-handled, bladed and spiked gardening tools wrapped in razor-wire.

"We can take them," Ignacio declares through gritted teeth.

"I think you're right. But they're not the problem."

"Then what is?"

"Them." I point to the approaching, rolling cloud of dust and sand on the horizon. "These kids here are just trying to slow us down until the rest of their army arrives."

"Then we better win," Mattea snaps. "*Fast.*"

We've been training for a few months now. These Unsettled have been fighting for their entire lives. But we have our weapons. We also have ample fear and plenty of desperation.

I slip my Serpent Blades from their holsters and hold them at the ready.

Next to me, Libra draws her sledgehammer, Sara slips four throwing darts from her bandolier, Arlo grips his scythe in both hands, and Ignacio pulls out his shillelaghs and begins to twirl them in a slow, even spin.

As I'm scanning our opponents, Mattea thrusts her hands deep into her pockets and walks toward a group of three of them with her head down but her eyes up.

Arlo reaches out to grab her arm, but she's already ahead of him.

I'm sure she's about to get hacked to pieces.

Dragging her feet in the dirt and sand, she absently and casually kicks away pebbles and small stones as she approaches what seem to be the three Unsettled in charge.

Flanked by two muscular boys with bladed weapons, a tall girl with a bare midriff and clumped, blond-streaked dreadlocks steps forward.

Unarmed, she raises her hand, her palm facing us. Her words come out as if she's puking up a bowl of alphabet soup.

"Her dead her go don't leave!"

Mattea puts her own hand out, palm up, and flicks her index finger, summoning the girl to come closer. The girl obliges, and Mattea leans toward her across the ten feet or so of space still separating them. Mattea's voice goes soft and slightly guttural "Her have no stopping, no stopping her dead."

Like me and the rest of my Cohort, the girl and the two boys stare. Behind the girl, the boys lower their weapons a few inches.

Mattea points her pinky finger to each of them one at a time. "Even on her dead, her not stopping. Her's families roams and goes and gets them's revenge."

The dreadlocked girl starts to step even farther forward, her head on a curious tilt, almost like she recognizes Mattea.

"See," Libra says to me out of the corner of her mouth. "Mattea can get us out of all kinds of trouble."

I'm just about to let go of the breath I've been holding when the tall girl stops mid-step and shakes her head hard enough for a puff of dirt to launch from her thick mass of dreadlocks into the hot, open air. She reaches back and snatches the long-handled weapon from one of the boys and swings it in a huge, looping arc right at Mattea.

Mattea ducks but the thin iron nail tied to the end of the stick catches her off guard and lodges in her shoulder. She shrieks in pain as I leap forward.

In a frenzy and under a small storm of sand, Mattea yanks the weapon out and rolls away as fast as she can, clutching her bleeding shoulder and calling out to us for help.

His twin shillelaghs clenched tight in his fists, Ignacio's eyes close in a furious squint.

Crisscrossing arcs of blue and white light flash in the air. Behind the Unsettled, the engines of two of their Skid Steers burst into a bright blue flame.

Clutching their heads in their hands, three of them shriek and bolt out into the open desert where they quickly drop to the ground.

Panicked now, some of the others from the chase-down squad dash over to what's left of the Skid Steers while still others choose to stay and fight.

Ignacio leans heavily against my side and starts sliding to his knees. Like a drowning man, he looks up at me for help before offering up a pointless apology. "That's all I've got," he pants.

I haul him to his feet. "Ugh. You weigh a ton."

"It's all muscle," he groans through a strained grin.

With the city-sized Army of the Unsettled lumbering toward us from under a fiery red setting sun, my Cohort and I draw together in a tight, six-person cluster.

Without a ton of time working together, we don't have the automatic sense of strategy I've seen first-hand from Kress and her Conspiracy.

We do our best.

It's not good enough.

The remaining members of the chase-down squad regroup, and I remember what undisciplined, savage fighters they are.

They swarm us with rabid abandon, screaming and swinging their array of clubs and bladed weapons in a stunning onslaught.

I take down two girls and disarm another one before I get dragged down by my wrist.

Three of the unarmed boys rush at me, separating me from my Serpent Blades in the process. I'm fast and pretty strong, but I've got a few hundred pounds of swinging elbows and flying fists on top of me.

Ignacio shouts for me to hang on as he cracks one of the boys in the head with his shillelagh and tries to pry the rest of the pile of bodies off of me.

A few feet away, Libra is backing up as three boys advance on her, driving her right into the arms of a tall girl who loops her arm around Libra's neck in a constricting chokehold.

Ignacio manages to lift me to my feet, and we join Sara who's standing, bloody-knuckled, over a boy whose face she just bashed in.

Arlo picks up his scythe and swings it wildly, but the two attackers—one of them even bigger than Ignacio—just laugh and skip around him, spitting at him and taunting him with half-lunges.

The remaining Unsettled don't seem satisfied to wait for reinforcements anymore, and they level their weapons at us and attack as one.

The blade of a knife wrapped with twine to the end of a long wooden handle whistles through the air.

I duck as the weapon zips over my head, but I don't have time to celebrate my evasive move as the razor-sharp edge catches Arlo in the face, slicing a huge gash from the corner of his eye all the way down to his neck.

Shaking it off like it's nothing, he raises his scythe, but he doesn't attack anyone with it. Instead, he plants it in the rocky sand, both hands gripped tight to the handle with him leaning on it like it's all that's stopping him from falling to the ground.

He clamps his eyes shut, and a powerful wave rips through the air around us. The blades and clubs of the Unsettled slow to a mid-swing crawl and then lodge to a dead stop in the air like twigs in wet cement.

For a second, we're all frozen as well, trying to figure out what the hell is going on.

It's Libra who snaps me and our Cohort to life, shouting at us to run as what's left of the Unsettled slump to the ground.

She clamps onto the sleeve of my jacket and drags me toward the tree-line just a hundred yards away, with Mattea, Arlo, and Ignacio close on our heels.

We plunge from the edge of the desert into a thick forest of very dead trees.

On the other side, Ignacio claps a hard hand onto Arlo's shoulder. "That was quite the trick you pulled back there, Mr. Reaper."

Arlo gives Ignacio a dark, squinty glare. For a second, I think he might take a swing at him with that long-handled scythe of his. But he just steps away and grips the top part of the handle with both hands, steadying himself as the rest of us try to catch our breath.

"Uh oh."

"What is it?"

"Where the hell is Sara?"

The tangled branches of a cluster of dead trees crack and bend, and the rest of us jump back, startled.

We all relax our shoulders and breathe a sigh of relief as Sara steps through the bramble and into the small clearing.

She's not alone, though. She's dragging the tall, dreadlocked girl from the Unsettled behind her by the ankle.

Blood gushing from a cavernously deep gash under her eye, the girl stares up at us, teary-eyed and stunned.

Sara grabs her by the shoulders and hauls her to her feet, but the girl's legs give out and she crumples back down to the ground.

Sara flicks her thumb back the way we came. "In case you're wondering, we're not being followed. The ones who aren't dead decided to hightail it toward their big, moving city." Sara kicks the dreadlocked girl in the ribs. "I thought maybe we could get some answers out of this one."

The girl groans as we all turn to stand over her.

"We're looking for a man. Thin. Tall." Ignacio runs his finger and thumb along his cheek. "A man with a beard. And a bird."

The girl's eyes go wide, and it doesn't take a mind-reader to know she knows exactly what Ignacio's talking about.

"Her knowing only," the girl stammers. "Her go, her tell."

"She'll tell us if we agree to let her go," Mattea translates.

Ignacio nods to the girl, who looks relieved but also a little suspicious. Like she's trying to figure out who we are and why we haven't killed her already.

Good question. I wouldn't have thought to look to anyone from the Unsettled for information. I hate to say it, but Sara may have just saved the day.

The girl goes on to spew out a bunch of what sounds like total nonsense. But Mattea nods and talks back to her like every word is clear as day.

At last, Mattea stops her interrogation and turns back to our Cohort.

"She says the man we're looking for is in a town not too far from here. A town called Sanctum." Mattea points to a spot off in the distance where five sharp peaks rise up to form their own crown-shaped mini-mountain range. "She says it's in a valley just before those peaks."

"Sanctum," I repeat.

"You know it?"

"I've seen it. From the outside. I've never been in the actual town." I glare down at the dreadlocked girl. "If what she says is true, I guess that's about to change."

34

CAUGHT

"SHOULD WE LET HER GO?"

"What's the alternative?"

"Well," Sara grins, drawing out one of her small darts and pressing it far too hard under the girl's already-wrecked eye, "we could kill her."

I actually contemplate this for a second. I've killed before. But always to escape, in self-defense, or in defense of others.

"We wouldn't be killing her," I say.

Sara grins at me over her shoulder. "Then what would you call it?"

"Murder."

"Branwynne's right," Libra says, stepping forward, her voice rich with an air of seriousness, authority, and finality I don't think I've ever heard from her before. "There's got to be a line we don't cross."

"What the difference between killing and murder?" Sara asks with a shrug. This time, she presses her small dart deep enough into the girl's cheek to draw a small, meandering stream of blood.

"Good guys kill," I tell her. "Bad guys murder."

Pretending to be disappointed, Ignacio smacks his thigh. "Frack. I kind of always wanted to be a bad guy." I ignore him because I know he's joking. He's a wanker, but he's hardly a killer and *definitely* not a murderer.

"Listen," Mattea urges, her eyes glued to our bleeding and helpless prisoner. "We got what we needed. We need to get out of here before the rest of her army tracks us down."

"Absolutely," Ignacio agrees. "She was nice enough to point us in the right direction. I say we accept her generosity in the spirit it was given and hightail it out of here."

In the middle of our group-nod, I catch Mattea giving Ignacio what I think is a pretty affectionate look of appreciation for backing her up, and I wonder if there's anything going on between them.

With our destination settled, we're just turning to make our way in the direction the girl pointed when Sara stops and zips a trio of throwing darts at the wide-eyed girl on the ground.

Two of the darts find their mark in the stunned girl's shoulder while the other lodges itself deep under her collar bone.

Shrieking, the girl crabwalks back, her eyes even wider than before and riveted on the silver barbs jutting out of her body.

As the girls scrambles to her feet and plunges through the thicket, I grab Sara's arm and whip her around.

"What the frack did you do that for?"

"Just a going away present." Sara yanks her arm from my hand and pushes me hard enough to knock me into Libra. "Just hope I'm not in such a giving mood with you."

Libra and Ignacio wedge between us with Ignacio shouting at me and Sara to knock it off and stop bickering. "We've got to get moving!"

He's right—both about the need to get moving and the need to stop fighting with each other. After all, we have more than our fair share of enemies out there we know we'll have to face.

Together—physically anyway—we race across some overgrown and uneven terrain. We hike for a long time, leaping over chasms in the earth, scrambling up hills, following overgrown hunter's trails, and shouldering our way through thick fields of spiky thorns.

The entire time, we do our best to keep our eye on the five tall peaks the girl from the Unsettled pointed out to us.

"I wish we had Trax with us," I tell the others in a breathy huff.

"I bet you do," Libra teases as she jogs along next to me.

I give her a good whack to the arm. "He's a tracker, you brassy scrubber!"

Libra laughs as Arlo, who's taken the lead, comes to a stop and barks out for us to do the same.

The six of us duck down at the top of a small hill and behind a thick barrier of leafless bushes and dead, fallen trees.

Arlo tilts his scythe toward the valley laid out in front of us and to the cluster of buildings making up the small town nestled in the long shadows of the five rocky towers.

We're close enough to the town to see most of the details: the wooden-plank sidewalks, the weather-beaten buildings, the dirt roads, the rows of two-story structures with white laundry hung over brass railings running the length of the shallow balconies.

"Yes," I tell the others. "Sanctum. This is the place I remember."

Arlo asks, "From where?"

"Five years ago. After we left you guys back in D.C., this was one of our last stops before the Academy. We drove near here in the Terminus." I point to a ridge far off in the distance. "There's a little compound way off in that direction. Over there...on the other side of the five peaks. That's where we stayed with the Cult of the Devoted."

"The ones Kress and the others warned us about?"

"It's not that bad."

"Then why—"

"We were told not to stay any longer. We were told something bad was going to happen to us."

"Told? By who?"

"A boy. His name was Matholook. He helped us sneak out in the middle of the night."

"So, for all you know, there was no real threat, and he just wanted to get rid of you."

"No. I know he was telling the truth."

"How?"

"We talked. Separately. A lot." The others stare at me, so I feel forced to explain. "Look. We were there for a week. I got bored. He showed me around. We got to know each other."

"I bet," Ignacio sneers.

"It wasn't like that, you grubby git. I was *twelve*. We just talked. He told me things about the Devoted."

"Things?"

"How they refused to join the True Blues. How they got kicked out of Sanctum."

"Kicked out. For what?"

"That I don't know. But he snuck me down there a couple of times. We would spy on the people from a ridge over the town." I point to a high rock formation across from us on the other side of the valley. "Just over there. We weren't supposed to. But he wanted to show me."

"Show you what?"

"That there was more going on in Sanctum than just a

bunch of hicks trying to wait out the apocalypse." They stare at me some more. "There are labs down there. Tunnels. Secrets. I think..."

Libra's eyes go wide. "What?"

"I think maybe they're trying to do what Krug couldn't."

"What's that? Recruit Emergents?"

"Not exactly."

"What then?"

"I think...well, Matholook thought they might be trying to make their *own* Emergents."

"What—like in a lab?"

"I guess. We never actually went into the town."

"So you don't know."

"No. But it adds up, doesn't it? A closed-off, secluded town. They set themselves up down here in a valley not too far from the very same mountain where Granden and his team built the Academy. They kick out anyone they don't like or who refuses to help them, including the people who became the Cult of the Devoted. And now, a mystery person breaks into the Academy and steals Haida Gwaii—one of two ravens that can communicate with an Emergent—at the exact same time when Kress and her Conspiracy just happen to be gone?"

"It's a little thin," Mattea says after a moment's contemplation.

Libra says she disagrees. "It's got enough meat on its bones for me." She turns to me. "So, Branwynne...what do we do now?"

I wish I had an answer, but I don't, so I suggest the most obvious course of action. "We need to sneak into the town, find the infiltrator, rescue Haida, and then get back to the Academy without being spotted and wait for Kress and the others to get back from their mission."

"Oh, is *that* all?"

"What choice do we have? If we go back to the Academy now, we'll have no answers, no Haida, and a whole lot of really pissed off teachers when Kress gets back."

"And we still won't know what they did to Wisp and Granden," Arlo reminds us.

I nod and give him a mental "Thanks" for understanding.

Libra raises her hand like we're in class. "One problem."

"What is it?"

She points to the fleet of small, scissor-shaped Patrol Drones circling the town in big, lazy loops. "How are we supposed to sneak in?"

Mattea's eyes glitter. "Maybe Ignacio can disable them?"

"And let everyone know we're here?"

Ignacio drops his eyes and stares at his boots. "I don't think I could do it, anyway."

"What are you talking about?" Sara teases. "You killed half the Unsettled back there in the desert!"

I tell Sara to stop it, but she brushes me off with a wave of her hand. "I think he may have even made some of their heads explode!"

Now, Libra and Mattea both jump in, telling Sara to shut her trap. She doesn't look too happy about being confronted or told what to do, but at least she stops talking.

That gives me the time I need to think of a plan. "Mattea and I will go first. We'll pretend to be lost travelers. People come and go around here all the time, so that'll be believable. Mattea can use her language skills to deal with anyone suspicious."

I glance over to Mattea who's looking at me like I'm crazy. I ask her what's wrong.

She swallows hard. "It's just...you're asking me to use abilities I don't really know how to control all that well, yet. You saw what happened back there with that girl. I tried to communicate with her, but it didn't work."

"Maybe not at first," I remind her. "But your interrogation went great. We couldn't have understood a thing that girl was saying without you, and we never would have found this place. And listen, we might not even need for you to do it again. If you and I can at least sneak in close enough to get us some intel..."

"Okay," Mattea nods. "We can do this."

We're just getting ready to put my great plan into action when we hear the sliding click of metal on metal, a sound I'd recognize even without our recent Weapons Training classes.

We whip around to see eight well-dressed men and women in matching black suits with crisp white shirts and starched yellow ties. They've got their rifles cocked as they surround us with murder in their eyes.

A million scenarios flash though my mind in a split second. Most of them involve me and my Cohort, heroically and with blinding speed, putting our training into action and taking down our eight assailants.

The scenario that actually happens, though, is a lot different.

Yes. We draw our weapons.

Yes. We leap into combat positions like we've been taught.

But that's about as far as we get.

One of the women in the group sweeps her hand in front of her as if she's wiping morning dew off a pane of glass, and it's like the whole world's dropped out of normal gear and down into neutral.

My body wilts, and my Cohort and I drop to our knees.

Without a word, four of the men in the circle around us fire their weapons.

Each weapon unleashes a hail of tiny barbs that pierce our skin and release an excruciating electric charge that causes our muscles to seize up.

So much for fearless leadership, Branwynne. After all this time and all the faith everyone's put in you, you should really be better at this.

It's the very last thing I think before my entire body goes completely slack, my eyes roll back, and unconsciousness washes over me in an endless, suffocating wave.

35

GALAXY EYES

I'M STANDING.

No. Not standing.

I'm...*floating*?

If I'm floating, how come I'm not wet?

I wiggle my fingers and toes. My hands, feet, arms, legs...it feels like they're attached to my body but a mile away at the same time.

It hurts, but I manage to open my eyes.

Instead of relieved, I'm blinded by a sudden explosion of white light that sears through my brain like an electric current.

Wincing hard, I do my best to blink away the pain. The bright burst clears to reveal three things:

I'm alone.

I'm suspended in some sort of glass bubble.

And there's someone on the outside looking in.

It's a man, maybe forty or fifty years old. He's bald. But not old-man bald. And not bald like War. It's like he never had any hair on his head in his life. And not just on his head, either. He's got no eyebrows or eyelashes and no hint of stubble on his sharp, angled jaw.

His broad, powerful shoulders contrast with his lean lower body to give him an overall sculpted, triangular shape.

Under his gold-colored jumpsuit with black trim around the neckline and sleeves, the exposed, gray-veined skin on his face, neck, and hands is stone-white but still tight, almost polished.

Finally. Someone found a way to animate a marble statue and wrap it up in a banana peel.

After a quick scan of the room, I don't see my Cohort and can't make out more than shadows, so I swing my eyes back around to his.

At first, I think maybe it's a trick of the light or a distortion from the curved glass or the aftereffects of getting my sight back so suddenly.

But no. The man's eyes, like his skin, are *white*. No irises. No pupils. Just white with tiny specks moving around in dark clusters, like someone sprinkled black pepper over a hard-boiled egg.

Basically, the opposite of mine.

I can't tell if this man is earthly handsome or alien eerie.

With his hands clasped behind his back, he leans forward and stares through the glass.

"Welcome back. It was a close call between life and death. I'm glad you chose the former."

His voice—a smooth, even baritone—is nothing like his looks.

I squint away the last bits of pain shooting through my head and try to talk, but nothing comes out.

The man shakes his head and leans even closer to the glass.

"So, it's true. You have Galaxy Eyes." He puts a finger to his face and tugs down the lower lid of his own eye. "Takes one to know one, right?"

I know I'm the one being held captive, but I want to interrogate this strange man. I want to ask him a million questions, but

I force myself to ignore him while I try to have a look around and assess the place and the situation like I've been trained to do.

Focusing past the marble man and his speckled eyes, I take in as much as possible.

I'm in a bubble, and I can't move. There are panels missing in the white drop-ceiling, and I can make out what I think is a surface of jagged rock. Am I in a cave? There are banks of quantum computer consoles, holo-displays, and input panels running the length of the walls on either side of me. There's a long table behind the man, and a silver door behind that. Is this a lab? A low-tech Processor of some kind?

Wait...

Galaxy Eyes?

I repeat the words. No sound comes out, but the man, reading my lips, smiles and nods.

Gathering whatever strands of strength I can find, I start to ask him who he is, where my Cohort and Haida Gwaii are, what he's talking about—the normal questions under the circumstances—but my voice catches in my throat. The room spins, the man pixilates, and a searing forest fire of pain blazes through my head.

I wake up to the same white-eyed, marble-skinned man, still peering intently at me like I'm a cluster of bacterial cultures in a petri dish. He pats the curve of glass between us. Chalky and threaded through with gray veins, his hand looks thick and strong.

"Going to try to stay with us this time?"

I shake the fuzziness from my head.

Did I just faint?

I'm embarrassed when all I can do at first is float here and try not to cry from the seething rage boiling up inside of me.

Take it easy, Branwynne. You've been drugged or something. That's all. When it passes, you'll be fine. Then, you'll tear off this guy's giant marble of a head, gather up your friends, and be back at the Academy before anyone knows you've been gone.

"I'm Epic," the man says and then breaks into a little laugh. "That sounds so...grandiose, doesn't it? I'm sorry. I don't mean to imply that I'm some vast, mega-legend. My *name* is Epic."

I try to glare at him, but right now, even the act of grinding my teeth and scrunching up my face hurts like hell.

The man spreads his arms wide. "Please believe me. I wish all this weren't necessary. I really do. But I'm not the bad guy here. I'm all about bringing people together. It's time to unite this country like it should have been united all along."

"And how...," I stammer, "how are you planning to do that?"

"By picking up where Krug left off and finishing what he started."

"I don't..."

"Oh, right. Of course. You're a Brit, aren't you? You weren't here for Krug. Shame. If being a narcissist was a superpower, he'd be Emergent Numero Uno. But he managed to do it all with nothing but good old-fashioned divisiveness, cruelty, and greed. Oh, and with a nice dose of stupidity thrown in for good measure. He managed to spread enough lies, scare enough people, play on enough fears, and keep us all ignorant enough so we wouldn't notice him dividing us up and gathering up more and more power for himself. All for the glorification of his own short-sighted little pea-brain."

"Krug's gone."

"That he is." Epic looks sad as he makes finger quotes in the air. "But his *legend* lives on. What I'm doing here—what *we're* doing—is for the benefit of others, not for ourselves. We're going to usher in a new age of peace, order, and evolution. A new era of connectedness. Darwin introduced the world to natural selection. That's all this is. Just subsidized."

"Sub...?"

"You know. Helped along."

I clamp my jaw tight and narrow my eyes. "I know about Krug."

"Then you know he was a divisive, self-absorbed sociopath."

"Takes one to know one." I try to make it sound like a courageously-delivered insult, but it comes out as more of a whining moan.

The corners of Epic's lips stretch toward his ears in a pair of sharp points. "I'll assume that's your attempt to look strong when I know you feel weak, so I'll let it slide. No. I'm neither self-absorbed nor a sociopath. If anything, I'm absorbed in *others* and am a philanthropist." He waves his hand in the general direction of the ceiling. "You see, unlike your friends up there, I don't want my country back. I want a better country than the one we had before all of this. I want a nation of cooperation, health, and peace. I want a new world to spring from the ashes of the old, a world without hierarchy."

"But with you still on top, right?"

This time, the smile breaks wide open, and Epic laughs—his boxy white teeth glistening on full display—like I've said the funniest thing in the world.

Dabbing the corners of his eyes, he pulls a mag-stool over and plops down in it with one leg crossed over his knee. "You're clever. I heard that about you. And before you ask, yes, I know about your Academy. I've known about it since before you were born. Since Quinn first started planning it."

"Quinn?"

"Kress's father."

Kress's...father?

"I worked with him. Me. Sadia. Caldwell. A bunch of others.

Deenays. En-Gene-eers. The occasional rogue computer hacker or techno-geneticist. We all had the same vision. We just saw it through a very different lens."

"I don't..."

"I'm sorry. I'm going pretty fast here, aren't I? Can't be helped. There's a war on the horizon. A war I need to stop. A war I need you to help me stop."

"You're the one who's planning a war."

"True. But *mine* is the right war." He jabs his thumb toward the ceiling. "First, I need to stop the wrong one."

"All wars are wrong."

Epic really enjoys that and tilts his head back far enough for me to see the tendons standing out on his neck under his gold jumpsuit as he laughs.

"Is that something they teach you at your Academy? All wars are hardly wrong, Branwynne. And you're far too old and too experienced with how the world works to believe otherwise. No. The war about to happen up here is just...nonsense. Fighting out of fear and hunger over scraps of land and poisoned rivers. My war will be the one to end all that. My war will liberate the enslaved, strengthen the weak, and topple the tyrants. You see, Krug wanted people like you to enhance his army. I want people like you...No, not people *like* you. I want you, Branwynne—you, specifically—to help me to enhance the world."

My mouth is cobweb sticky, but I manage to stay focused enough to keep my tongue and jaw working. "Kress's father died. A long time ago. She told me so."

Epic flashes a wide smile, his blanched, cube-shaped teeth standing out against the washed-out blue-grey of his tongue and lips. "Maybe. But she's not his only kid still hanging around."

Spinning halfway around on his mag-stool, Epic reaches back and taps a glowing button on a small holo-display above the long table behind him. Nearly instantly, the door whooshes open, and a tall man—thin and with a scraggly beard—steps on slightly wobbly legs into the room. Like Epic, he's wearing a gold jumpsuit, only his is faded the color of melted wax and is stained with spots of what looks like dirt and oil.

He's angled, a little grungy, and he's not alone.

He's got Haida Gwaii tucked in his folded arms.

It burns my throat to shout, but I do it anyway, screaming out to her and calling her name.

She lifts her head a little, but otherwise, she doesn't move, and I'm not sure she even recognizes me or knows I'm here.

Gazing fondly at the white raven, the thin man drags a finger along her back as Epic summons him forward.

"Branwynne. I'd like for you to meet someone."

The man stands next to Epic and offers me a brown-toothed but overall pleasant smile. His voice is soft, but I can't tell if it's muffled by the glass or by his tangled, wire brush of a beard.

"I'm Micah," he says, his eyes glittering with more life than he has in his shabby body. "I'm Kress's older brother."

My eyes dart between Epic and the man calling himself Micah.

Nope. Not possible.

"Nice try," I snarl with a head shake that makes me feel queasy again as the room spins.

Take it easy, Branwynne. It's not the time for heroics. Yet.

"Kress's brother died years ago," I say. "She told me so, herself."

Epic reaches over to rest a hand on Micah's shoulder. I can't tell if it's a gesture of affection, camaraderie, or if he's making sure Micah—who's twitchy-eyed and nervous looking—doesn't bolt from the room.

"Kress wasn't lying," Epic explains. "Not on purpose, anyway. As far as she knows, yes, every member of her family—including her brother—disappeared, died in the Valta, or else perished in the endless drone attacks that turned the rest of the world into the savage nightmare of death and desperation it's become."

Standing up from his mag-chair, Epic walks over and fiddles with a small holo-schematic hovering over a slanted console of black glass off to his side.

Micah's bleary eyes follow him before landing back on me. He absently pets Haida and opens his mouth like he wants to say something, but Epic stops him with a raised hand.

The two men—one fish-belly white, the other lanky and slightly feral—exchange a curious look before Epic swings back around to face me, his palm pressed flat to the glass.

"You're wondering where your friends are. You want to know why you're here and what I plan on doing with you." I open my mouth to answer, but he cuts me off. "Those are reasonable questions, Branwynne. But they're also beneath you." Epic turns again to hunch over the console. "You don't realize how important you are. Did you think you were recruited by accident? Or that you're just another Emergent, a member of some evolutionary avant-garde destined to live or die fighting an endless army of enemies over abstract, nebulous ideas like freedom and equality?"

Keep talking, you smarmy arse. When I get out of here...

With my head a little clearer now, I get a better look at Haida. She's quiet and still, practically comatose in Micah's wiry arms. She's not fighting or trying to escape, but that could be the result of a million things: fatigue, fear, being drugged, having her connection to me cut off by this gravity-defying bubble-cell I'm in...

But at least she's alive. Which means there's hope, and I remember one of the things War taught us back in the Academy:

Don't give up. Just because something looks dead doesn't mean it is.

I scan every inch of the two men standing in front of me. I'm taking detailed notes about everything from their eyes to their exposed necks to their beating hearts under their rising and falling chests.

Everything I'm going to hack to pieces once I'm free.

36

TRAPPED

Epic pauses for a second, and I'm guessing he's caught me sizing him and Micah up.

He locks his white eyes on my black ones like he's reading my mind. Who knows? Maybe he is. Or maybe he's just reading my intentions through my tense jaw, my clenched teeth, or my clamped fists.

After all, I'm not exactly keeping my fury a secret.

Epic grins and drops his eyes, his voice slipping into a casual cadence, like we're mates or something having a chat over morning tea.

"The bubble you're in is called a Mag-Grav Suspension Cell. A little something left behind by the Patriot Army when they were garrisoned not too far from here a long time ago. We modified this one a bit. It now emits a mild but effective electromagnetic pulse specifically calibrated to your neuro patterns."

Epic walks past Micah, dragging a bone-white finger over Haida's head and back as he passes. "Getting those patterns wasn't easy. It's why we needed her. As I'm sure you know, you're not just you, and your raven isn't just your raven. You're a connected unit. We needed her to get to you."

He paces around the bubble, and, with my body frozen in place, I have to turn my head halfway to either side to keep him in view. "That's why you keep getting migraines. Every time you try to access the Emergent part of your brain to connect to Haida, you run into the cell's firewall. It hurts, doesn't it?"

When I don't say anything right away—mostly because I'm not sure if he's waiting for an answer but also partly because I can't seem to make my jaw work—the door to the room slides open, and a woman walks in.

No. She doesn't walk. She *glides*.

She's average height, maybe five foot seven or so, but that's all that's average about her.

Her onyx hair hangs down to her shoulders in shimmering waves. Like Epic, she's wearing a set of black-trimmed golden-yellow scrubs. Unlike Epic, hers are form fitting, so the toned muscles in her neck, shoulders, and arms under her short-sleeved scrub shirt are on full display.

She looks like she just stepped out of a fashion magazine. Or maybe stepped down from an Olympic podium. Either way, she looks like she belongs somewhere other than in what I think is an underground bunker most likely designed for the capture, experimentation, and torture of people like me.

The exotic-looking woman has high cheekbones, olive eyes, and the smoothest honey-colored skin I've ever seen.

But it's her legs that draw my eyes. Long and shapely, they taper down to her knees where they stop abruptly and lead into a pair of tall metallic-black boots with what look like silver tank treads at the bottom. Only they don't quite touch the floor. Instead, they hover an inch or so in the air over a wavy distortion.

"This is Aubrielle," Epic announces with a casual wave of his hand. "As you can see, she's a Modified."

Aubrielle reaches down and pats the side of her leg. "Magnetic propulsion system," she says with a smile way too pretty to belong to someone on the same side as an evil arse like Epic.

She taps the back of her head and smiles again. "I've got a few transhuman things going on up here, too. But there's plenty of time for all that. We've been waiting for the two of you for a long time."

Her eyes flick between me and Haida, who is still tucked quietly, as if paralyzed, in Micah's arms.

"Aubrielle is the third part of our triumvirate," Epic says, his voice brimming with barely restrained pride.

"We always work in threes," Aubrielle explains. "Epic handles the big picture stuff. You know...planning, strategizing, coalition-building. All the things it takes to start and win a war." She gestures over toward where Micah is standing on a weird angle and looking oddly out of touch. "You've met Micah. You might say he's our Inside Guy. The one who knows how to get in and out of places. A handy ability to have when it comes to reconnaissance missions, wouldn't you say? And me...well, I'm a lot of things. But the one job I have you might be most interested in is 'bird wrangler.'"

She reaches over and scoops Haida Gwaii out of Micah's arms, tucking the white raven against her chest.

Haida's eyes flutter, and her head and wings shuffle a little at the motion, but otherwise, she doesn't react.

I feel my nails digging into my palms as my fingers curl around into tight fists.

"What did you—?"

Aubrielle gasps and puts her hand over her heart, like even the thought that I may have my doubts is enough to offend her. "We didn't hurt her if that's what you're worried about."

"I'm worried about a lot of things," I snap from behind the curved wall of my glass prison.

Epic steps forward. "We wouldn't hurt Haida Gwaii any more than we'd damage a key we were about to use to open up a lock."

"Honestly," Aubrielle adds, "she's at least as important to us as you are."

"Kress is the key to what I'm looking to accomplish," Epic says. "But you're the key to Kress. With you on our side, we can counter her and any other Emergents she and her so-called 'Conspiracy' manage to get their hands on. And yes. Before you ask. We know they're out on a recruiting mission. I'm not the only one who knows what's coming. As for the rest of your friends, well, we'd like them on our side, too."

"But they won't join us without you," Aubrielle sighs.

"They won't join you at all," I growl, lashing out as best as I can toward the glass.

Instead of being startled, offended, or intimidated like I'd hoped, Aubrielle just beams her pretty smile at me and brushes a swoop of her thick hair behind her ear. "Don't be so sure, Branwynne. After all, how long have you known your fellow Emergents? And how well?"

"I know them well enough to know they'll do whatever it takes to help Kress and stop you."

"Really? Did you know that two of your friends are mass murderers?"

I stare daggers at her, but she still doesn't react.

"Or that one of your friends has already betrayed you?"

Don't let her manipulate you, Branwynne. Remember your training: Stay focused and in control.

I take a deep breath and try to connect with Haida. Maybe if I can channel her senses again—even just a little...

The lightning strike searing its way through my head is twice as powerful as it was before. Only this time, it's not only me who suffers.

Still in Aubrielle's arms, Haida shrieks in agony and strains her wings but fails to fly as Micah launches himself over and joins Aubrielle in clamping their arms over her.

I don't know if I hear her screams in my ears or in my mind. Or maybe both. It doesn't matter. All that matters is that my white raven companion, my *friend*, is in excruciating pain.

And I can't even move far enough to bang on the glass.

Epic waves his hand in the air, and it's like he's sprinkled magic dust or something over Haida, who settles into Aubrielle's arms with a fading series of light clacks.

Micah releases his grip and shuffles over to stand just behind Epic.

"There's a place called the *Lyfelyte*—" Epic begins as he takes a few steps toward the bubble.

"I know about the *Lyfelyte*," I pant, my lungs, mind, and entire body brimming with rage.

Epic comes to a screeching halt. "You do?"

"I've seen it."

He strides the rest of the way over to the cell so fast I think he's going to crash into it. But he stops and slaps both of his palms onto the glass. "You've *seen* it?"

"Uh huh."

A deep crease forms at the bridge of his nose between his white eyes as he scans me up and down. Apparently concluding that I'm off my trolley, he grins and takes a half step back. "I don't believe you."

"I'm not surprised. You're an idiot."

The groove grows deeper but then his entire face softens, and his bone-white smile returns. "You think you have leverage now, don't you?"

"I think you have me and Haida trapped, but I have information you want, which means you're trapped too."

"Hardly."

"If you let me go, I'll tell you what I've seen. And I've seen a *lot*."

"Counter deal: You tell me what you've seen—tell me everything you know about the *Lyfelyte,* including how to access it—and I won't have *them* snap all your bones and toss what's left of you out into the desert for the Unsettled."

On cue, two men and one woman in matching armored amber-yellow and black motorcycle racing suits march single-file into the room and line up behind Epic.

"This is one of our Trio of Sanctum Sentinels. As you can see, like us, they travel in threes. And they have the toughest job of all of us. You see, they're tasked with keeping you here. That's the easy part. But they've also been assigned to making sure they don't kill you if you try to escape. I think you'll admit, it's quite the balancing act we're expecting of them. But I believe they're up to the task."

"Where are my friends?"

Epic rolls his eyes at me. "Why? So you can start planning your great escape? And where would you go, exactly?"

My eyes have a mind of their own and glance up at the ceiling. Epic notices.

"The Academy? We'll follow you. Or did you mean out there in the desert? The Unsettled would love to get their hands on you."

"More likely their *teeth*," Aubrielle chuckles. "Food's been scarce out there for a long time."

Epic gives a nod to Micah, who taps the cashew-shaped comm-link in his ear and says something I can't hear. Epic turns back to me and fixes his eerie eyes on mine.

Do my black-with-white-speckled eyes look this creepy to other people?

"I'm sorry, Branwynne," Epic sighs. "But this isn't the movies. There's no cavalry coming to help you, and I'm not some moustache-twisting evil genius who's going to tell you all my plans and leave the room unguarded while you make your escape."

"You're right about one thing."

"Oh?"

"You're no genius."

Epic tilts his head back and laughs. Wiping a tear from his eye, he chuckles, "I didn't expect this."

"Didn't expect what?"

His face goes oddly serious. "I've known about you for longer than you've been alive. I expected great power and great stubbornness from you. I just didn't expect to like you quite so much."

Without turning around, he waves his hand to Micah and Aubrielle, who turn and begin walking past the three guards toward the door.

On their way out, I catch a glimpse of Haida's barely-open eyes from where she's secured on Aubrielle's forearm.

I've seen Haida hungry, angry, bored, overprotective, and deadly.

This is the first time I've ever seen her scared.

37

STRONGER

I DON'T REMEMBER FALLING asleep, but I must have, because when I open my eyes, Epic is sitting in front of me on his floating mag-chair.

He smiles but also grumbles a little as he stands, like he's been waiting for me for a long time.

On the long lab table behind him, Haida Gwaii is perched on top of a silver, mushroom-shaped platform.

She gurgle-craws and clacks her greetings to me from across the room.

It's nice to hear her voice.

I pin my eyes to Epic's. "Where are my friends?" I'm too tired to bark it out, and it comes out as more curiosity than an angry question.

"They're being held in a different part of the compound. We can't have you collaborating now, can we? Frankly, Branwynne, we're not interested in them. They can't do what you can do."

"I can't do anything."

"Not by yourself. That's true." Epic swings around to stand behind Haida Gwaii, his hands pressed flat to the table on either side of Haida's perch. "You are one of a very few people who can talk to her."

"Haida?"

"I meant what I said before," Epic says. "I'm all about connections. And you have a very special connection with this very special white raven."

Haida yelps a series of weak clacks before hanging her head in helpless defeat.

"What I want is the telempathic bond you and your raven share."

"You want our bond?"

Epic smiles. "Kind of. You see, Branwynne, human beings have spent thousands of years elevating ourselves over everything around us. Plants. Animals. The air. The earth. Each other. You name it. We've hardwired ourselves to survive at the expense of everything outside of us. It's what we've conditioned ourselves to do. And what's worse, we've brainwashed ourselves into believing we're unique. Separate. Individual. We go around breaking bonds. Well, you and Haida are the key to reconnecting."

"I don't know what you mean."

"Didn't Kress teach you anything?"

"Kress taught me *everything*," I snap.

Micah laughs at this, which makes me furious since I'm not even close to joking around at the moment.

"From what we've heard, she's teaching you to fight."

"How do you know—?"

Epic puts up a hand to interrupt me. "And she's teaching you how to connect with Haida. It doesn't matter how we know. We know."

My heart races, not out of fear or desperation. It's out of frustration. If this were a regular cell, I could pace around, smash my fists against the walls. I could dig, scratch, and claw to try to find a way out.

Whoever designed this maddening bubble knew what they were doing. I'm free, helpless, and powerless at the same time. I can feel my muscles and my will getting weaker by the minute.

In front of me, Epic drags the backs of his fingers along Haida's wings before walking around the table to stand behind his mag-chair.

"Emergents have abilities to varying degrees. Some of you are quite powerful. Others aren't. What makes all of you special, though, isn't what you can do. It's *how* you're able to do it. You're not an evolutionary leap forward as much as you are a return to a natural state of connectedness. By tapping into what you and your raven here share, I can bring that connectedness back to the world."

"You know," I tell him in my snarkiest possible voice, "you could've just *asked*."

"And what would you have said?" he laughs. "If I had tracked you down in your hidden fortress and asked you to let me into your head so I could put an end once and for all to this hell on earth we created..."

"I would've called you a barmy loon and told you to bugger off."

"*Exactly*."

"And then, I would've busted up your bloody face and chivvied off to bed without giving you a second thought."

Nodding, Epic eyes me up and down. "From what I understand, you could do it, too."

He reaches into his pocket and draws out a red disk not much bigger than his palm. Stepping toward the bubble, he slaps it to the glass where it sticks and starts to shimmer in a kaleidoscope of color.

"You see, when it comes to being connected, humans are on a spectrum. We bounce back and forth between wanting to be with others and wanting to be left alone. We dream of living in safety and isolation in a big house—or, in your case, a big school —high up on a mountain, but we can't resist the pull of others. We're in orbit around each other."

I'm trying to focus on Epic, but the swirls of reds, blues, greens, and yellows from the disk on the glass keep drawing my attention.

"Way over on his end of the spectrum," Epic says, spreading his arms wide, "Krug was the ultimate human being. And way over on the other end, there's you."

"I don't..."

"I'm going to find out exactly what's happening between you and Haida. Then, I'm going to replicate it. And then, I'm going to use it as the glue to put back all the broken pieces of the world."

He steps back to the console in the table where Haida is perched.

"It's time for some tests."

Only, there are no tests. No challenges. No questions or interrogations.

There's just pain.

I scream and beg to black out, but I can't seem to lose consciousness.

Across from me, Haida starts to quiver and cringe. She spreads her wide white wings and tilts her head back, *crawing* to the ceiling and snapping out a string of anguished barks.

As casually as I might slip on my boots, Epic taps out a flurry of codes into a scrolling holo-display floating in the air between him and Haida.

A sizzling, green-hued dome of light materializes around Haida, trapping her inside.

Everything that happens next happens in about five seconds. Or is it five weeks?

It's impossible to tell. I've lost all sense of time and space. I've lost all sense of myself.

I'm not me, and I'm not Haida.

Somehow, as impossible as it sounds, I've become the connection between us.

I start out as a dot, a pinprick of light, bouncing around in the vast black of outer (or is it *inner*?) space.

The dot I am turns into a line, which turns into a criss-crossed patchwork of streaks and contours. The contours become a web that bends over onto itself until it forms a sphere, like someone wrapped a planet-sized soap bubble in a giant spider's web.

As quickly as it seems to happen, the disorientation gives way to a strange calm, which gives way to pure fury when I finally open my eyes to discover that I'm still floating helplessly in Epic's spherical suspension cell.

Across from me, Haida is still under the crackling dome of energy on the lab table.

Her head perks up when she notices me noticing her.

I take a quick look around. The three guards are still stationed just inside the door, their eyes glued to me.

But no Micah, no Aubrielle, and no Epic.

A noise that starts as static and turns into language startles me to full attention. It's Haida Gwaii, and her voice in my head is the best sound I've ever heard in my life.

~ Gone.

Epic is gone?

~ Yes.

Are you okay?

~ Yes. Are you?

Yes. What did Epic do to us just now?

~ *He tried to access our connection.*

Did it...did it work?

~ *Yes. But not how he planned.*

What happened?

~ *He accidentally made us stronger.*

38
_____

ESCAPE

With Epic gone, I figure it's now or never.

Hovering a foot in the air and ignoring the nasty looks from the three amused guards, I thrash around inside the bubble.

I stretch my arms as far as I can, but I can't reach the sides of my glass cage. I can kick my legs, but it's pointless. I can't reach the glass, and even if I could, I don't see how I could possibly break it. And if I managed to break out, I'd still have the three guards to deal with.

And even if I managed to do all *that*, I'd still need to free Haida Gwaii, locate my friends, escape from this facility, and somehow get us back up the mountain to the safety of the Academy.

In my seventeen years, I've been shot at, beaten up, and kicked around.

But nothing guts me like feeling helpless.

Furious, I thrash around some more until it feels like all four of my limbs are about to come unhinged.

How can moving be so easy and so impossible at the same time?

If I could get free, maybe I could find a way to channel

Haida. Or use what Kress has been teaching me to walk right through this thing.

I do my best to concentrate, but my mind is a swirling storm of anger, helplessness, and frustration—all mingled in with a whole lot of embarrassment over having gotten caught in the first place.

The three guards stationed in the lab are trying to look professional, but they keep exchanging amused looks and swapping smiles at my frantic and pointless attempts to escape.

Seeing the smug looks on their smarmy faces makes me want to get out of here even more—even if it's just to rip their bloody heads off and juggle their disembodied skulls right out the front door.

One of the men leans back against the wall and starts talking to the woman. The other man doesn't look too pleased, and I'm in the middle of processing what the relationship might be between the three guards when a voice from out in the hallway catches my ears.

It's a girl's voice. A voice I know.

Sara?

"She's going to betray you."

Yes. It's definitely Sara's voice. But how...?

"You've seen the doubt in her eyes. You've heard her hesitate. She's manipulating you."

The two male guards swing around and face the female guard, whose eyes go wide with terror.

"She's going to betray Epic," one of the men says, drawing an old-style handgun from his holster. "She's going to let the girl go."

His partner nods his agreement and draws a brown-handled, fixed blade knife from a sheath on his belt and begins to advance on the woman.

She takes two full steps back until her back and both palms are pressed to the wall.

The man with the gun fires his weapon twice. The first shot pings into the wall right next to the woman's head. The next shot strikes her square in the thigh.

She cries out and clamps her hands to her leg as blood burbles between her fingers, seeping into the fabric of her pants.

"She's trying to help the girl escape!"

It's Sara's voice again, and the man with the gun repeats it word for word.

With the desperate, feral eyes of a cornered cat, the woman lunges at the two men.

Swinging and flailing wildly, the three guards go crashing into one of the smaller lab tables. Together, the two men and the one woman fall into a rolling, tangled knot of kicking and punching bodies on the floor.

Shielded by the commotion, two figures slip into the room.

I can't help saying their names out loud. "Sara! Ignacio!"

Sara rushes over to the bubble while Ignacio turns his back and does something I can't see to the input panel on the wall.

The bubble lowers to the floor and peels open like a transparent clam shell.

Sara reaches in, grabs my wrist and hauls me out.

"Wait!" I cry. "Haida!"

I sprint to the table where Haida is bobbing her head under the shimmering green dome of energy.

Taking her from under there could hurt or even kill either one of us. But there's no choice and even less time to figure it out.

Thankfully, I'm able to slip my arm under the green hood and slide Haida safely into the crook of my arm.

Dashing over to the door where Ignacio is hurrying us along, we skirt around the three guards who are now clambering to their feet—apparently oblivious to our presence—and slashing at each other with long steel military knives.

The woman guard is still bleeding badly from her leg, and her hair is a mess of matted sweat and blood. She's got her back pressed up against one of the standing lab tables with one of the guards brandishing his own knife while their partner, the third guard, lies dead on the floor between them.

That's all I have time to take in as Ignacio throws his arm around me and together, he and Sara drag me out of the room in a full sprint.

39

RUN

TOGETHER, the three of us dash full speed down the corridor, through an open doorway, and up a narrow set of stone stairs.

Along the way, we sprint past glass-walled rooms filled with lab tables and all kinds of diagnostic equipment.

There are cubbies, lockers, and closets along the wall on one side of us and a railing looking out over a dark courtyard on the other.

The floor is an uneven combination of polished stones, natural rocks, and very old bricks.

It's like an older, more beat-up version of the Academy!

I turn to Ignacio as we bolt down the next hall and around a corner. "How the hell did you—?"

"Long story!" he shouts back.

"I'll take the short!" I call out over the din of alarms and the thunder of boots coming from overhead, down the hall, on the stairs behind us, and basically all around.

"Let's just say they underestimated our girl Sara here!"

Sara waves off the compliment and shouts, "We've got to get to the others!"

"Others?"

"Libra, Mattea, and Arlo!"

I'm about to head up the next flight of stairs when Sara shouts out from behind me. "Wait! Our weapons!"

I turn back to see Sara and Ignacio huddled in front of a glass door leading into one of the labs.

Ignacio slaps both hands to the input panel embedded in the rock wall next to the room and slams his eyes shut.

The input panel and most of the rocks and stones around it burst into a crackle of blue flame. It's not hot, but the cave-like wall still blisters and turns black before our eyes.

Ignacio's hands drop to his sides, and Sara and I catch him as he stumbles backward.

"I'm okay," he mumbles.

Regaining his balance, he bursts into the room and over to the wood-topped table where our weapons are lined up in a neat row.

In a flurry of motion, he passes the weapons back to me and Sara, one by one.

Sara slides her bandolier and its arsenal of throwing darts over her head, and I slip the holster and my Serpent Blades around my waist.

Ignacio tucks his twin shillelaghs into his belt and tosses Libra's sledgehammer, Mattea's bear claws, and Arlo's long-handled scythe to me and Sara.

We tuck the weapons into our belts and under our jackets as best we can....and then we bolt from the room and run like hell.

Dashing up an inclined walkway, we cut over to an open doorway leading to a dark, narrow stairwell.

Shouts of "This way!" and "They're over here!" echo around in the long, low-ceilinged corridor behind us.

The doorway to the stairwell is low enough so even I have to duck down to get through. In front of us, the stairs are old, gray, and brittle with several of them missing.

We bound up anyway, leaping over chasms leading down into a very bleak darkness I'd rather not fall into.

At the landing, Ignacio shouts for me and Sara not to fall behind as he thunders his way up the next flight of stairs—this time a wide set of stone steps leading to a wide wooden door with daylight streaming between its crooked slats.

Ignacio slams his shoulder into the door, sending it smashing outward and halfway off its hinges.

Holding my hand over my eyes against the blazing sun, I'm braced for a firing squad of Epic's guards. Instead, we're greeted by toothy smiles and happy hugs from Libra, Mattea, and Arlo.

From her perch on my forearm, Haida belts out a series of gurgly barks.

Leaping over, Libra hugs me hard enough to crush me and Haida if she's not careful.

"The family reunion'll have to wait," Ignacio barks as he hauls Libra off of me. "Did you find transportation?"

"Over there!" she cries and then dashes off to where a small fleet of military mag-jeeps is parked on grav-pads next to a windowless bunker-like building.

Sara and I distribute everyone's weapons as the six of us pile into a battered green jeep with Mattea sliding into the driver's seat.

"It won't start!" she cries, her hand pressed hard to the starter on the glossy black access panel.

"Is it the parking pad?" Arlo asks. "Are the mag-locks engaged?"

"No!" Mattea yells, "I deactivated them!"

Libra leaps from the vehicle, tearing away from Ignacio who tries and fails to hold her back.

She drops to all fours and dives headfirst under the mag-jeep while behind us, one of the Sentinel guards bursts from the doorway we just came through and fires wildly in our direction.

By the time I jump down and crouch to the ground, bullets whizzing over my head, Libra has already rolled out on the other side.

"Let's go!" she hollers.

I dive halfway into the jeep with Sara and Arlo hauling me in the rest of the way by the seat of my pants.

With Mattea at the controls, we speed off, bouncing over a barrier of steel angle-iron before hurtling up onto a long, curving road of hard packed dirt.

Behind us, their three-wheeled dirt-bikes kicking up a storm of dust, the Sentinels are in hot pursuit.

There's no time for calculations or risk-assessment. Even with our training and weapons, we're no match for whatever battalion of Epic's Sentinels are bearing down on us.

Mattea steers our jeep off road toward a distant tree line. The ground under us is a combination of pebbles, sand, jagged stones, and long cracks in the dry terrain. Not exactly the best conditions for a high-speed getaway.

We're all bouncing high enough to go flying out of the jeep and onto the ground if we don't hang on.

After another mile of bone-rattling, tooth-jarring flight, the jeep clunks to a pathetic, grumbling stop in the middle of a stretch of land in between two long heaps of human remains— some skeletal, some only partially decomposed.

The smell of death and decay washes through the open sides of the jeep in vomit-inducing waves.

The Unsettled have been here. Which means we need to be anywhere else.

Ignacio hops out of the passenger's seat and sprints to the back of the jeep.

He slides to a stop, his boots kicking up a spray of red dirt. He stands, legs planted and shoulders squared, facing our pursuers.

I leap out after him and grab his arm.

"We can't make a stand here! They'll kill us!" I tug his arm harder and point off toward the distant tree line. "We have to make a run for it!"

Instead of following me, he plants his boots even more firmly into the ground. Reaching out toward the fleet of Sanctum Sentinels, his golden-amber eyes flicker and glow.

In the distance, every Sentinel vehicle is bathed in a crackling blue light followed by an explosive, blinding flash of white.

Reeling back, I feel like my eyes have been flash-fried.

When the haze of white clears, Ignacio takes my hand and starts sprinting back to the jeep.

"What did you do?" I shout.

"Just disabled their jeeps," he calls back over his shoulder.

Mattea vaults herself from the driver's seat and lands gingerly on the ground with Arlo and Libra leaping out after her.

"Branwynne's right. We have to run!"

"I'm sorry!" Libra sobs. "I thought I fixed it!"

"You fixed it enough to get us out of there!" Mattea says, grabbing her by the hand. "Come on!"

Haida bursts into the air, banks hard, and glides out and over the distant treeline.

The rest of us bolt along over the uneven ground after her.

As we sprint off, I look back, expecting to see the Sentinels trying to chase us down on foot.

Because of my renewed connection with Haida Gwaii, my senses are jacked up ten times over.

But I don't need our amplified telempathic bond to see the piles of charred bodies behind us or to hear the last screams of the remaining Sentinels as they die.

40

SAVIOR

WE'RE IN A PANICKED, full-on sprint across a large patch of barren desert before finally closing in on a long stretch of black trees leading up to some gradually sloping cliffs and rocky foothills.

My head spinning, I scramble with Ignacio and the others up a hill of red dirt and sparse, dead grass and dive through the tree line. The dried vegetation from the bushes and slanted trees flakes away and crumbles into finger-sized clumps of charcoal and puffs of wispy ash as we go crashing through.

Seeing more hills and high overhanging cliffs of red stone in the distance, none of us is prepared for the steep drop-off into a deep ravine on the other side of the tree line.

Arse over elbow, we go tumbling down the ravine, crashing into each other and smashing against every razor sharp stone and boulder on the way.

Raking across jagged shards of rocks over what feels like a mile, I skid to a stop at the bottom of the chasm, the skin on my hands, wrists, and forearms shredded and bleeding.

If this were a cartoon, I'd have cute little stars dancing

around my head. Instead, I lean over to the side, blood pooling at the corners of my mouth, and throw up.

I drag a sleeve across my face, spit, and try to snap the world back into focus.

A few feet to either side, the other members of my Cohort are moaning and checking themselves for cuts, sprains, and broken bones.

The front of Libra's once-white shirt is a patchwork of orange dirt and scarlet blood.

Through my blurred gaze, I see Mattea roll to her side and hand Arlo his scythe. He braces it against the ground as he pulls himself to his feet and returns his hood to its usual position over his head.

Sara coughs and sits up as Ignacio calls out to me, asking if I'm okay.

I spit again and tell him I think so, as I look up at the cliff edge high overhead. "But I could have done without the three-hundred-foot fall."

"Speak for yourself," Libra jokes through a strained groan. "That was the most fun I've had all day."

The world around me is just shifting back into focus and I'm contemplating which way we should run when I'm startled by the unexpected intrusion of a shadowy figure standing inches away.

Hovering over me, a teenage boy reaches out a hand, offering to help me to my feet.

I follow the crisp black army boots up to the gray canvas cargo pants and to the striped red, white, and blue heat-resistant compression top.

The boy has dirty-blond hair, longish and swept back on the top with the sides cropped close. His thin beard is trimmed on a sharp angle to match the long slope of his defined and tapered cheekbones.

Under dark, downturned eyebrows, his eyes are glassy: somehow sad and bright at the same time.

And they're green.

Emerald green.

Neon emerald green. And I'm pretty sure they must glow in the dark.

Squinting up at him, I work out the stiffness in my aching jaw. "Matholook."

I catch a teasing glint in those glistening eyes as he says, "Branwynne."

It's been five years, but I remember him like it's been five minutes. He's the boy I spent a week together with once when we were both twelve years old.

I was with Kress and her Conspiracy when we stopped at his compound, the home of the Cult of the Devoted.

During our stay, Matholook kept me company when I felt edgy or alone. I was a long way from home, after all.

Sneaking from building to building and shadow to shadow, he showed me around New Harleck, the compound where the Cult of the Devoted settled when they got kicked out of Sanctum. He showed me their school, their church, their armory, and some of the meeting rooms where the adults had strategy sessions and made decisions on behalf of the community.

We had a weird, instant bond that surprised and excited me as much as it scared the hell out of me.

But that was five years ago when he was vaguely interesting, a little exciting, and sort of cute.

Now, five years later, he's tall, chiseled, and...gorgeous?

Get him out of your head, Branwynne. There's barely enough room in here for you.

Matholook grins and thrusts his hand forward again. "It *is* Branwynne, right?"

"Uh..."

"It's been a long time."

"Five years."

"You're safe," he assures me. "You and your friends. But we have to go. Now." His eyes flick back up the steep rock face before turning back to me, full of desperation and pleading urgency.

I've read enough fairy tales to know this is how it's all supposed to happen: Girl gets in over her head. Danger ensues. Girl teeters on the brink of death. Dashing heroic boy with hypnotic green eyes swoops in to save the day.

So, according to the myth, everything's going according to plan.

There's one problem, though: It's not *my* plan.

I swat Matholook's hand away and push myself up to one knee, brushing dirt off my pants and pushing up the sleeves of my red leather jacket in the process.

"I don't need help," I snap.

Matholook throws his hands up and gives me a cheeky grin that makes me want to kick him in the head. "Wouldn't dream of helping an invincible warrior such as yourself. I just thought you might prefer leaving with me rather than getting hunted down by *them*."

He points back up the towering cliff toward the top of the rocky plateau and the desert beyond where we just escaped with our lives.

"Don't worry," I groan, glancing over toward Ignacio and Libra. I marshal every ounce of strength I have to push myself the rest of the way up. "We took care of them."

"I saw. That was...impressive." Matholook crosses his arms and lets out a pretend, casual yawn. "But did you think that little platoon is all they have? There's a whole other battalion that'll be here in about two minutes. If you don't believe me, just listen. You can hear them."

He's right. The rumble vibrating through the air is impossible to miss.

And so is the dusty red-hued cloud rising up in the distance and blocking out the sun.

"We can be polite and wait for them down here, where they can easily pick us off from up there on the ridge," Matholook says, "or else we can be smart and, you know, run like hell."

Dabbing at her badly cut lip, Libra tugs on my sleeve. "You know this guy?"

"I do."

Sara tugs on my other sleeve. "You *trust* this guy?"

I look back into Matholook's happy-sad, mesmerizing eyes.

Who are you, really?

"So...you just happened to show up here?" I ask him out loud.

"What can I say?" He gives me a knowing, playful wink and flicks his thumb back and forth between us. "You and me...we're inevitable."

Libra leans in, her lips nearly grazing my ear. "Is this the one who made you feel right?"

"Um..."

"Thought so," she whispers through a breathy chuckle.

Arlo limps over to us, his face buried in shadow. "I think maybe we should go with him."

"We're fine on our own." I snap. "Inevitable or not, I don't need a savior."

Matholook thrusts his hand out once again. "Then...how about a friend?"

Ignacio shoulders his way between me and Arlo and clamps Matholook's hand in his own. "Sounds good right about now."

Her eyes ping-ponging between Matholook and the top of the practically vertical cliff we just plunged down, Mattea nods her vigorous agreement. "He's right about one thing," she calls out over the growing rumble in the air and the vibrations quaking through the ground, "something is on its way, and I doubt they're friendly. I say we get the frack out of here!"

With a gurgle-craw from high above, Haida announces her agreement.

"Ah," Matholook beams, his eyes flashing skyward before landing back on mine. "We've got a consensus. Democracy in action! Follow me!"

Without waiting for any more discussion or debate, he bolts along the rocky ravine with the six of us pounding along behind him.

I don't know if we can trust him. But one thing we *can* be sure of, if he's telling the truth about there being more Sentinels on their way, going with him is bound to be better than falling back into the hands of Epic and his lunatic confederation of tyrannical techno-geneticists.

With the distant rumble of the Sentinels' jeeps, bikes, and dune-buggies coming closer and closer from somewhere high above and behind us, we bolt along the dry, winding canyon.

After a few hundred yards of skipping through what seems to be a very old and very dry riverbed, Matholook cuts hard to one side and scrambles on all fours up a steep escarpment.

We follow him, kicking up clouds of hot dust as we spill out onto a flat stretch of land between rolling hills of waist-high, camel-colored grass.

The sun is high and hot. The dry air rising off the fields of sand and stone burns into my lungs until it's next to impossible to breathe.

The others are panting, too, gasping for breath and dragging the backs of their hands across their sweat-soaked foreheads to keep the sting of salt and the stickiness of blood from their eyes.

Overhead, the mountains loom, teasing us with the safety of

our Academy at the top and the impossibility of getting there any time soon.

Twenty feet ahead now, Matholook doesn't seem to be having much trouble at all. Sprinting over the flat parts of a plateau and skipping over the rockier sections, he launches himself over a jagged crevasse in the ground before darting through a cluster of towering boulders rising up from the crimson ground like the world's biggest bowling pins.

"Come on!" he barks, his hand waving us on in a bout of frantic impatience. "We've got to go faster!"

Sure. Easy for you to say. You weren't just locked in an underground bunker by a trio of villainous psychopaths.

Gathering every ounce of strength I've got left, I follow him as fast as I can with the other five members of my Cohort thumping along behind me.

Haida Gwaii must still be overhead somewhere and close by because I feel a surge of energy and speed blast its way through my body.

I can't always control when the connection happens, but I'm always happy when it does. Especially at times like this when I really need the boost.

With my Cohort struggling and lagging behind, I just wish I could share it.

Haida Gwaii's voice pings in my head:

~ *Someday, you will.*

I try to reach back to her, but the connection fizzles, and I wind up exhausted and fighting against the sting of lactic acid build-up in my muscles.

It's not fair. Kress and Render are practically a single unit, working in total harmony at all times. Meanwhile, after five years of training, my bond with Haida remains patchy at best.

"Come on!" Matholook urges as we chug along, desperate to

put as much distance as possible between us and any Sanctum Sentinels who might be on our trail.

I keep looking back, half-expecting to see a second wave of them thundering up from behind.

But so far, it's just us.

After another twenty minutes of scrambling along a narrow trail and then through a field of crisp, waist-high grass, we grind to a stop in a natural clearing filled with a cluster of sun-bleached animal bones and ankle-deep clumps of ash, all surrounded by an interlocking ring of fallen trees.

Matholook leaps up onto one of the tree trunks and peers off into the distance. Cupping his hands around his eyes, he scans the flats and the foothills behind us while the rest of us lean over, our hands on our knees as we struggle to catch our breath.

At last, Matholook hops down and brushes dirt from his shoulders and arms. "We're safe."

"That's great," I pant.

Unless you count the fact that we just got led to safety by a boy whose entire cult—and that's literally what they call themselves—is devoted to recruiting those they can trick and killing those they can't.

41

ENEMIES

SETTING my doubts aside for the moment, I continue to trudge along next to Matholook with the rest of my Cohort nervous and clustered in a shoulder-to-shoulder bunch behind me.

Matholook leads us up a hill and deeper into the woods until it becomes pretty clear that he's as lost as we are.

"Where's Trax when we need him?" I groan as we weave through a dense section of leaning and splintered trees.

Matholook gives me a side-eyed look. "Trax?"

"He's an Emergent. Like us."

"Oh, right. The boy with the sister who was always writing and drawing? I remember him from when you came to New Harleck all those years ago. Quiet, shy kid, right?"

"That's the one."

Only not so quiet anymore and not so shy.

Huffing, Libra clambers over a range of steep, uneven terrain and strides alongside me and Matholook. "Trax can find his way through unfamiliar territory like this."

Matholook peels back a curtain of dry vines hanging from a partially uprooted tree and ducks through. "I should know my way around better, but the truth is, we don't make it a habit of leaving New Harleck. Too many ways to get killed out here."

We hike along for a few more minutes, up some old trails and over what's left of some very old, very rusty railroad tracks.

The remnants of a wood and steel bridge sit far below on the rocky floor of a steep canyon.

"We can't cross here," Matholook tells us as he continues leading the way along the edge of the canyon. "I'm sure we can get across farther along."

He doesn't sound sure in the slightest.

Mattea, usually cool under pressure, clears her throat three times and raises a shaky hand before asking, "Is it true that the Unsettled…"

"Eat people?" Matholook scoffs. "Not *live* ones."

"Thanks," Sara sneers. "That's very reassuring."

"Sorry."

"Don't mind her," I tell him as we duck and weave through a scraggly thicket of dry underbrush. "Sara doesn't do humor."

Matholook pushes a thin branch aside as we crouch under the thorny vines draped over it. "What's it like?"

"What's what like?"

"Being an Emergent." When no one answers right away— mostly because we're almost too out of breath to form words— Matholook adds, "I'm what your people call a 'Typic,' right? Just a normal, boring human being."

"I don't know about the human being part," Libra huffs with a breathy laugh, "but you risked a lot back there to save us. I don't get the sense that you're boring or normal."

Matholook says, "Thanks" as he clambers up a steep embankment and leans against a tree, his hands on his knees, as the rest of us scramble up to join him.

"He didn't save us," I protest, swinging around to stand face to face with Libra. "Arlo got us away from the Unsettled. Sara and Ignacio got us out of Epic's little underground prison-lab. You and Mattea got us away from the Sentinels. And we'd have been just fine and found our own way after that."

Libra beams and throws her arm around my shoulders, pulling me into a very tight, very unwelcome embrace. "Aw! You love me, don't you?"

"Sure," I smile back. "If by 'love,' you mean that I barely tolerate you and really wish you would stop hugging me."

Libra drops her arms, kicks at a small stone on the ground, and pretends to be mortally wounded by my rejection of her before breaking into a happy chuckle. "Come on. Let's see where we are."

From our elevated perch, we can easily see out over the distant tree line, down to the foothills and out to the expanse of snaking chasms and open, rocky desert far below.

Ignacio remarks on how high up we are. "I didn't even realize we were climbing so much."

"Well," Mattea reminds him. "It *is* a mountain. It's pretty hard to get to the top of one of these things without climbing."

Ignacio manages to squeeze out a laugh, even though, like the rest of us, he's clearly feeling the combination of fatigue and pain from the whole running-for-our-lives thing.

As high up as we've come, we're still hours away from getting to the Academy. And that's if we don't get followed, caught, or killed along the way.

There are no roads or paths around, which is good because it means we're not likely to be tracked down by anyone in a motorized vehicle. But it also means having to carve our own meandering path through some pretty rough landscape. Because of a few impassable rock formations and a couple of wide gullies, it seems like we spend half our time going back *down* the mountain.

I tell my Cohort I remember reading about some guy in a

myth who had to keep rolling a big rock up a hill only to have it roll back down over and over again for all eternity. None of us can remember the guy's name, but Sara asks how come he didn't just kill himself.

"That's the real torture," Arlo tells her. "I think he was already dead."

Sara glares at Arlo for a second, and I think he's going to say something snippy to him, but she just grunts and keeps walking.

A cloud of anxiety seems ready to engulf us. We're lost, exhausted, possibly being hunted, and we could still have a whole host of problems waiting for us back at the Academy. So it's no wonder everyone's a little on edge.

If we could find our way to one of the old mining tunnels, maybe we'd have a chance. But without Trax and with no clue about where the tunnels are from here, we're in more than a bit of trouble.

"What now?" Ignacio asks after we've all taken another minute to catch our breath. "I don't think anyone's following us."

Out of nowhere, Sara whips around toward me. Her jaw is clamped, and her face is tight and flushed with anger.

"You got us into this mess, Branwynne. How, exactly, do you plan on getting us *out*?"

Although I'm too stunned to respond, Libra and Ignacio step forward to form a protective wall in front of me.

"It's not Branwynne's fault," Libra barks at Sara. "There was an intruder, and they took her raven. What did you expect her to do?"

I'm not used to Libra being anything but gushing and happy, so to see her with her back up throws me off a little.

Ignacio takes a small but still menacing step toward Sara. "Leave her alone. No one forced anyone to leave the Academy. We all agreed to come. Branwynne and Haida are connected.

Branwynne did what she needed to do to save them both and to protect the Academy. Any of us would've done the same."

Sara's fingers curl into tight fists. "Maybe that's the problem. Maybe the Academy shouldn't *be* protected. If Epic wants it so bad, why not let him have it? What does it matter to us?"

Now, it's Mattea who steps forward, planting herself next to Sara.

"Sara's got a point. But I think we'd all agree that getting back to the safety of the Academy is a better outcome than getting tortured by Epic, killed by the Sentinels or *eaten* by the Unsettled."

We all stop and stare at Mattea. Her wide, brown eyes dart back and forth as she waits for our response.

Sara's face and eyes soften, not a lot, but enough so we know she's on board. Her fingers uncurl, and she shoots a side-eyed glare at Matholook.

"So, where to now, Mr. Savior?"

A voice in my head says, *I can help.*

I scan the sky overhead. "Haida Gwaii?"

I might not have the smooth and instant communication that Kress has with Render, but I *do* know the sound of my white raven's voice as well as my own. I hop onto a flat-topped rock and swing my head from side to side as I try to reconnect with her.

Where are you?

~ *Don't go back. Not yet.*

Why not?

~ *Enemies.*

What enemies?

~ *The worst kind. The ones from within.*

Within? Are we in danger?

~ *Yes.*

Haida's voice crackles and fades, but the intention, the emotion, and the feelings of fear linger in my head.

"What is it?" Libra asks. "What did she say?"

"I couldn't understand it all. But she doesn't want us to go back to the Academy. Not yet."

Sara smirks, but Mattea snaps around in a rage. "Is she crazy? We need to get out of here! We need to get to safety!"

"That's her point. I don't think the Academy is safe at the moment."

Arlo gulps from deep within the shadow of his hood. "Cohort B. Are they...?"

I shake my head. "Haida doesn't seem to be in panic mode. And I'm not sure if it's the Academy that's in trouble or if she's warning us about something else. Or *someone* else between here and there."

"The Sentinels? Epic and the Civillains?" Ignacio asks, looking more nervous than normal for him.

"I can't tell. But it's a reasonable possibility. We know Micah knows where the Academy is..."

"Which means Epic knows, which means they'll try to cut us off," Ignacio finishes. "Or worse—follow us and wait for us to lead them right through the Academy's front door."

"What about Kress and the others?" Arlo asks. "Maybe we can hide out until they get back?"

"Except we don't have supplies, and we don't know when they'll be back. It could be hours. Or days. Or longer."

Mattea bites her lip. "Or they could be in as much trouble as we are."

"There are a lot of things I'm worried about," I tell her. "Kress and her Conspiracy getting into trouble they can't get out of isn't one of them."

"Branwynne's right," Libra says. "Kress can take care of herself. If the Academy's not in immediate danger, then the only thing we have to worry about is us."

"And the enemies Haida says are out there," I remind her.

"Then we don't have a choice," Matholook declares. "You'll have to come with me."

Mattea frowns. "Come with you where?"

"Back home to New Harleck."

"Forget it," I tell him with as much finality as possible.

"Unless you'd rather stay out here and get tracked down by Epic's Sentinels."

"I'm not going back to a town that's two feet from the one we just escaped from."

"Sanctum may be close. But there's no way Epic will look for you in New Harleck. He wouldn't dare."

Libra makes a dramatic show of stepping between me and Matholook. "Or maybe you'll just turn us over to him to save yourself. After all, you're still at war, right?"

"I wouldn't do that."

"And what about the other Devoted," she asks. "What would *they* do?"

"There aren't enough of them to do anything."

"What do you mean?"

"You said it yourself. We're at war. Literally. Most of the cult is off fighting the Unsettled a hundred miles from here."

In the space of Matholook's half-second pause, a million scenarios flash through my mind. Most of them end up with me and my friends back in the clutches of Epic and his Civillains, imprisoned by the Devoted, or hacked to pieces and snacked on by the Unsettled.

All I wanted was to get Haida Gwaii back and maybe help protect the Academy in the process.

Instead, I just led my Cohort into the middle of a three-way war.

Nice going, Branwynne. So much for being a superhuman leader. Kress would be so proud.

I do a quick calculation in my head before swinging back to Matholook.

"You're as lost as we are. Can you even get us to New Harleck?"

Matholook's eyes dart upward to where Haida Gwaii is bouncing on wind thermals high above the tree line. "No. You're right. I'm as lost as you are. But I bet the two of you can get us there."

Nodding, I wince past a streak of pain in my head and connect with Haida, who confirms that she can get us from here to Matholook's compound.

Okay. Take us to New Harleck. We'll follow you. Just remember, we can't fly!

Overhead, Haida *clacks*! and banks hard to the side, slicing through the air and screeching at us to follow her.

Arlo nudges me as he walks past. "Nice to have someone around with a bird's eye view."

Libra heaves a heavy sigh. "Here we go."

"Hey, Sara," Ignacio calls over his shoulder as we start our march back through the woods and along the steep slope of the mountain. "What do you call it when you escape from the lion's den and decide to look for safety in a den of tigers?"

"Stupid," Sara says as she pushes past me. "Really, really stupid."

42

CHURCH

IT'S dark by the time Haida leads us to Matholook's compound.

It's a good thing, too. Otherwise, everyone in my Cohort might see me shaking.

It's my second time in New Harleck. Other than the fact that it's eerily empty, it's not much different than it was five years ago.

It's still got the patchwork buildings of wood and stone rising up from the combination of dirt paths, broken concrete walkways, and rough fields of weeds and jagged rocks.

Looming up like giant tombstones under the ghostly light of the blood-red moon, a collection of archways, pillars, and wood scaffolding for partially-built additions rise up in clusters around the perimeter.

A wide road of hard-packed dirt runs through the middle of the compound with smaller footpaths branching out toward the one and two-storey structures making up the small, outlying town.

In my brief travels across the country, I've seen giant cities—some as big as London—toppled by drone strikes, poisoned by radioactive fallout from the Atomic Wars, and emptied out by the Cyst Plague. War and Mayla once told us about what cities like Chicago used to look like a long time ago. They described jam-packed busyness, endless fleets of vehicles, and towering skyscrapers of glistening steel and stone with millions of crystal-clear windows looking out onto the world.

With its quiet, rustic calm and apparent lack of anything modern about it, I don't think New Harleck ever looked any other way than it does right now.

Matholook asks me to thank Haida for him.

I tell him I will. "She definitely doesn't like to fly at night."

"Then give her a super special thanks. Without her, I don't think we'd have found our way back."

"Those leaders of yours...?" I start to ask, but Matholook, his neon green eyes finding mine in the dark, shakes his head.

"They're out on the front lines. They're the only ones the rest of the Devoted will follow into battle against the Unsettled."

The fact that Justin and Treva—the leaders of the Cult of the Devoted—aren't here doesn't make being behind enemy lines any less creepy.

While it's true that we've never been attacked directly by the Devoted, Kress swears they were hours—maybe *minutes*—away from doing something terrible to us when we stopped here on our way to find the Academy five years ago.

"Trust me," she said during one of our training sessions. "Render can sense trouble, which means *I* can sense trouble. If we can get you and Haida to the same depth of telempathy, that same level of connectedness could one day save your life. Of course, it helped to have Matholook on our side."

On our side.

From Kress, those three little words and the vote of confidence they imply mean everything in the world.

That doesn't mean I'm going to let my guard down, though. Matholook may be helpful. And he may be cute. But he may also be the enemy. And what was it Haida said about an enemy within?

Could she have meant Matholook? No. She wouldn't have agreed to lead us here if there was danger.

Summoning us deeper into the compound, Matholook leads us through the front double-doors of a dark church. Our boot-steps sound like thunder against the wobbly wooden floor-boards lining the aisle.

Matholook nods toward the pews and the ring of folding chairs set up in a semi-circle in front of the low stage. "We'll wait here in the crossing."

Leading us to the open space in front of the altar, he taps a small input panel on the dais, and a thin band of holo-lights on the walls to either side struggles to life, casting the whole front part of the church in a weak, hazy glow. "We'll be okay here until services start in a few hours."

I'm happy to see how empty the place is. It reminds me of a smaller, much creepier version of our Assembly Hall, and I'm suddenly nostalgic for the Academy.

While the rest of us gather at the front of the church, Ignacio drags his finger along the back of one of the front pews. "Is everyone really out at war?"

"Not everyone. But most of us. Yes."

"Is this a normal thing around here?"

"Unfortunately," Matholook sighs, gesturing for the six of us to join him for a very welcome sit-down in the small ring of chairs.

"I don't know how you live like that," I tell him. "Constantly at war."

"The alternative is sitting back and getting slaughtered. What would *you* do?"

Sitting at last, Ignacio leans back, his legs crossed at the ankle. "You've got a point."

"Relax," Matholook insists. "The Devoted who are still here are asleep on the far side of the compound. The rest of us—Justin, Treva, and our military detail—will be gone for hours. Maybe even days."

"We can't stay here for that long," I remind him.

"I agree. It's too dark now. And too dangerous. First thing in the morning, though, we should work on getting you all back to your Academy."

Libra surveys the rows of empty pews in the dark church. "Preferably before people start swarming in for service."

Matholook scratches at the scraggly part of his beard along his jawline. "There aren't enough of us left in the compound to 'swarm' anywhere. But yes, we'll definitely get you out of here before they start *trickling* in."

"What about Haida's warning?" I ask.

"Since we're here, whoever's out there looking for us won't find us. If it's the Sentinels, they'll figure you got away and headed back to the Academy. If it's the Unsettled, they'll be too busy fighting against my people to worry about you."

"And if it's *your* people out there looking for us?"

Matholook shakes his head. "We hardly ever go up the mountain. Not even when we're *not* fighting against the Unsettled."

Ignacio clamps his hands to his knees. "Okay. We camp here. But then we're out of here first thing in the morning, right?"

"First thing," I promise before swinging back around to Matholook. "Hey. Whatever happened to that really tall boy... what's his name?"

"Bendegatefran."

"Right. Where's he? And what about that mean little half-brother of his? He was a beastly little piece of work as I recall."

"Efnissien. The two of them are out on the front lines against the Unsettled. They're Vindicators."

Sara's eyebrow goes up. "Vindicators?"

"Warriors," Matholook explains. "Fighters. The advance guard of our military detail. They're the ones trained to inflict pain on others and ignore their own."

"And you?" Sara asks.

"I'm what's called a Caretaker."

I lean forward, my elbows on my knees. "And what, exactly, do you take care of?"

Matholook doesn't answer. I'm about to press him when Libra interrupts with a cavernous yawn.

"Sorry," she laughs. "I don't think I've ever been quite this tired."

"We're all tired," Sara tells her. "But I don't think falling asleep right now is the wisest idea."

"I agree," Ignacio says. "I say we help each other to stay awake all night." He turns to Matholook. "No offense."

"None taken. I didn't bring you here to put you at more risk. We've only got a few hours before morning. So stay awake as long as you like. But at first light, we've got to go."

Ignacio opens his eyes wide and promises we'll all get through the night together, only to be the first to drift off.

Shifting over to one of the wooden pews, Libra falls asleep next. Sara and Mattea aren't far behind.

Under his hood, Arlo's eyes are the last to flutter and close. His legs are stretched out and crossed at the ankle. Even in sleep, he grips his scythe close to his chest like it's his favorite stuffie.

As it turns out, there are only two of us who manage to stay awake:

Me and Matholook.

In the gloom of the dark church, he and I continue to talk, our voices breathy and barely above a whisper.

"What did you mean before?" I ask. "About us being...inevitable."

"The Mabinogi," he murmurs, and I have to ask him to repeat the word.

"Oh," I say. "I know those stories. It's where our names come from."

"More than just our names. Our destinies."

I start to chuckle, but I stop when Matholook seems offended. "Sorry. But what does a set of thousand-year-old stories have to do with us or with any of this?"

"In the old stories," he tells me, his voice hesitant with caution and thick with awe, "you were a kidnapped princess. I was a kidnapping king. Our nations went to war over us. There was death, deception, betrayal, and mutilated horses."

"Mutilated horses?" I ask, sitting bolt upright in my chair.

"Your parents didn't tell you about that part?"

I shake my head, embarrassed that this emerald-eyed boy sitting across from me seems to know more about me than I know about myself.

Check that. He knows more about the *myth* behind my name. That's all. That's a million miles away from knowing anything about *me*.

"In the old stories," he continues, "the prince my brother is named after mutilated the horses of the king I'm named after. He cut off their lips. Their tails—"

"Ugh. That's terrible."

Matholook gives me an apologetic shrug and taps his finger-tips to his chest. "I agree. But *I* didn't do it."

"So what happened after that?"

"Oh, you know. The usual."

"War?"

"Yes."

"Betrayal?"

"Naturally."

"Romance?"

Matholook grins. "Inevitably."

"Do you think those things really happened?"

"The things from our myths?"

"*Our* myths?"

"Sure. We have them in common, right?"

I scoff at this. "We're from two different worlds. Literally. Anything we have in common based on a million-year-old myth isn't anything more than coincidence." I don't feel the least bit bad when Matholook blushes a crimson red I can see in the near dark.

Hunching forward in his wooden folding chair, he laces his fingers together and rests his hands on his lap. "Are you asking if I think myths are real?"

"You're right," I admit, tucking my legs under me on my own chair. "Dumb question. Myths and reality are opposites by definition, right?"

Matholook stares at me for a long time before he answers. "Maybe the mistake is drawing such a dark, thick line between the two."

"You're saying the myth you think is about us is...real?"

"No. I'm saying it *will* be."

"You talk about reality and myths and about the past and the future like they're all the same thing."

"Maybe they are."

"I once knew a girl who'd agree with you."

"One of the ones you came here with?"

"Her name was Manthy."

"I remember. She mostly hung out with that redhead."

"Cardyn."

"Right. Whatever happened to them?"

"They...left."

Matholook nods and says, "Oh" but doesn't press me to explain any further. Which is fine with me.

I still don't totally understand the worlds that Kress and the twins—Lucid and Reverie—have been working on accessing over the past five years. All I know is that five years ago, I personally watched two seventeen-year-old human beings—Cardyn and Manthy—walk into a circle of light and disappear. I didn't understand it then, and despite all the lessons Kress has given me, I still find the whole idea of it pretty baffling.

Matholook leans back and smiles at the sleeping forms of Libra, Sara, Mattea, Arlo, and Ignacio. "I like your friends."

"Oh," I scoff. "They're classmates, not friends."

"Remember that dark, thick line...?"

"That's not the same," I protest. "Friends are people that you like and care about and share experiences with. Classmates are just the kids you go to school with."

"It sounds like being at the Academy together is the least of all the important things connecting you."

I think about this for a second, and I'm about to agree with him, but I stop myself.

No sense giving this boy the upper hand in my weird, evolving relationship with my Emergent friends. I mean, classmates.

I grin as Libra mumbles something unintelligible before she rolls over and drops back into a deep, snoring sleep, curled up on the pew with her knees tucked up to her chin.

I slip my jacket off and drape it over the back of my chair before turning back to Matholook. "It'll be morning soon."

"I know."

"Haida could lead us to the Academy, but we wouldn't be able to follow her. The terrain is way too rough, and I don't fancy running into any of Epic's Sentinels who might still be out there looking for us."

"I know. But there are access ports to the underground mines."

"And you know where they are? You can really help get us back to the Academy?"

He closes his eyes for a long time. When he opens them again, he takes a deep breath like he's getting ready to dive into the ocean. "I have a confession."

"What is it?" When he doesn't answer right away, I press him harder, my voice low but firm under the gloomy high-ceiling of crisscrossing wooden beams. "What *is* it?"

"I didn't bring you here to New Harleck to save you."

A lump rises in my throat, and my heart revs in my chest. "Then why—"

He shakes his head and presses his lips together.

"Matholook," I whisper-hiss in the cemetery silence of the church.

He answers by standing up and resting one hand on my shoulder before walking over to the far wall off to the side of the church.

He presses his palm to an input sensor pad. A concealed wooden panel—about the size of a small door—slides open. One by one, a dozen, blinking and disoriented kids steps out into the dark chapel.

The kids shuffle into a compressed knot behind Matholook who rivets his pleading eyes onto my very stunned ones.

"I brought you here to help me save *them*."

43

GATHER

I DON'T THINK my gasp is all that loud, but the other five members of my Cohort stir, moan, and then snap to full attention as if I've just announced at the top of my lungs that the church is on fire.

Ignacio rubs his eyes with the heels of his hands before leaping to his feet like the Army of the Unsettled is about to come storming in.

Libra, Sara, Mattea, and Arlo—as if they were four bodies with a single mind—snap themselves from the depths of sleep and jump into defensive postures in a semi-circle behind me.

Their weapons—sledgehammer, throwing darts, bear claws, and scythe—are drawn, poised, and ready for action.

Matholook seems surprised by the sudden burst of motion. I'm not sure why. It's not like we're accustomed to getting startled awake by the sudden presence of a group of haggard kids who've apparently been trapped inside a small room hidden behind a wall in an old church.

Ignacio says, "What the hell—?" and spreads his arms out—a shillelagh in each hand—to form a protective screen in front of our Cohort.

Ducking under Ignacio's arm, I step forward and do a quick head count.

The twelve blank-eyed kids—probably all between thirteen and seventeen years old—gather in an even tighter clump behind Matholook.

The boys and girls range in shape and size, but they're all wearing the same rumpled blue outfits with the Eagle crest of the Devoted embroidered on the breast pocket.

Without turning my head from this unexpected group of quivering kids, I flick my eyes toward Matholook.

"Who—?"

"I'm sorry. I really sprung this on you, didn't I?" I stare daggers at him as he stutters on. "They're Devoteds. We call them the Set-Asides. They're the ones we think might be Emergents. Maybe even Hypnagogics."

"Where did they come from?"

"Some were born right here in New Harleck. Most once lived in Sanctum."

"With Epic?"

"Yes."

Libra gives my sleeve a frantic tug, but I hold up a wait-a-minute finger and tell her it'll be okay.

"I doubt that," she mumbles.

"Epic was using them?" I ask Matholook.

He nods, and his eyes go sad. "Like he was trying to use you."

"How...how'd they get here?"

Matholook actually blushes. "I um...I saved them."

I'm about to ask how he managed to do that, but he cuts me off, his words tumbling out in brisk, crashing waves.

"They've demonstrated some exceptional but also some pretty dangerous abilities. You're not the only ones Epic is after. We like to take care of our own. But in this case, 'our own' don't belong to us. They barely belong to themselves. If they stay here..."

"They might be killed?" I ask.

His eyes flit from me to the group of kids behind him and then back to me. Dropping his voice, he says, "No. They might kill *us*."

Pointing a dagger-like finger at the opening in the wall behind the kids, Mattea's acid-laced voice spills out from behind me. "And your solution is to keep them trapped in there?"

"For their own good, I promise. Our examiners...they test them. But they never hurt them or experiment on them. You have my word on that."

Libra stands in fist-clenched defiance next to Mattea. "It's hard to accept the word of someone who keeps a bunch of kids locked in a closet."

"It's not a closet," Matholook insists. "And I didn't keep them there." He brushes loose strands of hair away from his eyes and turns to me. "You can ask Branwynne. I'm the one who just let them *out*."

I have to give him credit. He's being awfully brave for someone who's outnumbered six Emergents to one Typic. But he seems sincere.

"They're really...like us?" I ask.

With a small shrug, he tells us most of them are Emergents. He reaches into the cluster of kids and draws one of them forward with delicate care by her elbow.

With what looks like a pair of needle-nose pliers for hands, a bald scalp like a curved circuit board, and a single camera lens for an eye with the swollen socket of her other eye stitched closed, the small girl is more of a junkyard collection of spare parts than a human being.

"This is Valinda. As you can see, she's a Modified. She's one of the ones I need you to save."

Libra opens and closes her mouth, but since nothing comes out, I ask for her. "Save? Save them from *what*?"

"From *us*." We all stare at him for a second before he explains. "There are plenty in the Devoted who think we should kill these Emergents before they kill us. Look. Epic isn't the only one who's afraid of what you represent. Years ago, we all lived in Sanctum down in the valley. The Devoted and the Civillains didn't exactly see eye to eye."

"About Emergents?" I ask.

"About anything, really."

"So you splintered off and came here," I continue for him. "I know that part of the story."

"The part you don't know is this: The Unsettled have gotten involved in Epic's search for Emergents. Emergents are the new weapons of war. And, believe me, there's a war coming."

With my eyes still locked onto the ragtag group of stunned kids, I give him a confrontational shake of my head. "We know that, too, Matholook. The Devoted and the Unsettled are out there right now. You've told us as much."

Matholook shakes his head and gives a casual flick of his hand in the general direction of the big double doors at the front of the church. "Not *that* war. What they're doing out there...that's nothing. That's just...territorial stuff. Jockeying for position. Revenge killing to trim down the ranks. All so we can get ourselves prepared for what's to come."

He ushers the kids closer, and they gather around him, shuffling and clearly too stunned—or too abused—to speak.

"What's to come?" Arlo asks.

"The *real* war. Not the war for food, water, space, land, or safety. That war's over. We lost. We all lost. Two-thirds of the population's been wiped out with everyone else scared and starving. No. I'm talking about the war over *you*."

"Emergents," I say. "You're talking about Epic's war." It's not a question.

Matholook gives me a sad half-nod as Ignacio offers up a half-hearted chuckle of his own. "Not bad," he says, his lower lip pressed forward in a contrived pout. "I never figured we were worth fighting over."

But his joke falls flat under Matholook's pleading gaze. He turns back to the quiet, dead-eyed bunch behind him, and, just for a second, he reminds me of Render and Haida Gwaii when they were going through an especially over-protective stint with their brood of six young ravens a few years back.

"They look like kids," he says. "I know that. But trust me. They're not."

"Then what are they?"

Matholook points back into the dark room they just emerged from and then back to the twelve kids. "That room is a weapons depot."

"And?"

"And...these kids...they're the weapons."

I'm torn. I want to grab my Cohort and run. I want to punch Matholook in the face. And I want to help these kids and make Kress proud.

After all, this is exactly what we've been training for.

I hate feeling indecisive almost as much as I hate feeling helpless.

"What do you want us to do?" I laugh. "Take them to the Academy with us?"

Matholook doesn't answer, and I can tell he hasn't really thought this through.

"First of all," I explain, "the Academy isn't a day camp where you just pop in and out. It's a school. We're in training to *stop* people like you."

When Matholook squints and his cheeks go red, I clarify my point. "Not to stop you, personally. To stop the Devoteds. To stop the Unsettled. And Epic and his Civillains. And every other faction in the Divided States who'd rather see the world end than saved."

Next to me, Ignacio nods and reminds everyone about how we have a very real, very urgent mission. "We're going to save the world," he boasts, his chest puffed out. "Whether the world likes it or not."

Matholook's eyes bounce between me, Libra, Sarah, Mattea, Arlo, and Ignacio. "These kids are like you," he insists, his anxious eyes wide and wet. "Without proper guidance, they'll turn into people on the wrong side of the apocalypse. They'll become the very weapons we're trying to turn them into."

"And *with* proper guidance," I remind him with a sweep of my eyes over the interior of the church, "they'll turn into people dedicated to bringing down all of this, bringing an end to *you*."

"I know."

"You're willing to help bring down your own people?"

"My own people shouldn't have been brought *up* in the first place. People like us, people with ambition and power and the willingness to use it...we've run the world for a long time. I'm tired, Branwynne. I'd like that time to finally be over. If we succeed, if the Devoted—or the Unsettled or Epic or if any of the other rogue factions gets an upper hand—then the whole country's at war."

"And if *we* succeed," I remind him, "you and I will technically be at war."

Through a cheeky grin, Matholook says, "I can live with that."

"No," I tell him with all the sincerity I can muster. "You can't. And you won't."

"I can get you back up the mountain."

"The mining tunnels?"

"Well, one of them, anyway."

"Fine. Where?"

"At the far western edge of the compound, there's an opening in a steel gate. Three hundred feet past that is a very large, very dead tree leaning against a small hill of red rocks. At the base of the ridge is a small opening. You'll need to squeeze in. It leads to a buried mining station and three tunnels. From there, you can take the middle tunnel back up the mountain. It ends and then starts up again in places, so you'll still have to navigate parts of the mountain from the outside. And the mines won't get you directly to the Valta, but they'll get you close enough."

Glancing from the kids to the open doorway, Matholook's glistening green eyes go twitchy with panic. "But you need to hurry. It's almost dawn. The Devoted will be here for church in less than an hour. And the rest of our army—the Vindicators—could be back as soon as nightfall. If any of them catches you here..."

"We'll take the kids," I announce on behalf of my Cohort. "But you need to know...you're just giving us the weapons we're going to use to destroy you."

"I'm counting on it."

"I'll come back," I tell him. Even as I say the words, I don't know if it's a promise, a question, or a threat.

Matholook asks, "Come back? For revenge?"

"No," I tell him. "I'll be back for you. After this, you can't tell me you'll be safe here. The Devoted—Justin and Treva—they'll know you let these kids out. They'll know you're a traitor. And they'll kill you for it."

"Not if they think you overpowered me," he grins. "What if I'm just an innocent victim of a rogue band of powerful Emergents who nearly killed me before taking off with our own collection of precious, rescued Emergents?"

I know exactly what he's asking, and I only hesitate for a split second before obliging.

I strike out with a quick jab to one side of his gorgeous face and then a second jab to the other side. Smiling, he tells me I need to do better than that. So I throw one more punch, clipping him on the jaw and follow that hit with a knee strike to his midsection that leaves him doubled over and gasping for air.

He doesn't so much as raise a hand to defend himself.

Nice job, Branwynne. You just beat up a childhood friend and a possible soulmate.

"Come on," I say to the group of kids who strain to switch their gaze from Matholook to me. Urged on by Libra, they snap into a hazy-eyed, partial focus and scramble out of the room with Sara, Mattea, Arlo, and Ignacio.

I'm the last one to reach the open doorway. Before I step through, I turn back to Matholook. He's on his knees, his cheeks red, the corners of his mouth cracked open and dripping blood.

"I'll be back," I promise. "For you."

"That'd be nice," he grins. "But why?"

"Well...you said it yourself. You and I...we're...*inevitable*. And I believe you."

Wincing and with one hand wrapped around his ribs, he raises his other hand and mouths the word, "Inevitable..."

I dash through the open doorway and sprint to catch up with my Cohort and the liberated kids who are already shuffling their way through the waning darkness toward the edge of the compound.

I keep my eyes forward and focused.

I don't need to *look* back to know that someday, I'm going to *go* back.

44

COHORTS

WE STARTED out as a class of eleven.

That was three months ago.

Now, with the kids from New Harleck and the ones rescued by Kress and her Conspiracy, we're up to thirty.

Because of the way the Emergents of New Harleck were revealed to me, I'm barely surprised when the Terminus doors open in the Sub-Basement hangar, and Kress leads seven kids—none older than about twelve or thirteen—down from the truck.

She and her Cohort beam in triumph. Terk brags about their successful mission, and Rain squeals about how great it is to be home.

As War and Mayla start relaying their supplies out of the massive rig, Brohn strides over to Wisp, who leaps into his arms, hugs him tight, and tells him she and Granden have got a *lot* to fill him in on.

"So it wasn't too boring around here while we were gone?" he asks.

I know all eleven of us original students want to burst out laughing. But Wisp and Granden weren't exactly happy with us about our little excursion outside of the Academy, so we hold our tongues.

"It definitely wasn't boring," I mumble at last through a suppressed smile.

"Great," he grins. "Can't wait to hear all about it."

"Well," Kella drawls, standing protectively behind the seven overwhelmed and stunned-speechless kids, "here's seven more students to add to our little school."

"Seven?" Ignacio crows, his raised thumb pointed toward the ceiling, his voice full of the bluster of an over-embellishing fisherman. "*We* got twelve!"

Kress and Brohn exchange one puzzled look, a second one with their Conspiracy, and then a third with Wisp and Granden, who nod their confirmation.

"They're upstairs waiting for us in the Infirmary," Granden tells them.

Clearly still not happy with us, Wisp gives us a withering glare. "Apparently we have some junior recruiters of our own." When Brohn holds his sister at arm's length like he's inspecting her for a concussion or brain damage or something, Wisp slips her arm around his waist. "Don't worry. We'll explain everything."

"Come on," Granden calls out, his words echoing in metallic waves through the expansive hangar. "Let's get everyone cleaned up, fed, and rested. I think we *all* have quite a few stories to tell."

AFTER KRESS'S heroic return and a full week of discussions and debriefing, Wisp and Granden divided the Academy's thirty students—the original eleven of us plus the twelve we brought back and the seven Kress and her Conspiracy rescued—into five Cohorts with six students in each group.

One of the new students—a pigtailed, thirteen-year-old prankster and practical joker named Prairie—was assigned to be the sixth person in Cohort B, which had been getting by with only five students since the beginning.

Along with our two original Cohorts, each of the three new Cohorts has been named after the term for a group of animals, mostly found in the mountains outside of the Academy. In keeping with traditions started by Kress and her Conspiracy and by Mayla and her family of the Unkindness back in Chicago, each Cohort is assigned the alphabetized group-name for a specific species of bird.

So now we have...

A Committee of Vultures

A Descent of Woodpeckers

An Exaltation of Larks

Cohort B, Prairie included, is now called a "Battery of Quail."

And my Cohort, Cohort A, has been given a name Wisp was sure we'd object to but which we unanimously cheered for when she assigned it.

Libra, Sara, Mattea, Arlo, Ignacio, and I are now formally known throughout the Academy as the "Asylum of Loons."

It wasn't long before we all dropped the bird part of our name for the sake of convenience.

That makes my Cohort known mostly just as "Asylum" and Cohort B mostly referred to as "Battery."

(Roxane—who still doesn't say more than a handful of words every few days—apparently thought our Cohort being called "Asylum" was the funniest thing in the world, because she laughed until she cried and then had to run out of the room to pee.)

Thanks to Chace's designs, each Cohort is going to get its own Academy patch featuring its very own animal representative.

She won't show them to us yet, but she promises it won't be long before we can see her pictures and read her stories.

It's been funny to see how quickly each Cohort has come to rally around its assigned mascot.

"It's like each individual in the Cohort combines to give them a single personality," Arlo points out as we're gathered together in the Lounge, watching the younger kids from Descent and Exaltation hooting and hollering in a rowdy darts tournament on the far side of the crowded, buzzing room.

Arlo's comment launches us into a whole new conversation about whether or not a *group* can have a personality in the same way a *person* does.

Leaning back on the orange couch, Sara claims it's impossible for a group of people to have a personality. "It's in the word, itself," she insists. "Personality means the character of a *person*. A group can't have a single personality any more than a bunch of raindrops can be called a puddle. It's one or the other."

"I disagree," I tell her. "I think it's possible for six people to behave differently as a group than they would as individuals."

"So what's *our* personality, then?" Mattea asks, her hand making a sweeping arc in front of the six of us.

I survey the Asylum and remember all the problems we've encountered, the arguments we've had, the dire situations we've escaped, and the things we've achieved over our first months at the Academy. "Well, we're not exactly the best bunch in the world."

"Or the nicest," Ignacio adds with totally inappropriate pride.

Libra snorts through a perpetual smile, which I'm now sure she simply can't control. "Speak for yourself!"

Mattea rests her chin in her hand like she's deep in thought. Then she grins and nods, apparently in agreement with herself.

"Okay. For this bunch, I'd say an 'Asylum of Loons' is about as accurate as it gets."

"See!" Arlo beams from under his hood. "Together, we're more than we are."

With my elbows on my knees and my head down, I tell my Asylum, "Listen. There's something Epic said to me when I was trapped underground in that bubble-cell of his."

"What did he say?" Ignacio asks.

"I haven't even told this part to Kress."

Feigning anger, Libra stomps her foot. "What *is* it?"

"He said the natural state of people is to be connected and that basically everything that's gone wrong with us as human beings is from us resisting that natural state."

Sara's ears seem to perk up at this. "So now you're saying even things that are totally opposite—good and evil, right and wrong, human and animal, Emergent and Typic—are really connected?"

"I'm saying that's what Epic said. Yes."

"And you agree with him?"

"I don't know," I shrug. "It was a strange thing for him to say. But I know it's important. I can feel it. Anyway, it just got me thinking."

"Ugh," Ignacio grunts with an exaggerated eye-roll. "*Thinking*. What a waste of time."

We have a good laugh, and Libra tugs at my sleeve. "Let's go show those little ankle-biters how to play darts."

I laugh again, not at Libra's use of my term for the younger Newbies, but because going over there with her as my partner and taking those little chabbies from the Exaltation of Larks down a peg or two is *exactly* what I both want and need to do right now.

Technically, this is Sara's wheelhouse. She's the darts expert, after all. But she seems content to sit in her armchair and look sour while the rest of us chat, gossip, and have fun.

For the next couple of hours, Libra and I lose ourselves in the thrill of harmless, painless competition.

Naturally, Libra and I destroy the little tossers. We finish the last set with a flurry of spot-on double bullseyes and a couple of high-fives just for good measure.

We're merciless in battle but gracious in victory, and we offer our younger opponents encouraging, overlapping rounds of "Not bad," "Good match," and "Better luck next time."

Libra takes me by the hand and half-drags me across the Lounge to plop back down with our Asylum for a few more minutes of rest and relaxation before we finally head off to bed.

Tucked in and preparing myself mentally for the new challenges we'll face tomorrow, I whisper my "Thanks" to Libra for prodding me into the diversion of a good game of darts.

After all, the last few weeks haven't been all fun and games.

Soon after our return from New Harleck and just a few days before Kress and her Conspiracy returned with their new recruits, my Cohort and I got yelled at for three days straight for leaving the Academy.

Wisp and Granden took turns slamming their fists down on the table in Wisp's office and storming around the room, promising that if we ever pulled a stunt like that again, they'd feed us to the Unsettled, themselves.

I tried to remind them that we rescued Haida, got *great* intel about Epic, discovered and brought back a dozen new students, and that Cohort B took care of the Academy and saved Wisp's and Granden's lives while we were gone.

But, thankfully, the words lodged in my throat.

(Who knows what Wisp would have done to me if I'd have been that brassy?)

A few days after that—and about two seconds after Wisp and Granden filled her in on everything that had happened in their absence—Kress pulled me aside and gave me a private, one-on-one afternoon of more yelling.

After that, it was back to school for a whirlwind of classes, training, private instruction, and more classes.

Plunged back into the routine of the Academy, the days and weeks flew by.

Things didn't always go smoothly—a few days ago, I failed Terk and the Auditor's Digital Tech seminar, and now I have to retake it with one of the younger Cohorts.

I passed Mayla's Communications Skills class...barely. I aced Part Two of Kress and Brohn's Unarmed Combat class, and only broke my arm twice.

With so much activity and so many kids darting from class to class, scarfing down quick meals in the cafeteria, crashing in the Dorms, or getting patched up in the Infirmary, the Academy feels closer to what I imagine school must have felt like before the end of the world.

The Academy also seems a little smaller now.

The enormous complex I first walked into more than five years ago is still enormous. But it's also filling up with life and chatter.

The empty echoes have been replaced by bootsteps on the stairs, the shuffling of bodies, buzzing conversations in the Tavern, bouncy play-fighting in the Dorms and in the Lounge, and a litany of complaints about who's got the hardest schedule, the toughest teachers, or the most injuries.

With five Cohorts on the go, it's been a tempest of energy and activity around here.

Libra knew the name of every new kid after about two days.

I still don't know most of their names, and I'm not eager to learn.

Besides, I don't need to know their names to know how annoying they are.

(If one more of those slobbery plonkers asks me about what it's like to fight the Unsettled, escape from the Civillains, or talk to a raven, I'm going to make a dog's breakfast of their perky little faces.)

Classes are still painful sometimes, but they're manageable. We're learning a lot, but, as Mattea points out, "We're still a long way away from saving the world."

It's a mission Wisp and the other teachers make sure stays front and center in our minds. Practically every day, we're reminded that we're *not* an army.

"Not in the traditional sense," Wisp tells all thirty of us for the hundredth time from the stage at Morning Address. "You're being trained to use your abilities to help *others* to victory, *not* to gain victory for yourselves."

And then, as she does every day, she sends us off to class where we'll continue to learn how to survive in the world we've been assigned to save.

At least my Asylum and I are getting along okay. I'm less annoyed these days by Libra's prattling. Sara hasn't been throwing me quite as many dirty looks. Mattea and Arlo have been keeping each other company and staying out of my way. Ignacio still has moments of profound wankerdom, but he's also been making visible efforts to rein them in.

He even bawled out a few of the new recruits from the Committee of Vultures for leaving one of the communal bathrooms in a shambles. Since then, it's been spotless.

So...partial credit there.

My favorite days are when I have my personalized Emergent training sessions with Kress.

I thought telling her about Micah would've knocked her for a loop, but she took it in stride. I don't know if that's because she didn't believe her brother was really alive, that he'd be working with someone like Epic, or if she was just too tough to show that she cared one way or the other.

During one of our private sessions, though, she *did* step out into the hallway to talk with Brohn and Terk.

Patched into Haida, my hearing was acute enough to make out parts of their conversation. They were worried, and they were planning something...something *big*. I crossed my fingers and hoped they'd let me be part of it—whatever it was.

That was a couple of weeks ago, but so far, nothing's come of it, and Kress hasn't said a word to me or asked another question about Micah.

Today, Kress is teaching me how to connect more deeply with Haida Gwaii—on an emotional as opposed to a physical level—and how to merge our abilities in times of extreme stress or fear.

I know Kress gets impatient with me sometimes. I try to stay focused. I really do. But there's so much going on in the Academy, twice as much going on in the world, and about a thousand times more going on in my head.

I feel like I'm a racecar with a high-octane engine under the hood, but no one will let me get the bloody thing out of first gear. Honestly, I felt at my best when I was fighting the Unsettled or running from Epic's Sentinels.

Libra says I have a death wish. But I think it's the opposite. Since I was a little girl in the Tower of London, I've felt driven to *live*.

I don't know. Maybe it's the increased number of students or maybe it's just my imagination, but sometimes it feels like the walls of the Academy are closing in on me.

After six hours of Puzzles, Codes, and Game Theory—where I got yelled at by Rain and failed every challenge—I'm on my way to the Tavern when Libra tugs me aside.

"What's with you?" she asks.

"What are you on about?"

"You were a million miles away back there."

"I guess I'm a titch distracted," I admit.

"Did you get answers to *any* of the number sequence riddles?"

I shake my head.

"Are you still thinking about Epic?" I shake my head again, and we step aside to let three of the younger kids from the Descent of Woodpeckers scuttle past. "What then?"

When I don't answer, she asks, "Matholook?"

When I don't answer again, Libra says, "Thought so. And you want to go find him, don't you?"

"He's still down there at the bottom of the mountain," I explain.

"And you're up here. Maybe it's best to leave it that way."

"We're up here partly because we don't know who we are. With Matholook..."

"You felt like you did."

"Yeah," I confess. "I can't explain it. It's like we're...like we've *always* been...connected."

I feel like a barmy, brain-addled tosser saying that out loud. I'm half-expecting Libra to laugh or brush it off as some stupid, teenage girl infatuation.

She doesn't go quite that far, but she *does* sound a little annoyed with me. Or else scared *for* me. "Listen, Branwynne, just because your names come from the same story doesn't mean you're on the same page. His people are the Devoted. If they can't use you--"

Frustrated, I lean back hard against the wall, my arms crossed tight in front of me with one of our hardcover Game Theory textbooks pressed to my chest. "I know. I know. I just feel like..."

"Like what?"

"Like he's one of the keys to me."

Libra's eyes go sad, and she offers up a slow, quiet sigh but doesn't say anything.

"He knows a war is coming," I remind her. "He knows what Epic is planning, and he knows more kids like us are out there, just waiting to get scooped up and forced to fight for one side or another. He still wants to help. Even more than he already has. I know he does."

"Help who? Epic? The Devoted?"

"I think he wants to help *us*. But not just us. I think he wants to help us help the world."

"Helping like he did is going to get him killed. If not by his own people, then by the Unsettled or by Epic's Sentinels. Or Roguers or Plaguers or any number of desperate gangs out there willing to slaughter whoever crosses their path. And you being anywhere near him...well, you'd just be putting yourself in the same sights he's already in."

"I know that, too."

"Then why risk so much?"

"It's not *that* much," I laugh. "Just my life."

Libra clamps her hands onto my shoulders and locks her eyes onto mine. I almost don't recognize her: Her hair, her skin, her eyes...they're all still painfully pretty and perfect. But she's not grinning, bouncy, or perky. "It's not just *your* life, Bran-wynne. It's all of us. It's everyone in the Academy."

Nodding, I tell her she's right.

"Come on," she beams. "Let's get something to eat before we pass out. We have Intelligence Ops with Kella first thing in the morning. We need to be in top form!"

I let her drag me along to the Tavern where we grab a quick bite and socialize a little with the other Cohorts before heading upstairs to the Dorms to decompress and get a few hours of long overdue and very well-deserved sleep.

And for the first time, I'll be doing it among friends.

EPILOGUE

THAT NIGHT, I spend at least three hours staring at the ceiling.

I know Libra's right about us getting some rest and about the need for us to stay focused on our training, now more than ever. And I know she's just looking out for me.

But with the rest of my Asylum purring in the depths of some very deep sleep, I slip out of the Dormitory. I make my way all the way down to the Sub-Basement and along the labyrinth of secret access tunnels leading away from the Academy.

Once I'm through the first set of doors, it's a long walk down some very steep, very creepy mine shafts with curved walls of rock, wooden struts, and steel support beams looming over me from every side. Beams of rectangular wooden railroad ties are hammered into the path with iron spikes, but they're not exactly steps, and they don't make the steep descent that much easier.

I know the first part of this path from the last time I left the Academy with my Cohort on a mission to rescue Haida Gwaii.

At least this time, the holo guide-lights planted into the tunnel walls are functioning. And at least this time, I'm alone.

But this time, unlike before, at the third split, I go right instead of left.

At the end of the first branch of the middle mining tunnel, I tap in the code on the input panel and press my thumb to the fingerprint I.D. scanner. The round metal door glides open, and I step outside.

Behind me, the door slides closed, and the Veiled Refractor activates to make the surface of the door blend seamlessly into the surrounding rock face.

I trudge down a long, winding footpath, through a dense and seemingly endless section of dead and fallen trees. I cling to branches and protruding rocks for balance as I continue to scurry and lope my way downhill.

Where the land flattens out, I slog across a series of deep fields of mud and slushy, melting snow.

The air and the earth are somehow warm and cold at the same time. I'll never get used to how odd the weather is outside of the climate-controlled Academy. It's like I can walk from arctic to desert and back again in the space of half an hour.

A flurry of movement overhead startles me. From out of the murky gloom, Haida Gwaii swoops down and lands with a light bounce on a low branch of a scraggly, ash and frost-covered tree. Her blue eyes sparkle, and she ruffles her slick white feathers, reflecting the hazy glow of the moon-lit night.

"What are you doing flying around out here in the dark?" I ask her.

I still can't always pick up complete language from her. But I *do* get a flood of her emotions:

~ *Concern. Anger. Fear.*

"I'll be back," I promise her out loud. "I just have to go see a...friend."

~ *Why?*

To connect.

Flipping up the collar of my red leather jacket against the biting wind, I clomp the rest of the way down the crags and valleys carved into the steep mountain toward New Harleck and the Cult of the Devoted, determined to find the missing part of me and to reunite myself with the other half of my myth.

END OF *EMERGENTS ACADEMY* – **Book 1 of** *The Academy of the Apocalypse* **series**

NEXT IN SERIES

Coming Soon!

The next book in the series...

The Academy of the Apocalypse:
Cult of the Devoted

Feeling an overpowering pull she can't explain or control, Branwynne slips out of the Emergents Academy in search of Matholook, the mysterious and charming seventeen-year-old member of the Cult of the Devoted she first met five years ago.

Heading right into the enemy camp may not seem like the most sensible thing to do, but Branwynne has never been one to blindly follow the rules—or to shy away from danger. Especially when her instincts are screaming at her that Matholook may have answers to questions she's been searching for all her life.

Thrust into the middle of a bloody, three-way war for power in a bleak and ravaged land, Branwynne has her loyalties tested as she closes in on the mystery of who and what she really is.

What she finds may not change her life or her mind.

But it could just change her *heart*.

Cult of the Devoted is coming in March 2021.

ALSO BY K. A. RILEY

To be informed of future releases, and for occasional chances to win free swag, books, and other goodies, please sign up here:

https://karileywrites.org/#subscribe

Academy of the Apocalypse Series

Emergents Academy

Cult of the Devoted

Army of the Unsettled (Coming in 2021)

Resistance Trilogy

Recruitment

Render

Rebellion

Emergents Trilogy

Survival

Sacrifice

Synthesis

Transcendent Trilogy

Travelers

Transfigured

Terminus

Seeker's World Series

Seeker's World

Seeker's Quest

Seeker's Fate

Seeker's Promise

Athena's Law Series

Book One: *Rise of the Inciters*

Book Two: *Into an Unholy Land*

Book Three: *No Man's Land*